Only Wanna Dance With You

Only in Goose Hollow
Book 1

Lisa Shelby

Lisa Shelby Books, LLC

ONLY WANNA DANCE WITH YOU
PLAYLIST

Betcha ~ Chris Lane

Practically Strangers ~ Jack Gray

Let's Do It Again ~ J Boog

Forget Me ~ Lewis Capaldi

Breaking My Heart ~ Mitchell Tenpenny

Wishful Drinking ~ Ingrid Andress & Sam Hunt

When You look Like That ~ Thomas Rhett

Last Night ~ Morgan Wallen

Sad in the Summer ~ Diplo & Lily Rose

Lose Control ~ Teddy Swims

Catching Feelings (feat. SIX60) ~ Drax Project

Hotel Key ~ Old Dominion

Out of My Mind ~ little image

Friends ~ Tyler Braden

Willow (Taylor's Version) ~ Taylor Swift

Weight of Your World ~ Chris Stapleton

I Met A Girl ~ Sam Hunt

Dance With You ~ Brett Young

Fix (Acoustic) ~ Chris Lane

Missing You ~ Betty Who

Anything She Says (feat. Seaforth) ~ Mitchell Tenpenny

Rush ~ Troye Sivan

Naïve ~ The Kooks

Until I Found You ~ Stephen Sanchez

You Make My Dreams (Come True) ~ Daryl Hall & John Oates

Take My Name ~ Parmalee
Would Ya ~ Christopher

LISTEN WHILE YOU READ

READER NOTE

This book contains explicit language, sexual content, limited violence and the discussion of parental loss, and stalking. I do hope that I have handled these topics with the care they deserve.

For Amanda,

Thank you for your support and friendship.
Everyone one should have a person like you
in their life. Someone who fixes their crown
before anyone ever knows it's crooked.

Chapter One

Callen

Of course, Knox stood me up.

I finally make it to LA, and my big brother and his rock star life are too busy to make time for me. Sure, I saw him and our entire family last night at the awards show, where his band won Album of The Year and Song of The Year. We all celebrated and partied late into the night. But I was hoping to catch up on some one-on-one time with him. I'm sure he'll have some reason for bailing on me. Like Elton John flew him to London for a spur of the moment party or some crazy celebrity excuse only he could give.

He and his band, The Hollow Knocks, are having quite a year. Their big hit song "Goodbye" has been all you hear on the radio for the past year and a half. He rarely has time for the little people these days. And this afternoon is proof that I am assuredly one of the little people.

"Skinny margarita, please." A feminine yet confident voice pulls me out of my pissed off mood, my brother all but forgotten.

Next to me, leaning over the one empty stool at the bar with a perfectly manicured hand resting on the marble counter, the other hand holding a credit card, is the most breathtaking woman I have ever seen, and this is just in my peripheral vision.

"Sure thing." The server winks. "Want me to start a tab?"

"No tab, thanks. Just having the one."

I can't help but look over at her since she's less than a foot away from me, and when I do, the brightest blue eyes I have ever seen knock the air right out of my lungs. She looks at me, and our eyes lock. Neither of us says a word for the longest time, but I can't hide my smile. And my smile causes her to smile, and well, I'm a goner.

"This seat taken?" she asks, breaking what should be an awkward silence but isn't.

Before replying, I look over my shoulder to make sure my brother isn't walking into the bar at this precise moment. Because why wouldn't my rock star brother finally show up and ruin whatever moment I'm having with this beautiful blond with the electric-blue eyes? It would be such a Knox thing to do. He always seems to one-up everyone.

"No. Please, have a seat."

While she settles herself, I stealthily check her out. I don't want to be *that* guy, but even the manners gained from my small-town upbringing can't stop my quick perusal of her body.

She's tall, tan, and lean, but still curvy in all the right places. Her beige suit jacket is open, revealing a silky white blouse tucked into tight dark blue jeans along with an expensive-looking belt. The white top and layered gold necklaces look good against her bronze skin. Thankfully, no gold or diamond shines from her left hand.

Reaching out my hand to her, she doesn't hesitate to take it, but just as I'm about to introduce myself, the bartender slides her drink in front of her and tells her how much she owes.

She attempts to release my hand so she can pay him, but no way am I letting go of her.

"Put it on my tab, please."

"Sure thing." The twenty-something wannabe actor walks away before she can protest, and her hand is still in mine.

"Thank you, but you didn't need to do that."

"It's my pleasure."

"Where are you visiting from?" she asks, a sweet smile lighting up her face.

She finally slides her hand out of mine and takes a drink of her margarita. Her tongue darts out to lick the salt from her lips, and I nearly forget what she just asked me.

"Oregon. That obvious?"

"Don't take it as an insult. Most people in LA aren't from LA, and this *is* a hotel bar, so there's a high probability you're just visiting."

"Well, you wouldn't be wrong. I'm only here for two more nights. I leave Sunday afternoon."

"What brings you here to sunny California and the Sunset Marquis?"

"Visiting my brother." I don't dare say who he is. That never ends well.

Women find out I'm related to Knox, and it's all they see. She's clearly out of my league, but you never know. I may be good enough for her all on my own. At least that's what the sparkle in her eyes leads me to believe.

"What do you do back in Oregon?"

"Work for my family business. How about you?"

"Funnily enough, I work for my family business, too."

We're both being vague, but strangely, it's hot.

It occurs to me she could be meeting a date here. I better figure this shit out before I get ahead of myself.

"You meeting someone?"

"Nope. Had an appointment, but my client never showed up. You?"

"Same." I look down at my watch. "Was supposed to meet my brother here forty-five minutes ago, and he's a no-show."

"What is it with people? I can't imagine not showing up when you know someone is waiting for you. I mean, I should be used to people in LA and their self-absorbed attitudes, but even after a lifetime here, it still pisses me off."

She's talking to me as if we've had a million conversations in the past and not like a stranger she met five seconds ago, and I'm eating up every word.

"I don't think it matters where you live. It's rude. My brother couldn't even send me a text or, God forbid, call me." I lift my phone, and Ruby, my pit bull, flashes up on my lock screen.

"Oh my God, she's beautiful. Is she yours?"

"Uh, yeah. That's my girl, Ruby."

"I grew up with a blue pitty just like her." She sighs, lifting her hand to her heart. "She was the love of my life."

I. Am. Screwed.

It's been two minutes and somehow this woman is more attractive with every sentence that comes out of her mouth.

"I know how you feel. Ruby goes everywhere with me. I can't imagine going to work every day without her by my side."

"My Steve was a lot smaller. Your Ruby has a big, beautiful head, and look at that smile." She tilts her head to the side, admiring the picture on my phone. "She's a beautiful girl."

"Thanks. Steve? You named your dog Steve?"

"Not sure why. I just always knew if I had a dog of my own, it would be a Steve. From the time I was a little girl, I had always begged my dad for a golden retriever. One day, my dad came home and announced that he had found a golden retriever at the local shelter. I was so excited. I was finally going to have my very own Steve. When we got to the shelter, we walked past all the kennels, and we went by one that at first looked empty, but then this clumsy little gray baby came running out from under a blanket and jumped up against the glass, looking me right in the eye. I didn't make it a step further. My Stevie picked me, and there was no going back."

"Steve. I like it."

"Got any more pics?"

I open my phone and find the folder where I keep all of Ruby's pictures, then hand it to her. She doesn't give it a second thought as she gushes over my dog. All the while, I watch her smile and am captivated.

Dumbstruck as I am, I blurt, "Is it even possible that you're single?"

Ignoring me, she keeps looking through Ruby's pictures but seems to be scrolling back through pictures she's already looked at.

"This is my favorite." She slides the phone back to me, and the picture is one my brother Angus took of Ruby and me on my boat. And I happen to be shirtless. "And yes."

"Yes?"

"I am very single. And you?"

"I am, and honestly, never been so happy to be."

She smiles but shakes her head at my honest reply, then takes a sip of her drink.

"What are you doing with your time while you're here?"

"Well, I just met this fascinating woman and was hoping I could buy her another drink and see where the day takes us. It's only..." I touch my phone to bring it to life and flash the time for both of us to see. "Two."

"Is that so?" she questions, but her eyes and that goddamn smile of hers say she's definitely interested.

"Would you like another drink?"

Turning on her stool to face me, she catches her bottom lip between her teeth as her eyes dart between my eyes and my mouth. One of her legs is crossed over the other and bounces as she wipes her palms on her jeans. She looks nervous, but her smile says it's an excited kind of nervous.

At least I hope it is.

"I would love another drink." She holds a finger up. "On one condition."

Intrigued because her eyes tell me she would like much more than another drink, I turn my stool toward her, and her bouncing leg now sits between mine. "We just met, and we already have conditions?"

"Just one."

"Okay, hit me. What is this condition that may or may not prevent me from buying you another drink?"

One side of her mouth lifts in a sexy grin as the opposite eyebrow lifts, and her slender fingers play with one of her gold chains. I don't know what she's about to say, but whatever it is, I'll agree as long as she keeps looking at me like that.

"No names."

I tilt my head to the side, confused. "What?"

"I won't tell you my name, and you won't tell me yours. Let's just have another drink and see where things go. But, for now, let's just have the freedom of enjoying each other's company without the pressure of expectations or leaving any strings attached."

If it weren't for the blush creeping up her neck to her cheeks, her bouncing leg, and her shaky fingers still playing with her necklace, I would think this is nothing new to her, but something tells me that assumption would be wrong.

"You do this often?"

She sucks in a breath, and even though she recovers quickly, her cheeks burn hotter.

"Never before."

"Why now?"

"I have a lot going on and need to blow off some steam, but complications aren't an option at the moment."

Well, at least she's being honest.

"And you think exchanging names would be some sort of complication?"

Her smile turns wicked, and my cock begs me to complicate things for her.

"I knew the moment I sat down, you would be a huge complication."

"Is that so?" I say, repeating her earlier question.

"I think you know so." She releases her necklace and puts her left hand on the bar, leaning in a little closer. "Don't think I didn't see you give me a once-over when I sat down. I think we're both interested. I'm just not wasting time playing coy about what will happen after this next drink."

And... I'm hard.

She extends her hand in my direction, offering me what I think might be a night to remember. I didn't come to LA hoping for a one-night stand, but here we are.

"Deal?"

It's not really how I roll, but I would be stupid to pass up the opportunity to spend time with a woman like her. Smart, funny, straightforward, and, of course, stunning. I've never done the whole "hit it and quit it" thing. It's not a rite of passage that was ever an option for me. Maybe the ripe old age of thirty-four is finally the time to see how it works.

I can't imagine a night with her would be something I would regret, so without another thought, my hand reaches out to take hers. The moment I feel her skin on mine, I know I've made the right decision.

But I also know she's wrong.

There is no way this doesn't get complicated.

Chapter Two

Charlotte

"So, your dream job would be to flip houses?" my attractive mystery man asks.

We're still sitting at the bar, and I'm still on my second margarita. The goal is to drink enough for the courage and confidence necessary to do what I want without becoming a sloppy drunk, so I'm sipping slowly.

"Flip them, renovate them. Anything that involves tearing down walls, building furniture, or transforming the space. But I want to get my hands dirty. I wouldn't want to just be the money behind it. I want to be a part of the process."

"Like that couple in Magnolia, Texas. The ones with a show where they do everything you just described."

Dear God, this gorgeous man is adorable. His thick dark hair is begging me to run my hands through it, and his rich dark-chocolate eyes have a sparkle that draws me in. But how he can be so sexy and attentive one second and too cute the next is a combination I've never come across in a man before.

"You mean Chip and Joanna Gaines?" I chuckle. "Yes, that would be a dream. Minus the TV show and the fame."

"What about the husband? Would you want to do it with a partner or on your own?"

What I wouldn't do to share some of life's burdens with a partner. Of course, I don't say this out loud. I'm determined to keep things light and fun. No need to let too much real-world, serious-life stuff seep in.

"Why? You wanna be my Chip?"

Where this boldness of mine is coming from this afternoon, I have no clue, but I haven't had this much fun in I don't know how long.

"Sugar, I'd be your Chip any day of the week."

Oh my Lord, this man. The upper hand he would have if he knew what he was doing to me.

So far, there seems to be much more to him than just a cute guy in a bar. He isn't simply placating me to get into my pants. He's genuinely interested. In me. Not what I can do for him. Not for who I know. He seems to just be interested in me.

He asks questions. Listens. Pushes me. And is sexy as hell in his crisp white T-shirt, dark jeans, and sexy well-worn brown boots. Of course, I checked out the shoes. The shoes matter. And his are quite the turn on.

Somehow, this perfect stranger who I've known for two hours is pushing me in a way nobody ever has.

Pushing me to do what *I* want. To follow *my* dreams.

My dad never pushed me into the family business. That

was all me. Everything I've ever done has been for my dad. I've never really even considered doing anything else until recently.

Now, here comes this man from Oregon with no name, chestnut eyes, and a pillowy bottom lip I want desperately to bite, causing me to contemplate exactly what I'm doing with my life.

"So, you wanna be my Chip, do ya?" I say, leaning forward and touching his leg.

Just as I bravely take my flirt game to the next level, someone pushes me from behind, and what's left of margarita number two spills all over the front of Chip, soaking his white shirt and dark jeans.

"Oh, my goodness! I am so sorry."

He stands from his barstool, and I'm not sure what I expected, but his height, his build, all of him, far exceed my expectations. Only he doesn't seem concerned with the sticky mess all over the front of him. His focus is on the person behind me.

"Excuse me, but you owe the lady an apology."

"What?"

"You pushed her."

"It's crowded, man. Accidents happen."

Looking around the bar, I'm surprised to see how full it's gotten. We've been so wrapped up in our own little world I didn't even realize the Friday afternoon happy hour crowd had shown up.

Chip's hands form fists, and he looks like he's about to blow, so I intervene. "It was an accident, no big deal." I stand from my stool and grab my bag. "Why don't we find somewhere to clean you up?"

Tugging on his hand, I'm surprised, yet relieved when he laces his fingers between mine. Glad he doesn't mind how sticky my hand is from the drink it's covered in. But he doesn't lead us to the bathroom. Instead, we seem to be heading toward the sunshine lighting up the hotel lobby. Thank goodness he already closed his tab.

"Where are we going?"

"My room so I can clean up," he says, still sounding pissed.

His room.

Do I want to go to his room?

Do I dare go to his room?

It's now or never. Walk away and always wonder what might have been or go to his room and break every rule in my make-believe rulebook that says I'm not that kind of girl.

I don't pull my hand from his.

I don't tell him we shouldn't do this.

Instead, I let him lead the way.

We walk past the knowing looks of rock gods of the past that cover the lobby walls and out into the lush gardens that surround the outdoor paths of the hotel property. Neither of us speaks.

The Sunset Marquis is not just one of my favorite hotels, but also part of rock and roll history. Legends in music and the Hollywood elite have partied here, and some have not just stayed for a weekend but have made the hotel a home away from home. Many have lived here for months or even a year to hide from the paparazzi. Every room is a villa with no enormous towers holding hundreds of rooms and cliché hotel carpet. The entrances to all the rooms are outside, and you get to your villa through winding walkways surrounded by trees and flowers, Koi ponds and exotic birds.

"Fuck," he growls under his breath.

One minute, we're walking, and the next, we're in a dark alcove hidden behind the leaves of a short palm tree. He gently positions me, so my back is against the wall.

He lifts his hand, not holding mine, taking my face in his palm as his thumb strokes my cheek. "I didn't ask you if you wanted to go to my room. I'm sorry about that."

All I can do is remember to breathe.

His eyes glance down at my lips, and his tongue darts out to wet his own.

Kiss me. Please kiss me.

"Would you like me to take you to my room?"

"God, yes."

His lips crash into mine, swallowing my words and stealing my breath.

His kiss is purposeful. Powerful. And gone way too soon. The weight of his body lightly pressed against mine had felt safe, and I miss it already.

"Pretty sure we're already past complicated, sugar."

He's right. Nothing about the chemistry between us is ordinary.

This is gonna leave a mark.

"Come on. I'm not afraid of a little PDA, but what I want to do to you isn't proper for public consumption."

"I like the sound of that, Chip."

As the heat of him leaves me, he wastes no time guiding us back to the walkways that eventually take us to his villa door. As we stand out in the open air in front of his room, the sun highlights the rich auburn of his hair that hid in the dark lighting of the bar, letting me think he had dark brown locks.

Damn, he is the finest ginger I've ever laid my eyes on.

Not letting go of my hand, he pulls his room key out of his back pocket with his free hand and holds the piece of plastic with a picture of Bob Dylan on it up to the pad on the door. The sound of the door granting us access sets off alarm bells throughout my body. Not the alarms that tell me to run, but the kind that says tonight will leave me wanting more.

The door swings open, and the crisp air-conditioned air doesn't have time to cool my heated skin because as soon as the door closes, he has me against it, his body pressed against mine, his lips blissfully kissing me again.

This time, our kiss is frantic. All teeth and tongues and I can't help but take a nibble on his perfect bottom lip.

He moans into my mouth. "I've wanted you since the moment you sat that fine ass of yours down next to me."

"You always get what you want?"

"Hardly ever."

"Well, I'm happy to be an exception." My fingers grip the hem of his T-shirt, lifting it up his chest. "What do you say we get this thing off you?"

He reaches behind his neck and pulls the shirt off in one swift motion. I don't have time to check him out though, because his lips are back on me, and he grabs my ass, lifting me so my legs are around his waist.

Leaning forward, I trail kisses down the side of his neck and over his collarbone. "Mmm. You taste like complicated decisions." I lick my drink off his sticky skin.

"Tell me your name."

"Sorry, Chip, we made a deal."

I lick and suck my way back up his neck. When I reach his ear, he gently pulls back to get my attention. The copper dancing in his brown eyes pleading for me to go back on our deal.

"What if I've changed my mind?"

"There's nothing we can do about it. A handshake is a binding agreement."

I know it's not fair to either of us, but I would rather be up front with him. It will be easier on both of us if we can walk away with no attachments because I certainly can't give him more than right here. Right now.

"What if I give you permission to break said agreement?"

Oh, Chip. You have no idea how much I want to give in to you.

"How about I give you me instead?"

His eyes search mine for something. Anything. But I hold firm.

"I'd be a fool to say no to that." He kisses me long and soft this time. "If you give me you, then what can I give you?" he asks, with his forehead against mine.

"I'm tired of being in control of everything and everyone. Most of all... I'm tired of being tired. Would asking you to bring me back to life be too big of an ask?"

"You want me to take control, sugar? Show you what you need?"

"Please."

"Your wish is my command."

Chapter Three

Charlotte

We've finally come up for air, after hours of toe-curling orgasms and wishes being granted. He took control just like I asked him to, somehow knowing exactly what I needed. Playing my body like a finely tuned instrument only he knows how to play.

His mouth. His hands. His magnificent cock and the way the man moves his hips have ruined me. The bar has been set and I don't see anyone ever measuring up. It's more than the physical act. It's the care and the passion behind the sex. It's in the way he made sure I felt safe while simultaneously bringing me to the highest of highs as I screamed in pure ecstasy each time he made me come. My pleasure was his priority.

After what I've been through, I swore I would never let anyone control me in any aspect of my life.

This was different.

He was in control, but only because I asked him to be.

Now, we're hydrating and snacking while we get to know each other with a little game of the classic, Never Have I Ever.

"Never have I ever... had cheesecake," Chip states, as though this isn't the most shocking statement he's made since we met at the hotel bar.

"What?" I screech, unable to comprehend how this grown man has never tasted my favorite dessert.

He shrugs. "Just the name of it sounds disgusting."

"You. Have. Never. Had. Cheesecake?"

"Nope."

"I... I... just... how is that possible?" My brain can't compute.

The scrunch of his nose may be adorable, but I need to fix this travesty right here and now. I pick up my phone, place my delivery order, and take a drink of my water.

He's in his boxer briefs, and I'm wearing what he said was his favorite gray Eastlyn Brewery Co. T-shirt. It's the softest cotton I've ever felt, and smells like him. We've raided the minibar and have our hoard of candy, crackers, cookies, and nuts spread out on the comforter. We've both given up alcohol for the night. I'm not sure of his reasoning, but for me... Well, I don't want to forget a second.

"What did you just do?"

"Ordered cheesecake from the best place in the city."

"You're barking up the wrong tree, woman. I'm not interested."

"We'll see about that."

"If ordering cheesecake means you're sticking around, you can order food I'm never gonna eat all night."

I hadn't even thought about whether I was overstaying my welcome. I'm relieved that isn't the case. In fact, I could hide out in this villa forever and be happy if these first few hours are any indication of what life might be like.

"Okay, this isn't my turn, because I've done it now, but I've never... slept with a ginger. That is, until this afternoon."

He turns his head to the side like a confused puppy. I can see him working it out in his head and my smile hurts it's so big.

"Hey now. I know you aren't talking about me! I am a lot of things, but I am not a ginger!"

"You are a total ginger!"

"No, ma'am."

"Look at these auburn highlights," I say as I run my hands through his hair. Our closeness changes the lighthearted atmosphere in the blink of an eye, and I pull my hands back. At the moment, I'm enjoying getting to know him.

"Highlights, gifted from the big man upstairs, do not make a soulless ginger."

"They do."

He throws a peanut M&M at me and takes his turn, skipping me.

"Never have I ever... had a one-night stand."

I take a sip of my bottled water.

His eyebrow lifts. "Is that so?" he probes.

"Well... I did go to college."

"Fair." A small smile crosses his lips.

"I see you didn't drink. Never? Not once?"

"Nope. Married my high school sweetheart." He sees me

tense and takes my hand in his. "She left me for my cousin a couple of years back."

"What a bitch."

He chuckles, but I'm not joking. What a fucking bitch.

"It was for the best. I dated after the divorce, but nothing I would call a one-night stand. More like friends with benefits."

"No crazy college years for you?"

"I went, but I was faithful."

"So, you were only with one person before your divorce."

"Nah, we didn't start dating until our senior year in high school. I had a couple of practice rounds before her."

"And since the divorce? Do you have a lot of friends with benefits?"

I'm not sure why I'm asking questions I don't really want the answers to. But I'm feeling irrationally territorial.

"I've spent time with people since my divorce."

"How many people?" I blurt out before I can stop myself.

"Are you asking me what my number is?" A devilish smile spreads across his face. "Do you have a burn book you're logging my details into?"

"Oh shit. I did just ask you what your number was, didn't I? How embarrassing." I laugh, throwing myself down on the bed, and pulling the sheet over my head.

Abort! Abort! This isn't high school, you idiot!

The mattress shifts, and I hear him pushing our expensive snacks to the side. Then he joins me, pulling the sheet over our heads.

"Whatcha doin' under here?"

He doesn't make a move. Instead, he lies next to me, taking my hand in his.

"Well, I was hiding from you, but here you are."

"Here I am."

He brings our hands up to his mouth and kisses the back of mine.

"You're a fan of *Mean Girls*?"

"It's a classic." He answers as if shocked I even had to ask.

Why do you have to be so perfect?

Why am I so embarrassed?

Quietly, I tell him, "I really don't want to know your number."

"Well, I'd tell you if you really wanted to know."

"I don't!" I blurt out.

He releases my hand and rolls on top of me, keeping most of his body weight on his elbows. The light shines through our sheet tent, and he leans to the side, lifting my shirt to place kisses on my stomach. "Stay the night."

"Okay."

He lifts my shirt and sucks one of my nipples into his mouth. "Stay the weekend." He moves to my other breast and repeats his previous action.

"Okay." My back arches subconsciously, pushing my breast against his mouth, wanting more.

He slides down my body, kissing and licking until he reaches my center, leaving me squirming underneath him. He lifts his head and extends his right hand to me. "Sugar, you're mine until they kick us out of here on Sunday. Shake on it."

With the heat of his words caressing my needy clit, I shake his hand. I pull the sheet over my head to hold above us, not wanting to leave our lust-filled cocoon as he sucks my sensitive bundle of nerves into his mouth without warning.

His tongue works its way across it several times before lazily lapping up the wetness brought on by him.

"And you can bet your sweet ass I'll be calling the front desk to ask for a late checkout." He inserts two fingers, curving them just right, and I'm ready to combust. "Now fucking come on my hand, sweetness."

And I do as he orders.

I come, and I come, and I come.

All weekend long.

Chapter Four

Callen

Staring at the circular white marble tub in the center of the gray-tiled bathroom while I shower behind the clear glass wall, last night's conversation runs through my head. We'd sat in that tub for two hours, talking until our bubbles dried up, the water turned cold, and our fingers wrinkled.

Last night, the tub was our confessional. I'd opened myself up to her in a vulnerable way I never have with anyone else.

We talked about her loneliness as an only child, and much to my surprise, I'd shared my feelings about being the middle son of a family of three boys and a girl. Feelings I had never verbalized to anyone or even admitted to myself until last night.

When one of your brothers is rock royalty, and the other

is a life-saving hero given the Congressional Medal of Honor at the White House, and you still live in your small town and work for the family business, it's easy to feel a little *less than*. Not that anyone has ever made me feel this way. It's just something I've kept in the deepest, darkest part of myself. But with *her,* it all spilled out of me. I shared my insecurities about taking over the business and she shared her feelings about one day having to do the same when it's the last thing she wants.

Somehow, we shared anything and everything without me mentioning who my older brother was or where I lived. I may live in a small town, but when your small town is the home of Knox McKinnon of the Hollow Knocks, people have heard it. When strangers hear Knox's name, their entire demeanor changes, and you can never be sure of their intentions again.

We covered topics everyone says you should never discuss, like politics and religion. We laughed our asses off telling childhood stories, discussing our favorite movies and music and the sex... the sex has been off the charts!

I could fuck this woman every day until the end of time.

She brings out a possessive control I've not experienced before. It's like she's made just for me, and I instinctively know exactly what she wants.

What she needs.

If there's one thing the last forty-eight hours have shown me is that there's much more than out of this world sexual chemistry between us. There's something real here.

And that's exactly what I told her a few hours ago, just before the sun came up and we finally fell asleep. I spilled my guts and asked for not just her name, but for more.

To give us a shot.

All she did was shake her head to there ever being an *us*.

But a couple of hours later, in the middle of an orgasm, she finally agreed to give me her name before checkout.

After what might have been an hour of sleep, I woke with her still in my arms, her head on my shoulder and her breath tickling my chest. I didn't dare move and risk waking her up. Needing the moment to hold her a little longer, to take in the softness of her skin, the lingering smell of our bubble bath in her hair, and her heartbeat against my rib cage. My brain strategized what I could say to make her change her mind about giving us a try.

I left her sleeping a few minutes ago to shower and clear my head before presenting my case to her once again. Turning off the water, I grab a towel and dry off, practicing my speech in my mind. Quietly, I brush my teeth, then call room service and order breakfast from the phone next to the tub. I slip on a plain white tee and a pair of shorts and reach for the door.

My stomach is in more knots than it was the day my parents left me in my dorm room at the University of Oregon. A small fish in a big pond and way out of my depth. This morning, this small-town boy, who knows he's not good enough for the big city woman on the other side of the door but knows his life won't be the same without her in it, will shoot his shot.

When I open the door, I don't see her in the bed. I saunter through the bedroom, hoping to find her in the kitchen wearing nothing but my T-shirt. But the villa is eerily quiet, and when I enter the living space, it's empty. As is the kitchen.

My heart sinks with a thud and I feel sick.

She's gone.

For a split second, I consider the possibility she just went to the hotel fitness center to get the nasty green juice she loves so much. But I know better. I go back into the bedroom, searching for any evidence I hadn't dreamed the encounter up. Her clothes and bag are gone.

I search the room from top to bottom for a note or any clues about her identity and come up empty.

The best weekend of my life. Certainly, the most intimate and by far the most vulnerable, and she couldn't even say goodbye.

Leave a note.

Or her fucking name.

Chapter Five

Charlotte

Two years, four months, and twelve days later.

There's something about the smell of freshly cut lumber. The faint hint of oil and earth settles me as I push my cart up and down the aisles, and I'm overtaken with beautiful memories of time spent with my dad. Most women prefer flowers but give me the nostalgic scents of a hardware store, and this woman is in heaven.

I'm staying at my client's lake house on an open-ended vacation. The house is perfect, but it doesn't exactly come stocked with the supplies to build the picnic table Knox is most definitely missing from his backyard. This means I *get* to buy all the tools and materials needed for my vacation project.

Sure, I love shopping for shoes, and I have an endless supply of face creams and hair products, but I'm just as happy shopping for lumber and power tools.

Knox, the lead singer of the Hollow Knocks, one of the biggest rock bands in the world and my number-one client, really undersold what he was offering when he said he had a little cabin next to a lake in Central Oregon. He made it sound like a shack, but it's absolutely perfect. A secluded wooden paradise right on the water, and the alarm system is next level. I haven't felt this safe in years. It's just what I need. But because I unfortunately have to work while I'm here, and the view of the lake from the back of the house is too breathtaking not to enjoy as much as humanly possible during my stay, I need a table for the backyard.

I could buy one, but none of the tables for sale at the town's small furniture store would complement the cabin. I'll just have to build him one. It'll be my gift since he refuses to let me pay him for my stay, insisting the place would sit empty if I wasn't there.

McKinnon's Hardware is far more impressive than the furniture store. I've been smiling since I pulled into the parking lot. My cart is full of screw bits, a power drill, several different saws, a tape measure, a wrench, a sander, wood glue, stain, and much more.

Now... the most important piece of the puzzle.

Wood.

Songs from my childhood have been playing in my head since I got here. Memories of me and my dad working on projects playing like home videos in my mind. Bouncing along to the soundtrack in my heart, I push my overflowing cart out the side door to the parking lot and the heat of the day, I turn left and follow the earthy smell of lumber to the rows and rows of wood planks stacked in the attached lumberyard. Taking it all in, I search for an employee, finding a bell on the wall above a sign that says *Press Here for Assistance* next to swinging doors marked *Employees Only.*

Without hesitation, I ring the bell with three quick little presses to the button that sounds more like a buzzer. While I wait, I wander around the stacks, taking my time and enjoying the easy breeziness of my day. I haven't felt this relaxed in far too long.

Come to think of it, when was the last time I felt this calm? Not worrying about my high-profile clients and the dozens of employees now my responsibility is more freeing than I expected.

If I'm honest, I can't remember the last time I felt like me. Today, I feel a bit of myself that I had lost somewhere along the way, popping her head out for a visit.

"Hello?" A deep, irritated voice interrupts my thoughts. "Did someone out here ring the bell, or are you just messing with me again, Loten?"

Moving my thoughts of inner peace aside for a moment I turn, heading back toward the bell as I yell, "Yes. Sorry. I wandered off."

Rounding a fifteen-foot stack of Douglas fir, I'm surprised to see nobody standing in front of the service bell.

"Hello?"

"Where'd you go?" he asks, his voice coming from some-where behind me.

"I'm back by the buzzer."

"You mean the bell?" His voice sounds closer.

"I guess so. Looks like a bell, sounds like a buzzer."

I plant my feet in front of the swinging double doors, so I don't get lost again but then I hear paws behind me. When I turn around, the cutest blue pit bull with a light pink collar wags her tail, watching me.

Reaching my hand out so she can sniff me and decide if I'm worthy of her time, she nudges my hand with her head, giving me the all clear to pet her. I squat and scratch behind her ears before sliding my hand down her back, watching her tail wag in delight. Wood and dogs, can this day get any better?

Boots shuffle against the pavement letting me know my new four-legged friend and I have company. I give the dog one last scratch before glancing up into the face of a man I never thought I'd see again, but have dreamed of the day I would.

The record scratches, and my entire world flips upside down.

Flashes of hotel bars, bed sheets, bubble baths, and hidden alcoves wreak havoc on my peace and slam me back into my turbulent reality.

Looking as shocked as I feel, he mutters, "It's you."

Chapter Six

Callen

It's her... the mystery woman who gave me the best weekend of my life before running out on me without a word. I would know that body anywhere. Skin littered with brown sugar freckles precisely placed by the heavens above, she's wearing cutoff shorts that reveal the long, toned legs I'd once had wrapped around me as she came apart in my arms. Her corn-silk locks are pulled back into a ponytail, reminding me of all the kisses I'd pressed against her exquisite neck.

She looks up at me and it feels like a kick to my ribs. Her eyes... dammit, they penetrate my soul. Can she see how often I've thought about her—how frequently I've dreamed about her—since she walked out of my life? I'd tried to find her, but without a name, I hadn't gotten far. Now, she's here like a mirage, crouched before me, scratching my dog's head.

Her hand stills and something akin to panic flashes in her piercing blue eyes.

"It's you," I blurt out before my mouth has a chance to catch up to my brain.

Her beauty smacks me upside the head as my heartbeat picks up pace and adrenaline shoots through my veins.

The excitement, however, is fleeting.

Her bright-blue eyes widen with shock and confusion. Perfect pink lips part as if to speak, only nothing comes out. She seems as dumbfounded as I am. If I had any hope she'd somehow figured out how to find me, it's shattered when she blinks her eyes shut and subtly shakes her head back and forth, as if hoping I'll magically be gone when she opens them again.

But when her eyes open... what do you know? That's right. I'm still here.

"Holy shit," she swears under her breath. "What a small world."

That's it? That's all she has to say about seeing me again? She clearly hadn't changed her mind about us. She didn't hire a detective to find me. She didn't care if she ever saw me again.

She drops her gaze back to my dog. "You must be Ruby."

"Why are you here?"

We both speak at the same time, but I don't miss that she remembered Ruby's name.

Where her statement is light and friendly, mine sounds heavy and bitter.

I'd always hoped to see her again, but knowing this reunion wasn't intentional brings the anger that's been building over the past two years right to the surface.

"This is your place, then?" Her attention is still locked on Ruby, and the traitor she is rolls onto her back, offering her belly in under five seconds.

I don't reply, but my heart stutters while my body heats at the memory of her breath on my ear, begging me to give her *more*. It feels like no time and a lifetime has passed all at once.

"It's been a while," she says, standing to face me.

I look at my watch to check the date. "Two years, four months, and twelve days."

Her eyes go wild with disbelief that I could have possibly remembered how long it's been with such precision. Doesn't she know she left her mark since she first spilled her drink on me? One I haven't been able to wipe away.

"What are you doing here?"

"Oh, um. I need to buy some lumber."

Not sure what I was hoping she would say, but did her answer have to feel like a punch to the gut?

"And why exactly are you buying lumber here, at my store?"

Her eyes narrow. "Well, I didn't know this was *your* store, but I'm pretty sure it's the *only* hardware store and lumber-yard in town. So here I am."

"And why exactly are you in *my* town?"

"Are you always this friendly with your customers?"

She's right. I'm being a dick. Because I'm still hurt, and knowing she isn't here for me and seeing her again is simply a coincidence really fucking sucks.

"What can I get you?" I grunt out. Fighting the animal-istic need to push her against the warehouse wall and kiss her until the crushing disappointment in my chest goes away.

She pulls a folded piece of paper out of her back pocket and shakes it open, but she doesn't need to look at it when she places her order like a pro.

"Pressure-treated cedar, Six 2 x 8 x 8's, six 2 x 6 x 8's, and three 2 x 4 x 8's."

I remember her love for building and take a stab at the project her lumber order might produce. "Table?"

"Yep."

"Why are you building a table in Goose Hollow?" It's none of my business, but I couldn't stop myself from asking anyway.

"I'll pay for everything inside, and if you can have someone bring the wood to the black SUV parked out front, that would be great."

And just like that, she turns and walks away from me.

Just like she did two years ago.

Only this time, she doesn't sneak away while I'm in the shower. This time, I get to watch her ass sway through my lumberyard with my dog following at her side. And as nice as her cutoffs fit, it doesn't feel any better this time.

I'd be lying if said her wood order didn't get me hard. Or that her confidence didn't still turn me on. As annoyed as I am that she didn't tell me why she was here, the knowledge she's in my town at least long enough to build a table excites the hell out of me. The mystery of her was always part of the attraction, whether or not I wanted to admit it to myself. The spark of hope I've never been able to smother flickers to a flame after our interaction.

Why I was such a raging jerk, I'm not sure.

Isn't this what I wanted?

Another chance with her?

Did I already blow it?

"Hey, boss," Loten, my right hand, interrupts my thoughts as he pushes through the doors leading out of the warehouse. "Livvy called back the lumber order for that tourist who's building a picnic table. I'll put it together and run it out to her."

"Okay, thanks. Appreciate it."

"Gotta love a woman who can build shit. Not most people's idea of a vacation, if you ask me. But she could build whatever she wanted if she were on vacation with me."

Loten worked here at the store with my dad for fifteen years before I took over. I know he's a good man—happily married with two grown kids—but I still don't like to hear him talking about her. Especially like that.

"Actually, I got this one," I yell after Loten, who is already on his way to fill her order.

I don't remember the last time I saw him move this fast.

I find him in front of the stacks of cedar, grinning from ear to ear. "No can do, boss man."

"Excuse me?"

"She said the tip would be extremely generous if anybody, but you brought it to her car. Seems you made a great first impression." He doesn't even try to wipe the smile from his face. "I usually hate when you get in one of your snits, but today... I thank you, sir," he says with a bow.

Any part of me that had just been heated and hopeful runs cold. Knowing that even here, in my hometown, at my place of business, she still thinks she gets to make all the decisions fuels my anger even more.

The only thing that matters to her is what she wants. Everyone else be damned.

Well, not this time.

Seeing red, I storm toward the parking lot, ready to tell her exactly this, when I'm stopped dead in my tracks.

A hundred feet away stands the one who walked away and the most important person in my life.

My mother.

Well, my mother and Petey, her cavapoo. *She's* holding the dog in her arms while dodging his kisses. She laughs and nuzzles into the back-stabbing canine. All the while, Ruby sits at her feet as though she is her person.

What the actual fuck?

Chapter Seven

Charlotte

If it were possible for a town to woo a person, I would say Goose Hollow was courting the hell out of me. This town has some big dick energy, and so far, the goods to back it up.

I've seen a Hallmark Christmas movie or twenty and assumed that's what I was getting when first arrived and caught sight of the historical downtown with its old-fashioned streetlights and family businesses. But this isn't the world of fiction, and it's not Christmastime. It's summer, and Goose Hollow wouldn't get a G-rating. The residents swear, occasionally stumble out of one of the local bars, and make out in public. There's no waiting for the kiss in the last scenes as the credits roll here, which makes this small town perfect, if you ask me.

In LA, the people you can call *locals* are few and far

between. And their personalities... well, let's just say they aren't as authentic as Loten at the hardware store who just had his appendix removed or Cheryl who told me all about her grandson's birthday as she rang me up at her floral shop. These Oregonians are kind and welcoming, and willing to share their life stories with anyone who will listen. They're curious about the new girl in town, but after my not-so-nice run-in at the lumberyard, I'm keeping my secrets and who I am to myself.

He doesn't know my name or where I'm staying, and as happy as I was in that first split second when I saw his beautiful brown eyes and the new beard covering his handsome face, his reaction left me feeling cold and depressed. After wondering what might have been for so long, his gruff displeasure at seeing me sent me into a bit of a spiral. But he is only one person, and everyone else I have come across has been nothing but kind.

As if the people weren't enough, the landscape is out of this world. With sweeping views of snowcapped mountains sparkling under the bright blue summer sun.

But my lake... oh, my lake. Surrounded by ponderosa pines and Douglas firs that cradle the setting sun every night as it makes its final descent, the sight is breathtakingly beautiful. After the sky put on a show for me on my first night, I've gone outside and taken it in every evening since.

Throw in the dreamy coffee and the orgasmic huckleberry ice cream, and I'm in love with the town.

Like I said, Big. Dick. Energy.

Today is day five of my break from reality and day three of waiting in line for the best soft serve ice cream I've ever tasted. I'm not sure what makes it so special, but I keep coming back for more. I've been here less than a week, and I already have an unhealthy addiction to the stuff.

It's only noon and already eighty degrees. Yes, it's hot back home in Southern California, but I work so much I don't get out to enjoy the weather nearly enough. I've made sure to spend as much time outside as possible while I'm here, and it's paying off in quite nicely. It's amazing what some sunshine and a view can do for a person's soul.

The park is full of kids on summer break, and the line to get my daily sugar fix was only five people deep when I arrived. It's finally my turn to order.

"Well, hello. Seems we've got a fan on our hands," comments the teenage boy with a sandy-blond mullet working the counter of the small stand called The Shed.

The Shed is bigger than a stand but smaller than a food truck. To be honest, I wouldn't care if they were selling the stuff out of the trunk of their car. I would still be here.

"I can't get enough. What do you put in the stuff?" I ask, leaning in closer. "I promise I won't tell."

He chuckles under his breath. "Sorry, ma'am. I've made a solemn vow. What happens in The Shed stays in The Shed."

"Well, whatever it is, I'll take a huckleberry cone, medium please," I say with a smile, pretending I didn't hear him call me ma'am. How old do I look? I'm only thirty-two, but I guess when I was a pimply teenager, that seemed old to me too.

He calls my order back, and by the time I've tapped my card on the payment screen and slid it back into my pocket, my new addiction is ready and waiting for me.

"Here you go—"

"Thanks!" I interrupt him before he can call me ma'am

again and make my way to the walking path encircling the park, setting a leisurely pace as I take my first lick of perfection.

Damn, that's good.

I've just turned the cone in my hand, ready to take a swipe at the other side, you know, to keep things balanced, when everything moves in slow motion. A blur of silvery gray fur appears out of nowhere and zooms around my legs, scaring the crap out of me. I jump and my cone falls to the ground. At the same moment, the smiling pup sits in front of me, tail wagging and looking like the best girl ever. I immediately recognize sweet Ruby, my friend from the hardware store.

"Sweetie, it's good to see you too, but you owe me an ice cream."

I bend down to her level and scratch her behind the ears. She's wearing a collar, but no leash. Did she get loose? The store isn't far from here.

She starts to lick up the ice cream splattered on the path. "No, no," I say, and she looks up at me with her big, beautiful eyes. "I don't know if your daddy wants you eating that."

Being the angel she is, she sits and keeps her eyes on me.

"Where is your daddy? Does he know you're out here scaring people out of their ice cream?"

"He's right here," a deep voice says from behind me. A voice that still sends a shiver of electricity down my spine when I hear it.

I've been wondering when I would see him again and if our next exchange would be more pleasant. I didn't recognize the cold man in front of me. His walls were up the moment he saw me, making it more than clear he wasn't happy to see me, and he made it crystal clear he didn't appreciate me taking up space in his town.

He was kind of a dick.

Actually, there is no kind of about it. He was a dick.

However, as he approaches me in his red McKinnon Hardware T-shirt, faded jeans, and sexy-as-hell work boots, I almost forget about our last interaction because, man, is he still as hot as ever. The addition of his full but well-kept beard adds to the manly package that is all him.

"Oh, good. Glad you found her. Looks like she got loose."

Just be pleasant. Maybe he was having a bad day, and his icy demeanor wasn't because of me.

"Sorry about your ice cream." He squints against the sunshine in his eyes. "We were on our usual lunchtime walk and she must have seen you and...." He trails off, shaking his head. "I guess you made an impression."

"Aw, that's nice. But where's her leash?"

"Hanging on a hook at home."

He crosses his arms over his chest, widening his stance, staring at me.

His demeanor pisses me off. Where is the man who shined a ray of light into my life when I needed it the most?

"What do you mean? You don't leash her? She could take off and scare a kid or get hit by a car. Or get lost. What if she wandered off into the forest?" I don't mean to sound so shrill, but there are coyotes in the area. I've heard rumors of cougars and bears, too.

"You underestimate her. This is her town. She couldn't get lost if she tried, and everyone in Goose Hollow knows her. You're the one who seems to be lost."

What the hell?

"Excuse me?"

"Why are you here?"

My instinct is to tell him. Tell him everything I was going through when I last met him and everything I'm going through right now, but this man is a stranger. And he's staring down at me like I owe him an explanation.

"Well, the plan was to have some ice cream, but your poor parenting ruined that."

He chuckles, but no smile accompanies the sound. "It wasn't me. It was all you. Something about you clearly makes people and, apparently, dogs act out of character."

Was that a compliment or an insult? His words are measured, and I can't read him.

I stand and Ruby turns her attention to my ruined ice cream. "What does that mean?"

"Nothing, forget I said it." He pulls his wallet out of his back pocket and tries to hand me a twenty. "Here, for your trouble."

"Thanks, but I don't need your money."

When I make no move to accept it, he slides the bill back where it came from as Ruby cleans up my ice cream. I guess it was okay for her to eat it after all.

"That's right. You don't need anything from anyone, do you?" He crosses his arms again. "You prefer to always have the upper hand. Silly me, how could I forget?" His weight shifts back and forth before settling. "So, what is it you want this time?"

His hurt is palpable, and guilt sits heavy in my belly. Deep down, the man I fell for so quickly is still there, but his walls are up. He doesn't trust I won't hurt him again. Or maybe because he doesn't know why I'm here, he thinks I must have malicious intentions.

"Chip, let me—"

"Don't you dare!" he growls low so only I can hear him, stopping me from using the nickname I gave him that weekend.

"I'm sorry if I—"

"No. We are not having this discussion. Not here and not now." He motions to the public area we're in. "Just tell me what you're doing here."

"So, no conversations about what I want to talk about, but we can talk about your topic of choice. That doesn't seem real fair now, does it?"

"Since when do you know the meaning of fair?"

Ruby moves to my side, ducking her head under my hand, looking for some love. It's like she knows how badly her daddy's words hurt my heart and she's trying to make me feel better playing the mediator. Welcoming her distraction, I move my attention to her. Stroking her head calms my racing heart enough to speak.

"Hey, sweet girl. I'm so sorry your daddy is such a stubborn butthead who doesn't give second chances." Daring to lift my eyes back up to his serious expression, I take my shot. "I sure hope he treats you better if you make a mistake you wish you could take back. Because sometimes doing something the right way hurts too much, and after something so perfect, you don't want to ruin it when you have to say goodbye."

His furrowed brow relaxes, and a flash of something shifts behind his eyes before his walls are back up. Thankfully, my sunglasses shade my stinging eyes. He doesn't need to see them filling with tears, like they are. I've already shown more than I should have, and he has a way of seeing all the way to the depths of my soul when he looks at me.

My heartbeat thunders in my chest as I wait for his reply to my confession. But he doesn't say a word. He continues to stare at me, arms still crossed over his chest. Not giving an inch. Punishing me for my past actions.

His stare is too much. It hurts because his chocolate eyes that once looked at me with lust and passion now hold no emotion at all. It would be easier to take if they held the slightest hint of disdain or even anger. The nothingness sours my stomach, and for self-preservation I need to remove myself from the situation.

"Well, you two have a nice day. See you around." I thank the heavens my voice stays strong and doesn't give away the anxiety I'm drowning in.

I don't bother getting in line for another ice cream cone, and I don't look over my shoulder to see if he's watching me. Instead, I walk a couple of blocks to my rental car and drive back to my little cabin in the woods where I'm safe from handsome men and adorable dogs who make me forget I made the right decision when I refused to tell him my name.

I'd felt the chemistry between us, just like he did, but it wasn't the right time for us. Not then.

He would agree with me if he only knew.

Chapter Eight

Charlotte

Enjoying my morning, I sit at the short diner-style bar in the section of Christie's Kitchen known as Cronies Corner. It's where all the locals sit and drink their coffee out of mugs with their names on them. The mugs are kept on a shelf on the other side of the counter. The first time I came to this boutique restaurant, only one seat was taken here at the bar, and since I was on my own, I figured I wouldn't take a table and made myself at home. I've lucked out and had an open spot at the counter every visit.

The restaurant's namesake is in the kitchen, working at a breakneck pace as she makes some of the best food I have ever had the pleasure of eating. I would consider this a brunch spot, but Christie hates the trendiness of *brunch* and insists she serves only breakfast and lunch.

My first time here, I watched a middle-aged woman pick

up her plate and lick it. That's right, a grown-ass woman licked her plate clean and then turned to her husband and said, "That just happened." That's how good Christie's cooking is. And don't get me started on her baking. Her pies are out of this world.

"Hey there, need a refill or anything else while I'm here?" Tina asks as she swings by to pick up an order. She's a single mom to two beautiful little girls. I've already seen pictures of Tina's girls. As well as today's hostess, Nicole's son and daughter and Christie's son, Jason. I fell in love with these women the moment I met them.

"I couldn't be better. Don't you worry about me."

She smiles and hustles on her way. The restaurant is an older two-story house Christie and her husband Gary converted into a restaurant. It's quaint but busy, and the employees here work their booties off, going up and down those stairs all day.

This restaurant was another must on Knox's list of local spots I needed to visit while I was here. And it's perfect since I'm avoiding any possible hostile hottie encounters by driving to Redmond, where I am now. Sometimes I even go to the bigger resort town of Bend to escape.

Whenever I do stick around Goose Hollow, I find myself looking for *him* wherever I go. I mean, it is *his* town, after all, and not a very big town on top of that. I'm not entirely sure what I'd do if I saw him. As much as I dread the possibility, disappointment sits heavy in my belly every day that I don't see his handsome face.

The cabin is still my fortress. I feel calmer and more relaxed than ever when I'm there. There's something about the winding, tree-lined road leading to the house and the fact that the only neighbors within view are on the other side of the lake. And that's just the part of the lake I can see. The lake goes on and on. One day, I need to explore just how big Goose Hollow Lake is. I've never felt this disconnected, in a good way, in LA.

Disconnected as I may be, it doesn't mean my mind hasn't wandered to *him*, our weekend, and how good his perfectly trimmed beard looked on him. I've distracted myself with building and staining the picnic table that I happily use as my desk in the backyard. I've taken lake swims in the scorching afternoons and read books in the hammock that I hung between two pine trees overlooking the water.

At night, after the sun sets, I have a glass of wine and watch terrible reality TV. The wireless connection is surprisingly great. I guess when you're Knox McKinnon, you don't have a problem getting great Wi-Fi, even if you live in the middle of a forest.

Unfortunately, there aren't enough picnic tables, books, or reality TV shows to rid myself of all the varying emotions I've felt since seeing *him* the first day I got here and then again at the park. A big part of me wants to seek him out. To see if the hot flashes of passion I haven't felt since that weekend still burn.

Who am I kidding?

I've never experienced chemistry like that with anyone else.

Never.

Our time together was incredibly intense and intimate, but also so natural. Easy. As strong as my yearning may be, I know I can't go there again. I may have been able to walk away once, but I'm not sure I could do it a second time.

Maybe it's a good thing he doesn't seem to be a second chances kind of guy. God, pissed off sex with him would be amazing, but probably not fair to my heart.

So, because I'm a coward, I drive twenty minutes out of my way to grab a bite to eat or do my shopping. Today, I'm hiding here in this restaurant that's beginning to feel like *my* place, eating a late breakfast before I hit up some antique shops in town. I'm not usually one for antiques, but Knox's place needs a little something. It's evident he spends too much time on the road because it lacks decor even though it's a fully furnished cabin. I hope to find hidden gems to add some life to my temporary home away from home.

Leaning back in my chair after finishing the best eggs Benedict I've ever had, a zap of energy tickles the back of my neck, and the atmosphere changes. In a split second, my energy transforms from relaxed and satisfied to *what the hell?*

When the seat next to me fills with a body I would know blindfolded even though I haven't seen it naked in years, the temperature dials up. I grab the menu to the left of me and start fanning myself.

"The usual?" Tina asks, reaching for the shelf of mugs.

"Yes, but to go, please."

"Sure thing. Where are you headed?"

He clears his throat before answering, and a couple of beats go by before he answers. "Headed down to Howard's place for a meeting in a couple of minutes."

"Everything okay—?"

"Just business stuff."

I would say he's trying to keep his personal life out of earshot because of my presence, but he hasn't so much as glanced in my direction. I would also say he didn't know I was sitting next to him if it weren't for all the other empty stools he could have chosen. Yet here I am, a hot mess because of his proximity. His broad shoulders have invaded my space, and even though there's a couple of inches between us he's close enough to set me on fire.

An inexplicable pulse of energy runs between us.

I feel it every time I'm near him, but today, it's making the little hairs on the back of my neck stand up.

Tina slides him his to-go cup, and he puts down a ten-dollar bill. "Keep the change. Christie looks busy. Let her know I said, hey."

"Will do. Have a good one."

She walks away and leaves the two of us alone at the counter. The silence is heavy. Not awkward. Just... heavy.

It feels like he's about to push up from his seat, but before he does, he turns his attention to me. I can feel his eyes burning into the side of my face. Unable to avoid the pull of him, I turn my seat so I'm facing him.

Big. Mistake.

With my chair turned this way, my knees rest against his strong thigh, and I have to tilt my head upward ever so slightly to look at him. His chocolate eyes—still the most complex I've ever seen—hold a storm of emotions. Searing into me as though he isn't sure if he wants to scream in my face or kiss me.

As our prolonged stare continues, my traitorous eyes can't help the quick glance they steal at his perfect lips. His mouth and how I know it can make me feel is something out of a dream.

And dream about his mouth, I have.

Daydreams sitting at my desk at work.

Driving in my car.

At night when I sleep.

And especially on nights I can't sleep. Those nights when I try to alleviate my insomnia with the help of my vibrator.

It's a mouth worthy of dreaming about. Only now, it's surrounded by a short beard with hints of red and even fewer hints of silver. I can't help but imagine what his beard would feel like against my inner thigh.

God, I wish he would take control like he did before.

What I wouldn't give to go back in time.

The moment my gaze leaves his mouth to meet his stare once again, I'm met with pure fire.

Only it's the wrong kind of fire.

He's pissed.

Could he still be this mad because I left without a proper goodbye?

And if so, that would mean I was right. He was different; no, scratch that, he was more than any man I have ever met. So much more.

Is that what's really put the fire in his eyes? His hate for me?

I mean, he couldn't be upset about the shirt I stole, could he? He joked it was one of his favorites, but I really didn't think he'd notice when I snuck it into my bag before I left.

He inhales slowly, exhaling as he looks away from me. My knees continue to touch his leg while my palms press against my thighs, and I force myself not to reach out to him. He looks down at the counter, and his chest lifts. His beautiful lips part as if he's about to speak, but to my intense disappointment, he stands and walks out the door without looking back.

A moment like the one we just shared is exactly why I snuck out of that hotel room. The anger aimed at me seconds ago is what I was trying to avoid when I behaved like a coward and fled our weekend of yes, sexual bliss, but it was much more than that. I found an emotional compatibility with him. It felt like I had stumbled upon something rare. I had never felt that kind of passion or shared my feelings about life with such honesty, and I had certainly never laughed so hard.

It's amazing what you can learn about a stranger with a simple game of Never Have I Ever when you both answer with complete and utter honesty without the worry of judgment, no matter the answer. When you know you'll never see a person again, it's much easier to be your true self.

At least for me it was.

What happened in that hotel suite was unique to the magic that ran between the two of us, and I knew I would never find it again.

Never.

And I still broke my promise to him and left without exchanging names. Granted, I gave that promise while in the throes of an orgasm.

He played dirty, and I lied.

What would his answer be today if we played Never Have I Ever?

Would our weekend still be his only one-night, well, one-weekend stand?

Have there been others?

The thought of him with other women threatens to ruin my breakfast, so I push it out of my mind. Instead, I focus on over-analyzing every second of what just happened.

He looks at me as though he can't stand the sight of me, yet he chose the stool next to me rather than putting space between us. More disturbing is that my body was so desperate for his attention that even his detest for me turned me on.

His eyes on me. That seems to be all it takes, and I'm wet and throbbing. Even though he did nothing to indicate he still wanted me.

Leaving money on the counter, I leave without saying goodbye to Tina. Playing the moment over and over in my head, I get in my rental and drive back to the cabin on autopilot.

Chapter Nine

Callen

What the fuck was that, McKinnon?

I've done my best to avoid her, but no matter how damn hard I try, she's every-fuck-ing-where.

First, she shows up at my store and cuddles up not to just *my* dog but also my mom and her dog.

Next, she infiltrates *my* ice cream stand and my traitorous dog's heart. Ruby never takes off. I can't remember the last time she left my side without permission. Not only did she misbehave, but she also forced me to interact with *her*.

To speak with *her*, dressed in her painted-on black yoga pants and equally body-hugging hot-pink workout tank. It's too much.

She's too much.

It's strange enough to see her out of Los Angeles and the

hotel where we created our own little bubble where the outside world didn't exist. But to find her in my neighborhood park, looking like sex on a stick is too. Damn. Much.

I've avoided the grocery store, Gracie's Café, and all my usual haunts. Preferring to stick to home and work, except for the mornings when I head to the ranch and work in the barn before going to the store. I haven't even ventured out to my brother's bar or been in touch with anyone in my family for fear they'll mention the new girl in town.

If she's in a relationship, I sure as shit don't want to see her in town with him.

So, it's the barn for me. That's where I clear my head.

I've gone out to the family ranch every day for the past week. There I've had no problem working up a sweat, but I'll be damned if I've worked out how to get her out of my head. Or why I even want to get her out of my head.

Shoveling shit, feeding and grooming the horses, and the quiet that comes with it usually does the trick. It settles me when nothing else does, but she has me rattled in a way that not even manual labor can relax.

My anger at her appearance is far from how I thought I would react if I ever saw her again. I had thought I was over her but seeing her brings all my anger and even hope back to the surface.

A reminder that I wasn't worth taking a chance on.

That I was disposable.

When she showed up at the store, I thought she had answered all my prayers. She'd found me. Oh, how wrong I was. Watching the shock, then fear flood her features was a punch to the gut. But the casualness with which she proceeded was too much to take.

Realizing she wasn't as happy to see me as I was to see her fucking hurt. I refuse to go through the bullshit she pulled last time.

But now I can't even go to my favorite restaurant in a neighboring town without running into her. And as much as it pisses me off, I am fucking drawn to her.

There are only two blocks between the restaurant and Howard's office. Two blocks to get my shit together. But how can I when I can still feel where her legs pressed against my thigh, and I can still see the eight perfect freckles sprinkled across the bridge of her nose.

She has this way of infiltrating every one of my senses and every thought in my head. I may have done a lousy job hiding her effect on me, but this morning, it was clear we were both still attracted to each other. Neither of us can deny there's something that runs between us.

Only this time, she didn't get to take control. I have no clue how long she's here or if I'll see her again, but if I do... she doesn't get to make the rules, and she doesn't get to have the upper hand.

She's on my turf and won't be bulldozing me or my heart this time.

Chapter Ten

Charlotte

Well, I made it a week.

One week of hiding out in my cabin and the resort towns surrounding Goose Hollow. Attending virtual meetings with the staff back home and the few clients I'm still handling on my own. All it took was one wordless encounter to get me all hot and bothered and desperate to run into him again. I could have gone to his store, but that would seem too obvious. Too desperate.

It's taken every bit of willpower in me not to find a million different reasons to return to McKinnon Hardware.

So here I sit—after changing my clothes at least ten times before leaving the cabin—in his brother's bar, talking to several locals as I hide in plain sight. I might as well run through town naked, screaming his name. But rather than get arrested for indecent exposure, I've opted to take the legal route. And I'm so glad I did because whether or not I bump into him, I'm still at one of the coolest bars I've ever been to, and I've been to a lot. When your clients are musicians and the Hollywood elite, you have a lot of unconventional meetings, many of which take place in bars, pubs, and taverns. Whatever you want to call the establishment, I've been to my fair share.

As cool as my surroundings may be, it's not enough to distract me from the information bouncing around in my head. It's only two words. Five simple syllables. His name.

Callen.

McKinnon.

Being the new person in town draws attention. And when I arrived tonight, it was only a few seconds before Angus McKinnon introduced himself and welcomed me to his establishment. The moment he said his name, the puzzle pieces of my world began to fit together. We started chatting and I figured out it was his mother I met in front of his family's store. It was then he mentioned his brother.

Callen.

At the sound of his name, my breath faltered, but I didn't let it slip that I knew his brother. I just let him keep talking.

Of course! How did I not put it together before this? I knew Knox had two brothers. One owned this bar, and one ran the family store.

That afternoon in LA we were both stood up by the same person.

Knox McKinnon.

His brother. My client. What a small freaking world.

Walking away before I knew his name was hard, but

now... the impact of simply knowing his name only reinforces why I had previously insisted we not share the information.

Having a name to go with his hard body and ruggedly perfect face makes the man I had almost convinced myself was fictional... very real.

Of course, I knew he was real, but with so much time between us, it was easy to think I had imagined the depth of his sex appeal. Dark rust-colored hair, long on top, but not too long, nearly straight nose, thick lashes that highlight eyes the color of strong coffee. I'd traced his jawline with my finger while he slept, admired a torso so perfect it looked carved by Michelangelo. There is nothing about him I didn't memorize that weekend.

Our close encounter this morning reminded me why I think of him every time I smell leather. Yet now there's a hint of citrus in his scent that wasn't there before. He smelled rugged yet refined, which is also how I would describe him as a man. He's tall and strong, outdoorsy and intelligent. Add his beard into the equation, and he is irresistible.

But now that I know his name, psychologically, everything has changed.

Callen McKinnon. The brother of one of my biggest clients. Knox McKinnon. The same man who not only stood *me* up that Friday in February but also left his brother sitting alone at Bar 1200 that same afternoon.

If only I had known. I might have thanked Knox for the best weekend of my life.

But then again, if I *had* known he was my client's brother, would I have had that second drink with him? Would our weekend have ever happened?

Would Callen have done anything differently had he known?

Regardless of what-ifs, our magical weekend happened, and we can't reverse time. Nor would I want to.

The real question is, what now?

What happens now that I do know who he is?

Do we carry on with silence and looks that could kill?

What had he been about to say before he walked out of the restaurant?

What does he want from me?

More importantly, what do I want from him?

He's Knox's brother. This could really screw up my relationship with one of my biggest clients.

Do I want a second chance with Callen?

Just thinking about it and my heart skips a beat and my stomach flips with giddy excitement. Of course, I do. I would be crazy not to.

But I don't want Callen. I want Chip, the sweet, sexy man who made me laugh until my cheeks hurt and held me in the bathtub. Not this cold, callous version of him.

But what I want doesn't really matter if he doesn't feel the same. Before our odd interaction at the restaurant, I would have said he had no interest in me. But then this morning happened. I know I shouldn't get my hopes up, but his intensity tells me he must feel something.

Right?

What if he's in a relationship?

Could that be the reason he's been giving me the cold shoulder?

Maybe I should just walk away again.

But there's a part of me that desperately wants to know

what might have been. Otherwise, I wouldn't be sitting here in his little brother's place of business, hoping he will magically appear.

According to Knox, one or both of his brothers is here on any given night.

And let's face it. It's a little less obvious than showing up at the store again.

The House is in an old fire station that Callen's brother, Angus, renovated and turned into the local hot spot. Knox listed The House as the number one place for me to seek out during my stay in Goose Hollow, and as soon as I walked in, I understood why. It's not what you expect in a small town, yet it's exactly what you would hope for.

Dark floors and ceilings paired with brick walls covered in massive framed black-and-white photos of old firehouses and fire trucks set the tone. The fireman pole is still in place, as are the two big truck bay doors currently rolled up, letting the evening summer breeze in. Booths line the walls, and tall tables—like the one I'm currently sitting at—are scattered throughout the room. The bar is huge, with a mirrored wall stretching at least twenty feet long and shelf after shelf of every price point and taste of alcohol a person could ask for.

The beer is ice cold, mozzarella sticks fried to perfection are already in my belly, and the three gentlemen hovering around my table are nothing if not entertaining, even if they are a bit overeager. Randy and Silas have both offered to get my next round, but I politely declined, not wanting to give the wrong impression. If there's a chance Callen might be here tonight, I need to have my wits about me.

"One more EBC for the lady," Angus, or Gus, as

everyone calls him, says, setting down a fresh beer, removing my old glass.

He's the youngest McKinnon brother and is shorter than his siblings, measuring an inch or two under six feet. His dark brown hair is buzzed to a barely there length, displaying a perfectly shaped head. He may not have the height of his brothers, but he is just as well-built, with arms covered in intricate tattoos. A black bar T-shirt snuggly hugs his muscled chest and broad shoulders while his jeans struggle to contain his thick thighs and impressive backside.

Yes, I looked.

He's hot.

But he's not Callen. "These idiots buggin' you?" asks the brother of the man I'm hoping to *coincidentally* run into.

"Not at all. They're being perfect gentlemen."

"Okay, well, you just say the word, and I'll get them out of your hair," he says, no humor in his tone. He's deadly serious.

"Come on, man. Why you gotta do us that way? We're just being friendly."

"David, your kind of *friendly* can come off as creepy. I'm just looking out for the lady. Knox gave specific orders to hover and make sure the local heathens leave his friend alone."

I'm a grown woman who doesn't need to be looked after, but I say nothing because he doesn't mean any harm, and it's sweet his brother asked him to look after me. Besides, when Knox McKinnon asks a favor, most people take the request seriously.

"And don't get me started on you two." He points between Randy and Silas, the two hot bull riders presently leaning on the table where I sit. "Did you tell her you're both in town for the rodeo over in Sisters and that you'll only be here through the weekend?" He wags his finger between the two cowboys who have been vying for my attention before leaning in and whispering, "No offense, but they're just here to hit and quit it, if you know what I mean?"

"No offense taken. I appreciate the heads-up," I say, with a smile in my voice as my mind strays to his brother. Is that what I did to Callen?

Did *I* hit it and quit it?

What would Angus say if he knew about my past with his brother? Bet he wouldn't be smiling at me like he is.

Angus heads back behind the bar and leaves me with two bull riders and an auto repair mechanic who hopefully are as harmless as they seem. Besides, I'm used to Hollywood hotshots and pop stars. Cowboys don't scare me.

"So, you two ride, huh?"

"Yes, ma'am. You ever been to a rodeo?" Randy asks, adjusting his cowboy hat as he stands to his full height instead of leaning against the table.

"Can't say that I have. Should I check yours out?"

"We ride on Friday and Saturday night. I can leave you a ticket at will-call if you're interested. And maybe take you out after?" Silas interjects, slowly making his way to my side of the table. He drapes one arm over my shoulders and tips the front of his hat down. I can't help but giggle.

"Well, the rodeo part sounds interesting, but I would be happy to buy my own ticket."

"At least promise me the first dance tonight?" he says, giving my shoulder a friendly squeeze.

"Dance? Where are we going to dance?" I laugh.

"Right where you're sitting. Eight o'clock on the dot, all these tables, including this one, will get moved out of the way, and easy peasy, lemon squeezy, you got yourself a dance floor."

"Really?"

"Yes, ma'am."

"Okay, sure. Why not?"

"Silas Cortland, remove yourself from that woman before I remove you myself," a deep brooding voice growls from behind me us.

Every inch of my body is on high alert because I'd know that voice anywhere. Hell, I've dreamed of it ordering me to come for years now.

Callen is here.

Obviously, I had hoped he would find me here, but hearing the possessiveness in his voice is unexpected. My gaze locks on the wall across the room while I give myself a moment to gather myself before facing him. I regret not wearing my hair up because the temperature in the bar has just skyrocketed with his arrival.

"Shit," the cowboy at my side says under his breath, holding his hands up as he steps away from me. "Sorry, Cal. Man, I... I didn't know she was your girl."

I open my mouth to correct him because I'm not anyone's girl, but Callen speaks first.

"Well, now you know. If I see the three of you within six feet of her again, you'll have me to deal with."

He's right behind me now, so close his breath tickles my bare shoulder. My entire body heats from the warmth of his nearness.

Oh, how he sets me on fire.

My panties instantly grow damp at the memory of the way I let him, no... needed him to take control in that hotel room. It takes all the discipline I can muster not to turn around and look at the man attached to the voice. The voice that would earn him a fortune if he took up a second job as a spicy audiobook narrator. Yes, I proudly read smutty romance. It's as close as I get to the real thing these days.

David, Randy, and Silas casually walk away, and I'm left alone with my beer and the looming presence behind me. Callen moves to my side, leaning on the table. I'm still looking straight ahead while his body faces me.

Standing close.

So. Damn. Close.

His stare burns into the side of my face, but he doesn't speak. Apparently, we're back to the same game he played this morning. Strategically, I dip my chin ever so slightly, letting my hair fall forward to shield me from his domineering stare.

This small action elicits a sigh from him, his breath moving wisps of my hair.

I take a sip of beer before finally breaking down and speaking first.

"I'm your girl?"

His silent treatment continues, and my anger bubbles to the surface. Who does he think he is? Not only am *not* his girl, but why the theatrics of scaring other men away if he's still going to act like he did this morning. I open my mouth to tell him as much, but he pushes my hair behind my ear, taking back his view of my face.

My body betrays me, melting at his touch, making me

even angrier. "What the hell do you think you're doing?" I say as I release my hair from behind my ear in defiance.

"Trust me, it's for the best."

His words are a low rumble meant only for me to hear. And trust me, I hear them. All the way to where he likely hopes I feel it, but it doesn't mean I'm not pissed. Especially when he pushes my hair behind my ear again. This time, he lets his hand linger, and his finger outlines the shell of my ear.

"Excuse me?" I shrug my shoulder up to my ear to push him away from me.

"No, excuse me." He drops his hand. "I didn't realize you wanted to spend your evening with two man-whores and a creeper."

I turn in my seat to face him, realizing my mistake the moment I lift my eyes to his. He's just as pissed as I am, and the heat between us is combustible. However, I refuse to let him get the best of me.

"Who I spend my time with is none of your business, thank you very much."

"Is that so?" He lifts a cocky eyebrow that makes me want to throat punch him. Or lick him like a lollipop. I'm so confused and frustrated, I don't know which way is up.

"Just because we had one exceptional weekend two years ago doesn't give you the right to say who I can or can't talk to."

He leans in, his lips brush against my ear when he hisses his next words. "That's right. How could I forget? You make all the rules. Everyone else be damned."

His unexpectedly honest reply feels like a slap to the face. A hot, angry blush spreads across my cheeks as he nonchalantly pushes away from the table. And because I can't help myself, I swivel on my stool and watch him walk away.

He only makes it two steps before spinning back around to face me.

"Glad you had a good time that weekend. But don't worry. I learned my lesson when it comes to you, and if you're looking for another exceptional weekend, plan to be incredibly disappointed because I won't make the same mistake again." He turns, takes another step away, and yells over his shoulder, "And you sure as hell won't find it with the numbnuts you were talking to when I walked in."

More than anything, I want to throw a smart-ass comment back in his direction, but I'm so flustered and upset nothing comes out. I have so many questions.

Why did he imply I was *his girl* when he's clearly not interested in rekindling what we once shared?

When did he become so arrogant?

Why does he seem to think he has a say in who I spend my time with? What I do and who I do it with is none of his business.

Why did it feel so good when he touched me?

And why did it hurt so badly when he said he had learned his lesson and wouldn't be making the same mistake again?

If he doesn't plan on making the same mistake again, then that must mean he isn't interested. And if he isn't interested, why is he making it a point to keep everyone else away from me? Is this his way of getting back at me?

The small flicker of hope that reignited this morning all but snuffs out, suffocated by the hollowness that's been following me around day after day. I should have stayed in my little cabin by the lake in my comfy sweats with my quart of chocolate peanut butter ice cream.

It's clear now how stupid this idea was.

The thing is, I've never been a quitter.

He doesn't realize I'm too stubborn to let his behavior send me fleeing. Unfortunately for me, my ice cream and sweatpants will have to wait. But I can't just sit here. Callen wasn't exactly quiet when he scared my new friends away, and people are watching me even more than they were when I was just the new girl in town. It's embarrassing. And I don't do embarrassed. I've got too much pride to feel this way.

Not knowing what else to do, I leave my table behind in search of the restroom. Angus is studying me from behind the bar while drying a pint glass. His raised eyebrow and tilted head says he witnessed our little interaction and is curious about my connection to his brother.

Me too, buddy. Me too.

My gaze involuntarily flickers to Callen's back. He's sitting at the bar with a man I don't recognize. The man says something, and Callen laughs.

The asshole is laughing. Sure, it sounds hollow, almost fake, but he is obviously handling this strange situation between us better than I am. For some reason, that stings and my eyes begin to burn.

Shit!

I frantically search for the restroom. When I can't find one, I look back to Angus, who's still watching me. He subtly tilts his head to my left, where I see the sign for the restrooms. I mouth a thank you. He nods, finally turning his back on me to fill a pint glass at the wall of taps.

My vision blurs with tears, but I blink them away, refusing to look back as I turn down a hall. I put one foot in front of the other until I'm secured behind the bathroom door and met with my reflection in the mirror. As always, my body refuses to keep my secrets, sharing my emotions like a flashing red neon sign all over my cherry red chest and face. As well as my one visible ear, the one he touched when he pushed my hair behind it.

Right before he scowled and walked away from me.

Who was that man? I think, as I pull my hair into a pony-tail using the hair tie I always keep on my wrist. Silly as it seems, the act of changing my hair feels like arming myself. After a couple of deep breaths and with my hair settled, I feel stronger. Ready to deal with whatever may come once I leave the confines of the bathroom.

The man I remember was kind and funny and, yes, he was assertive between the sheets, because I wanted him to be. Asked him to be. But this cold side of him hurts my heart. Is this who he really is, or has something about my presence provoked him?

Was our time together as life-altering for him as it had been for me? Yes, he'd wanted more than the forty-eight hours we had together, but I hadn't led him on. I was upfront we couldn't have more, because I knew the first night I had wanted it all.

Everything he had to offer.

Only my life wouldn't allow it.

At least that's what I told myself.

Before the first night was over, he said he knew it was more than a one-night stand. Of course, I felt it too. But I panicked. I offered him what I could at that moment to appease him, which was me. And promised to tell him my name at check-out.

In the end, my fear won out. I snuck out before the time came to keep my promise.

Flashes of our weekend vow, sealed with a handshake, invade my thoughts, and when I think of the sincerity in his eyes that night, I get why he has such disdain for me.

I didn't give us a chance.

But what he doesn't realize... is that I didn't just break his heart. I broke mine too.

Chapter Eleven

Callen

Owen talks about last night's shift, but I don't hear a word. He's a police officer in the neighboring resort town of Bend, and I usually find his stories entertaining. Tonight, I don't care about the transient who set fire to a field or the married couple he found making out in the back seat of a sedan in an elementary school parking lot. A married couple who, of course, weren't married to each other.

We've been best friends since we were toddlers. Our moms met at a horse show they both attended to support my mom's best friend, Joy. They hit it off, and his mom, Heather, a stay-at-home mom with two kids and a barn full of horses, has been like a second mom to me ever since.

Owen is family. He's also the only one who knows about *her*. Although, he walked in just as I was walking away from her table, he doesn't know *she's* here tonight. He knows she's in Goose Hollow, but has no idea she's in The House right now. He'll make the night miserable if he puts two and two together.

I don't have to look in her direction to know she's back in the room. I would feel her presence anywhere. Regardless, I steal a glance because she's impossible to ignore, try as I might. She's stopped in her tracks at the other end of the bar staring at the spot her table had been in when she left to hide in the bathroom.

My God, she is beautiful. Her light cropped jeans and her off-the-shoulder black top shows off not only her thin black bra strap but her bare skin. She's put her hair up and I'll be damned if seeing more of her exposed skin isn't a fucking turn on. When we had our moment over at her table, and my lips grazed her ear, I had to stop myself from leaning down to kiss her exposed shoulder as well. Instead, I kept up the asshole attitude I've had with her since she walked back into my life a little over a week ago.

Self-preservation and all that.

This woman, whose name I still don't know, crawled under my skin before my lips ever kissed hers, and she's been there ever since. I'm sure Angus introduced himself to her and likely knows her name, but I have no intention of asking him what it is. I've kept myself hidden at the ranch riding and shoveling shit or behind my office door at the store all week to avoid not only her, but the chance of hearing anyone else talk about her. When I get her name, I want to hear it come out of her mouth, not my brothers or anyone else's.

She may not have come to Goose Hollow looking for me, but this morning when her gaze moved to my mouth, and she bit her bottom lip, like she does when she's turned on, she gave herself away.

Like me, she had to be remembering how good we'd been together. Exceptional weekend, indeed.

And those damn sapphire eyes of hers said more than her words ever could.

My thoughts should be on my legal woes and saving the family business, but I can't get those goddamn gorgeous eyes out of my mind. When I caught those idiot friends of mine flirting with her, I'd nearly thrown her over my shoulder and carried her out the door.

She's mine. I know it doesn't make sense, we're barely speaking to each other, but she's fucking mine.

Sill watching her and anyone who comes within six feet of her, I notice when Tina, a family friend and server at Christie's Kitchen, sees her. She runs up to give her a hug. Relief washes over her face, likely grateful she knows somebody here besides me. A blond man trails Tina, and I watch her introduce him to *her*. My hackles rise. The three of them chat, and he says something that makes them laugh. When she does, her eyes flash in my direction, and her blush subtly returns.

Her gaze doesn't linger on me though, because Blondie says something to her. She nods her reply and accepts the hand he offers her.

Nope.

I don't give a damn that my barstool screeches across the floor before thudding to the ground when I stand to cross the bar and meet them at the dance floor. It's time I make it clear to everyone in Goose Hollow... she... is... not.... available.

Who knows? She may not actually be available to

anyone, including me, but I will not make it through the night if I have to watch her dance with other men. This is my brother's bar. *I'm* not going anywhere.

Her eyes widen when she sees me coming. Then fire ignites in her irises as her free hand clenches into a fist.

Is she gonna hit me?

Or does she want me to intervene?

Hell if I know. But I can't stand back and watch some asshole put his hands on her.

She's consumed my every thought today. Let's be honest, she's all I've thought about for the last week. I thought getting out of the house would be good for me. Have some beers, meet up with Owen and shoot the shit. All I needed was a couple of hours thinking and talking about anything but *her*. But the plan was a pipe dream.

Because she's here.

She's gorgeous.

And our chemistry is just as strong.

So why have I been such a dick?

I'm sure if you ask my friends and family, they'd say I've been a bit of a dick since I came home from LA, but my mood has darkened in these last six months. My life seems to be on a downward spiral and I'm taking it out on her. I've had enough heartbreak and anxiety. I'm not sure I would survive her luring me in, only to walk away again.

All I want is to cling to her like a life raft. Instead, I continue to push her away.

But tonight, seeing her with other men has been what I needed to shake some sense into me. The mere thought of anyone else touching her enrages me beyond rational sense. My need to protect her is overwhelming.

Because damn it, she's mine. I feel it in my bones.

So why am I treating her like she is anything but?

Blondie's just stepping onto the makeshift dance floor and is about to pull her into his arms when I grab her free hand. "I'll take it from here."

"Hey, what the hell—" he starts to argue with me, but I ignore him.

She doesn't fight me and releases his hand. Her eyes narrow, but I meet her glare head-on.

Without a word, I rest my hand on her bare shoulder blade. Her left hand slides to my shoulder while our opposite hands clasp. I take the lead and she follows but doesn't speak as we two-step around the floor.

After our first turn round the hardwoods, she hisses under her breath. "Who do you think you are?"

"I think you know exactly who I am."

"I thought I did."

"What does that mean?" I ask, even though I know precisely what she means.

She misses the fun, flirty man she met. She doesn't recognize this version of me. Neither do I. I'd give anything to be the carefree, lighthearted man I was when she met me, but he's buried somewhere deep down inside.

"You don't get to pick and choose who I do or don't talk to. Or dance with. I am not your property."

"Never said you were. Never would. But if you think you can come in here and dance with other men after... Well, it's not happening."

"Callen... I..."

Hearing her say my name sends a spike of adrenaline through my veins. My dick hardens, making it nearly impossible to focus on the anger that has me seeing red because she knows my name. Even though I still don't know hers.

"I see. You get to know my name, but I am not afforded the same luxury?"

I spin her out in front of me and then pull her back into my arms until her chest presses against mine. God, she's feels good. It's a mistake to have her this close. If I'm not careful, she'll feel how much I like having her in my arms.

"Did you know my name all along?" I ask. "Was this some kind of game to you?" What I really want to ask is if she knew where I was all this time, yet never tried to find me. But I don't.

"No." Her eyes search mine. "It was never a game. I didn't know your name until tonight."

Relief washes over me.

Still, I will not ask her for her name.

After all this time, she needs to volunteer the information. Freely.

We don't speak as the song ends and a country waltz begins. Taking her hand, I escort her to the center of the floor, pulling her against me once again. It's foolish to hold her like this, but I can't help myself. Her hands find their way to the tops of my shoulders and mine drop to her hips.

Our gazes meet and she studies me for a few seconds before asking, "Are you in a relationship?"

Her question surprises me, but I'm not mad about it. "No. You?"

She shakes her head as she bites her bottom lip. My hand moves to her lower back, pressing her flush with my body. Her breath caresses my neck when she asks, "Are you sleeping with anyone?"

What the fuck?

"I just told you I wasn't in a relationship. Contrary to our history and what we talked about back then, I am not a friends-with-benefits kind of man anymore."

Her reply is to wrap her arms around my back, hugging me to her as her cheek presses against my chest. Clearly, this was the answer she was hoping for, and I'm glad it was the only answer I had to give.

We stay like this until the song ends, and when it does, she releases me and lifts to her toes and whispers, "Charlotte. My name is Charlotte Carruthers. It's nice to meet you, Callen McKinnon."

Chapter Twelve

Charlotte

Leaving Callen on the dance floor with my name, I make a beeline for the bar.

I need a shot.

However, ordering a drink may not be that simple, judging by the way Angus is watching me with his arms crossed in front of his chest, just like his brother is known to do. His expression skeptical if not pissed.

Not letting his demeanor get the best of me, I place both palms on the edge of the bar leaning forward. "Tequila, stat."

He lifts a questioning eyebrow that also reminds me of his brother.

"Please?" I add, remembering my manners.

"So, you know Callen?"

"I do."

"And how do you know him?"

"Yes, that is the question of the night," the sandy-haired man who had been sitting with Callen earlier says as he slides up to my right side. His wide smile puts a pair of dimples on display. I have no doubt he gets a lot of feminine attention.

He's hot. But he's not Callen.

"He's just someone from my past."

"From your past?" Angus asks, even more skeptical. His brow furrowed.

"That's what I said. Now, how about that shot?"

His eyes narrow on me, but I don't miss the flicker of attention they shoot over my shoulder before he finally reaches for a shot glass.

The sandy-haired man leans in closer, extending his hand. "I'm Owen, Cal's friend."

I give his hand a firm shake. "Nice to meet you, Owen."

A flicker of movement in the mirror behind Angus catches my attention. Callen stands a couple of feet behind me. Our eyes meet in the mirror. His beard almost makes him look like a different person, but his eyes... I could never forget the storm clouds raging in those sexy, dark eyes. They've been haunting my dreams every night since seeing him at his store.

The shot glass slides across the bar. Without a moment of hesitation, I slam it back, gaining the liquid courage I need to get through the rest of what I have a feeling is going to be a long night.

"Two more," Callen orders, now standing directly behind me. If I were to turn around, I could bury my face in his chest.

If I wanted to.

But we need to have a serious conversation about the shitty way he's been treating me before I bury myself in him.

Angus doesn't question him like he did me. Instead, he silently pours two more shots and slides them directly in front of me.

Callen's chest presses against my back when he reaches around me to grab his shot glass. Our eyes connect in the mirror as he leans forward and whispers in my ear, "Bottoms up, *Charlotte*."

He holds his glass in the air in front of me, until I clink my shot to his. Then we slam them back at the same time. The back of my head bumps against his broad chest, and the heat rushing down my throat extends to the rest of my body.

He sets his glass on the bar, while I relish in the feel of his warmth against my back. The mix of his citrus and leather scent wreaks havoc on my senses. The anticipation of more lighting me on fire from the inside out.

"So, Cal," Owen says, slapping him on the back. "Who's your friend?"

"Owen, this is Charlotte. Charlotte, this is Owen, and he was just leaving."

Yes, please go away, Owen. Things are just getting good.

At least I hope they are.

"C'mon. Don't be like that. The night is young. The dance floor just got cookin', and I'm sure we'd *all* like to get to know Charlotte better. Wouldn't we?" he asks Angus, who gives a slow nod of agreement.

Callen's hands land on my shoulders. "Charlotte. How about we go somewhere and have a chat?" His tone is somewhat condescending, rubbing me the wrong way.

He's right. We need to talk. And I'd like a chance to clear the air, but I also need him to shove his icy demeanor up his very firm ass. I understand he's upset about the way things ended, but enough is enough.

However, he's still pissed, and I've got a buzz. I'm not sure now is the best time for a chat. The tequila has me feeling all warm inside. One more shot and it will only act as a truth serum.

"Isn't this somewhere?" I ask, using Angus and Owen's presence as a protective shield.

He leans more of his body weight against me, our eyes still connected in the mirror. I couldn't look away even if I wanted to.

"Somewhere private."

"Hey, big brother. You gonna introduce me to your friend, or you just gonna smother her to death?" a sweet feminine voice says from somewhere behind us.

He stiffens. "Fuck. Is there anyone who isn't here tonight?"

"Evening, Clover," Owen says to the beautiful woman standing on the other side of me. She sticks her tongue out at him, and he clearly loves her reaction because those dimples of his are back with the smile lighting up his face.

"Daisy," Callen corrects, pushing away from me. "This is Charlotte. Charlotte, this is my little sister, Daisy."

My heart lightens at his sister's name. She's just as adorable and petite as he had described her that weekend and Knox has described over the years. The sparkle in her light brown eyes says she's feisty, and I like her already.

"Daisy, it's nice to meet you. I've heard so much about you."

Her forehead wrinkles. "You have?"

"Yes, only good things, of course. Like how kick-ass you are at interior design."

"What the what? Why do you know so much about me when I've never heard of you?" She shoots a glare at Callen.

"Good question, sis," Angus chirps in from behind the bar. "Charlotte says she's someone from his past."

"His past?" Her eyes narrow further. "You've lived in Goose Hollow your whole life. We all know everyone in your past." Her expression turns thoughtful. "Wait a minute. College! Did you two go to college together?"

I open my mouth to correct Daisy's assumption and let her know most of what I know is from years of Knox bragging about her, but Callen speaks before I get a chance.

"How I know Charlotte is none of your business. Besides, we were just getting ready to leave."

Who does this man think he is? "Speak for yourself. I'm just getting started. Barkeep, another shot please. Daisy? Owen? Care to join me?"

"Yes, please!"

"You know it."

They reply in unison as Angus fills four shot glasses, and Daisy, Owen, Callen, and I toss them back, but I do my best to keep my attention on Daisy. Ignoring her brother is impossible, but I'll take her as a distraction while I sort through the multitude of feelings fighting for prominence inside me.

Where the McKinnon brothers are tall and broad chested, Daisy is only two or three inches over five feet and fit. With her shorter light brown hair that barely grazes her shoulders and big light brown, almost golden eyes she looks much sweeter than she is. Well, if Knox's stories are all true.

"So, tell me—"

"Nope. No storytelling tonight. Charlotte and I are catching up, so if anyone gets to ask questions, it'll be me," Callen interrupts his sister and takes my hand.

"Excuse me?" I ask, but don't pull my hand from his like I probably should.

"I think it's only fair that if you answer any questions tonight, they be mine." His dark eyes hold nothing back as they mirror the emotions bumping around in my chest.

He's right, but I'm not quite ready to tell any stories yet.

"Are all of you McKinnon brothers this bossy?" I wink at Angus.

He doesn't reply, simply studying me like he isn't sure what to think of me yet.

"Girl, you have no idea," Daisy commiserates.

Callen squeezes my hand. "Let's go."

That last shot is lowering my inhibitions, and Callen is pissing me off. The combination makes it impossible to hold my tongue. "Let me get this straight. You think you can tell me who I can or can't talk to or dance with, and now you get to decide who I have story time with?"

"You tell him, Charlotte!" Daisy encourages.

Pointing an accusing finger, I step toward the demanding man, but my brain does a little loop de loop, reminding me I had two beers before my shots. I grab onto the bar to steady myself.

"You okay?" he asks, concerned, gently grabbing my elbow.

I turn to Angus. "Check please."

Time to go. I should've known better. Stupid tequila.

Daisy's eyes are pleading when she leans closer. "Please don't leave me alone with my brothers. It's barely past eight!"

"Stay." Callen rests his hand gently on the small of my back. "But maybe no more shots?" He kisses me on top of the head.

I should argue with him. Tell him he doesn't have the right to tell me how many shots I should take. But that kiss! So gentle and full of sincerity and concern. Like the man from my past.

There's no way I can walk away tonight, but I'm not ready to *talk*.

"Okay, I'll stay."

"Yes!" Daisy exclaims, pumping her fist into the air.

"On one condition." I face the group.

"Oh, this is getting good," Owen says, rubbing his hands together in excitement.

"Of course," Callen grumbles beside me, but his hand is still on my back, his thumb rubbing circles on the bare skin he's found between my shirt and jeans.

"No story time about how Callen and I met." I turn so I can look him in the eyes. "No more scaring away people who are simply being nice to me."

"Sorry, I'm not able to make that promise. Because *I* don't break my promises."

There is no illusion of playfulness in his voice, and his possessiveness is sexy as hell. I may be staying, but I don't think I'll be dancing with anyone else tonight.

"Fine. But be nice."

"I'm always nice."

Daisy, Angus, Owen, and I all laugh.

"Whatever. Come on, let's throw some darts. Angus, get

Laurie to watch the bar for you. We need to show Charlotte how we do things around here." He tugs on my hand, and it's settled. I'm staying, and apparently, we're throwing darts. All while getting top of the head kisses and holding hands.

This should be interesting.

Chapter Thirteen

Charlotte

"Jenga!" Daisy and I scream over the music flowing into the outdoor area of the bar where there are firepits, two sets of corn hole, and a giant—you guessed it—Jenga game. Most importantly, there's Callen.

Tonight, he's back to behaving like the man I remember. His silent treatment is over, and while a multitude of questions linger in his eyes, all hostility is gone. Our banter has been teasing and playful, but also superficial. We'll have to talk at some point, but I plan to ride this wave of subtle touches and easygoing fun as long as I can.

Daisy throws her fist in the air. "Drink up, suckers!"

"Daisy, we saw your shoulder tap the tower when you leaned over to watch Angus pull his piece out," Callen yells over the music. "Nice try, sis."

I saunter closer to Callen. "What? You afraid I'm gonna get you drunk and take advantage of you or something?"

Between the heated looks he's been casting in my direction and the not-so-hidden touches he's taken every time he moves past me for his turn, he's far from trying to hide our attraction from his siblings. Of course, thanks to the liquid courage slowly fading from my system, I feel much more confident about how this thing between the two of us could go. Thus, my flirt game is picking up. Okay, I don't really have a flirt game, but I'm flirting to the best of my ability. And it's fun.

"Woman, do not threaten me with a good time." He smiles and he is absolutely beautiful.

"Why not?"

He chuckles, shaking his head. "You're lucky I'm a gentleman and respect you because if I had my way, I'd have taken you back to my place two hours ago."

Unable to resist his pull, I slide up to him, pressing one hand to the front of his shirt, unsure of whether to push him away or pull him closer. Fueled by need to touch him, my fingers trail up his shirt. "Oh yeah? And what would we do at your place?"

He traps my fingers, giving them a little squeeze until I meet his gaze. "Don't pretend you've forgotten the things I did to you in that hotel room. You know exactly what we'd do at my place."

"Is that a threat or a promise?"

"Oh, it's a promise, Charlotte."

Intertwining my fingers in his, I yell over the mess of fallen Jenga pieces and loud music. "Hey, Gus! Put all of this on Callen's tab. Something just came up." I wag my eyebrows at him to make sure he gets the pun, and his little brother smiles and shakes his head at me. Holy shit. I think I may be winning him over.

The bearded man promising me a good time tugs on my hand, stopping me before I can drag him out of the building. "You sure? Because I wasn't kidding."

Nodding, I look up at him from under my lashes. "I hope your place is close."

"What she said." He bends, grabbing me and throwing me over his shoulder as I let out a squeal. "I'll be by tomorrow to pay up."

"You brute!" I giggle as my hands take turns smacking him on the ass. "What are you doing?"

"Taking you home."

Home.

His home.

If I weren't hanging upside down right now, and laughing like a loon, the possibility might just scare me half to death, but I'm living in the moment.

And so far, living in the moment is paying off like it did before. I need to make spontaneity a regular thing. It's been a long time since I've felt this good.

As we hit the sidewalk in front of the bar, I hear Owen yell from the firepit where he's been cuddling up with a beautiful brunette. "Don't do anything I wouldn't do!"

Callen carries me to the end of the block, and after he makes a right down the next street, he sets me on my feet. Finally upright and catching my breath, my hair feels like an unruly mess. I try to fix it, but he pushes my hands aside and smooths the hairs that have fallen out of my ponytail away from my face, tucking them behind my ear.

"Charlotte, can I kiss you?"

"God, I wish you would."

His big hand cradles the back of my head as his thumb lightly skims over my cheek. As I wait with bated breath for his lips to touch mine, he looks at me like he knows me. Knows my innermost thoughts and feelings, and once upon a time, he did. But tonight, standing in the middle of the dark sidewalk waiting for him to pick things up where we left off, we're little more than strangers. We both know we need to have a proper conversation. But not now. Tonight, there's nothing but need between us. And my jumbled mess of emotions.

Anxious.

Excited.

Scared.

Happy.

Horny.

I feel it all. But most of all, I need what I know he can give. Grief and responsibility have been suffocating me since my father's death, but Callen can take it away. He's done it once before, making me feel free and detached from all my burdens. I'm desperate for that freedom once again. I know it's not fair to expect so much from a person, but he's the only one who's ever been able to do it.

To free me.

To take control the way I needed him to.

His mouth is a breath away from mine when he whispers, "I'm really glad you're here." Ever so gently, his lips press against mine in a barely there kiss. "I've missed you."

With his confession floating on the night air, both of his hands now hold my face as though I'm something precious, but this time, when his lips find mine, they're hungry for more. He greedily tastes me, as if he can't get enough.

I meet his fervor.

One of his hands tangles in my hair, the other sliding down my back to my ass pushing me flush against his body. All the while, his tongue outlines my upper lip, seeking permission that I give without hesitation.

Our tongues dance in a rhythm only the two of us can feel. I've never found it with anyone else, and I need more of it. My hand slides under his T-shirt. The heat of his skin under my fingertips is electric.

He gently grabs my wrist, pulling it away from his body. He ends our kiss and rests his forehead against mine. "If I don't get you home, we're gonna get arrested for indecent exposure. C'mon, my place is only another block and a half away."

He takes me by the hand, leading the way. My heart pounds in my chest. The anticipation of what's to come nearly unbearable. I've spent so much time wondering about this man and the mystery of who he was. Tonight, I not only called him by his name and shared mine with him but also spent the evening with those closest to him. Now, I'm going to his home. It's everything I've wished for, but the reality of what's happening is still scary as hell.

What if we were only meant to have one weekend, and outside our hotel bubble, we don't burn as brightly?

My worry abruptly spikes when he pushes through a short wooden gate attached to a fence that lines a perfectly manicured yard. It's dark, but lights line the walkway. The front porch is lit up by the beautiful light above the light blue front door. At the top of the steps a porch swing to the left catches my eye. A glance at it is all I get before he grabs my waist, pressing my back against his front door, his body pressed against me.

"You sure you want this?"

"Of course I want this." I pull back to ensure he sees the sincerity in my eyes. "I want you, Callen. I've wanted you since the first moment I saw you in that bar."

"You have a funny way of showing it."

He doesn't give me time to analyze his comment when he turns the doorknob, pushing the door open and wrapping his arm around my waist to prevent me from falling on my ass.

We're two steps in the door when he kicks it closed. He presses me so tight to him that all I see is the storm brewing in his eyes. A storm full of passion but also lingering disdain.

He maneuvers me so my back is against a wall and glides my hands upward until they're over my head. He holds them in place with one hand while his other slides down my neck and chest until he cups my breast.

"You know, I've told myself that I wished I had never met you."

His words send a bucket of ice water over me, and I try to pull away. When he doesn't release his hold, I turn my head to avoid his eyes, not wanting him to see how much his words hurt me.

Taking my chin between his thumb and forefinger, he brings my eyes back to his. "Because it hurt too much to know I would never have this again. Never taste your lips again." He kisses me deeply. "Never feel you under me again." He grinds against me, and the hard planes of his torso and his arousal press against me, washing away the momentary hurt. His words reignite the fire that had briefly singed to ashes.

Lips hovering over my ear, he whispers, "Never hear your moans again in anything other than my dreams."

My core aches at the sound of his confessions. If he reached between my legs, he would find me drenched for him.

Oh, how I want him between my legs.

Against my neck, his confessions continue. "Never hear you laugh again."

He licks my neck, and I can't help but giggle.

"Do you know what your laughter does to me, Charlotte?"

"No," I breathe out, practically panting.

"It brings me life. Makes me feel worthy."

What in the world?

"Because making you happy is all I wanted the chance to do. If I could make a woman like you happy, what else would a man like me need in life?"

"Callen..."

"But you took that opportunity away from me." His teeth gently bite at my collarbone. "You decided for both of us."

I want to plead my case and remind him we both agreed on the terms of our weekend, but I let him have this because as much as his words sting, he deserves to get this off his chest.

His frustration and anger means he missed me as much as I missed him. That and the way he's touching me feels so damn good.

Ruby barks for our attention. She's standing beside her daddy, trying to wiggle between us, but there's no room.

Pulling back to peer down at me, he continues, "As pissed as I still am at you, right now is not the time to hash this all out. We are going to talk about the bullshit you pulled last time. But we will talk about it tomorrow morning."

"Is that your way of asking me to stay the night?"

"I'm not asking. You've drank too much to drive. Besides, I plan to keep you up all night long." He releases my hands. "Do I hear any objections?"

I make the universal sign of zipping my lips.

His lips crash into mine, and his hands drop to my ass, where he lifts me, so my legs wrap around his waist. He carries me through the house, still kissing me, and I'm kissing him back with everything I've got. We're frantic. So desperate and careless for each other our teeth clank together, and he bites my bottom lip, but it's still one of the best kisses of my life.

In fact, all my best kisses have been with him.

Callen pushes us into a room that I only register as a bedroom when he pulls away, allowing me to take in the bed and dresser. The space smells like him, and I can't believe I'm here. This is really happening. He points at the dog, and she leaves the room. He closes the door behind her then his intense focus returns to me.

"Charlotte, I'm still the same man I was before."

"Good. I like that man a whole lot."

He kisses me lightly. "I'm real glad to hear that. But what I meant was I still don't do one-night stands. If we do this, I'm gonna want more than tonight. We'll have a conversation and get everything out in the open tomorrow in the light of day. Are we on the same page?"

I nod my reply.

"I need to hear you say it. Are we on the same page?"

Are we?

Am I ready to give him what I couldn't before?

"Isn't it too early to promise more? We've just found each other again. What if it's not the same?"

He grinds his erection against me, but I don't miss the seriousness in his eyes. "Does it not feel the same to you?"

A groan falls from my lips as he moves his hips to make his point. "It does."

"That's what I thought." He takes a step back, putting space between us. I instantly miss his touch. "I'll ask again. Are we on the same page?

Who am I kidding? The make-out session we've already had proves the chemistry between us is every bit as intense as it was before.

I want this.

I want him.

I'm in Goose Hollow to figure my life out. Why not start with being honest with myself? I'd like to see where this can go. I know we live in different worlds, but why not complicate my life this time around and see what happens.

"Yes."

"I'm gonna hold you to that. But right now, I need you naked."

Playfully, he tosses me onto his bed and kicks off his shoes. I reach down to do the same, but he stops me.

"No," he commands. "Don't you dare. I've been dying to take your clothes off you all night." He pulls his T-shirt over his head, revealing his defined torso. God damn, the man is still as hot as he ever was.

All I want to do is rip my clothes off.

To feel my skin against his.

"Need any help over there?" I say, leaning back on my elbows, watching him.

"You stay right where you are, woman."

"So bossy."

"If I recall, you liked it that way."

My cheeks heat. "Only with you." My reply isn't coy. It's straightforward and honest. Vulnerable. Like before, when I'm with him I don't need to hide my desires. My inhibitions fade away. For some reason, I feel more myself with this virtual stranger than anyone I've ever had any kind of relationship with at all. And apparently the beautiful man before me taking control is my kink.

Keeping his gaze locked on me, he pushes his jeans over his hips. His arousal bounces free, and oh, how glorious it is. Just like the rest of his body, his cock calls to me.

He growls as he kicks his pants away and takes me by the hand to pull me up from the bed. Barely on my feet, he has my shirt over my head and on the floor with his clothes. His mouth leaves a trail over my chest until he reaches my breasts. Slipping one finger beneath the cup of my bra, he sweeps over my nipple.

"Your nipples are hard, sugar. I wonder if the rest of you is as ready for me?" He turns me around but doesn't press me against him. Instead, his hands unbutton my jeans.

Anticipation deepens my breaths, making me sound like I've just climbed ten flights of stairs. But when he pushes my jeans over my hips and follows them down with kisses to my lower back, ass cheeks, and thighs, it takes every bit of my willpower not to reach into my panties to touch myself. I'm already so close. And knowing him, he is fully aware of what he's doing to me and how close I am.

I step out of my jeans, and he stands, pressing my back to his front. His fingers splay across my stomach, his pinky sneaking beneath the lace of my panties. Teasing.

"Fuck, I've waited so long for this. I'm gonna ask you one last time. We on the same page?"

"Yes," I say, frustrated. Placing my hand over his, I guide it under the soaked lace of my now useless panties. "Please touch me."

His fingers glide over my clit and part me as he moves his fingers through my wetness in painfully slow strokes. "Fuck, Charlotte." Two fingers press inside me, and I instinctually lift my leg to give him room. "You're so wet. So ready."

Much to my dismay, he withdraws his hand and reaches around me, grabbing the duvet and throwing it to the floor. "We won't be needing that." He kisses my neck. The warmth of his finger traces down my spine, sending a shiver through me. In one swift move, he unclasps my bra, then pushes it off my shoulders, and I let it fall to the floor. "Lie down, sweetness."

I do as he asks, and as insecure as I often feel in my now thirty-two-year-old body, I lay myself bare in front of him.

The hunger in his appraising eyes say he likes what he sees. "You are fucking beautiful, Charlotte."

"So are you."

He pulls my underwear off and holds them to his face, inhaling deeply.

"You are a maniac, you know that?" I laugh.

"You smell so damn good." There's a glint in his eye. "I can't help myself."

He drops them on his bedside table and pulls a condom out of the drawer, ripping the foil open with his teeth. With a barely there, knowing smile he slowly strokes himself before rolling the condom down his length as I marvel at his body.

Joining me on the bed, he crawls to me, positioning himself above me. His heavy cock rests on my thigh, his full body weight on his elbows.

Pushing my hair off my face, he says, "I can't believe you're here." His voice is tender, as are his lips when they meet mine.

He kisses his way to my breast, cupping it with his hand and pulling my nipple into his mouth, his tongue circling the tight bud. The friction of his beard is a new sensation that I don't mind one bit. His fingertips mirror the action on the other breast. My hands are in his hair as I moan my pleasure, but I need all of him.

"Callen, please. I need you now. We have all night for foreplay. I just want you to make me come. I want to feel you inside me. Make me forget the past two years without this." I reach for his sheathed cock and make it clear exactly what I want.

"With pleasure." He pins my hands above my head like he knows I like, and our eyes lock as he pushes into me. But they close as I adjust to the feel of him inside me. "My woman gets what she asks for. And don't you forget it."

His magnificent dick distracts me from thinking too much about him calling me *his woman* like a caveman. Because, at this moment, I am his, and he is giving me the only thing I want.

Him.

Chapter Fourteen

Callen

The space where the curtains don't quite meet emits a blindingly cruel light that has my eyes slamming shut at the same moment I attempt to open them for the day. I haven't slept as well as I did last night since I don't know when, and I'm not ready for it to end.

Rolling onto my side, the smell of vanilla and some sort of citrus hits my senses, and my heartbeat accelerates. My morning wood grows even harder when I realize last night wasn't a dream.

Charlotte is really here. In my bed.

I reach for her, but the space her body occupied last night is empty.

Sunshine be damned, my eyes fly open. Sure as shit, she's gone. The bathroom door is open, she's not in there, either.

Where the hell is she? Trying not to think the worst, I pull on my boxers and bolt out of the bed to hunt her down.

Ruby hears my feet storming down the hallway and whines, begging to be let out of her crate. She's not used to being locked up, not to mention me having someone in my bed besides her. She wouldn't stop crying outside the bedroom door last night, so I had to crate her. Ignoring her for the moment, I check the kitchen and the front room, just for kicks. I also check the spare bedroom and second bathroom, but there's no sign of her.

She fucking bailed on me again.

What the fuck is with this woman?

I'm pretty sure I made myself clear last night.

I don't do casual.

I told her I wanted more than one night. She not only said she understood this, but she seemed to want the same thing. More.

Yet here we are again.

We agreed to have a conversation this morning. And still, she vanished.

God, this woman is a damn coward.

I may know her name, but I don't know where she's staying, and I don't have her number. While this is a huge red flag, it changes nothing.

She. Is. The. One.

I know this in my gut. Just like I did two years ago.

It's not a sex thing, although I've never connected with another woman between like I do with Charlotte. It's a *her* thing.

We fit.

I know it.

She knows it.

This time around, she won't be the one who got away.

Now I have to figure out not only where the hell she's staying, but how to keep her from disappearing again.

Until I figure it out, I begrudgingly have to get on with my day.

"Come on, girl." I open Ruby's crate and lead her to the back door to let her out. "At least you like me enough to stick around."

I carry on with my mundane morning routine of feeding the dog and brushing my teeth while the shower heats up. As I wash my hair, visions of Charlotte gripping the sheets as she arched her back under my touch repeat in my head. My lips already miss the feel of her moans vibrating against them as we kissed. My ears miss the sound of her screaming my name as she came. The rage running through my veins prevents me from using my hand to relieve myself. I refuse to give her that much power.

Dressed and almost ready to leave, I start to make my bed like I do every morning, but I can't do it. As irate as I am, I'm not ready to erase the memory of our night together. Not yet anyway.

Chapter Fifteen

Callen

Ruby and I have been at the store for about an hour when my little brother announces his arrival.

"Where's my pretty girl?" Gus yells from the back entrance, letting himself in.

Ruby leaves the comfort of her dog bed beside my desk in my back office to run toward my brother's voice, making her the second female to run away from me this morning.

Of course, he shows up minutes before we open.

"To what do I owe the pleasure of this early morning visit?" I yell over my shoulder as I make my way onto the store floor.

"Can't your brother stop by the family business for a chat?"

Yep, he's about to piss me off. I can feel it coming. "What do you want, Gus?"

"Just stopping by to see how you're doing this morning."

"It's just another day."

"Last night was fun, yeah?"

Could he be more obvious? "Yep."

"Miss Carruthers is a nice little addition to Goose Hollow. Wonder how long she'll be staying here in our humble little town?"

"I have no idea."

"Wanna talk about it?"

"Talk about what?"

"Bro, I think you know exactly what. Or should I say who I'm talking about?"

"Nope." I pretend to check my imaginary watch. "Listen, I gotta open the doors."

Of course, Angus doesn't take the hint. Instead, he follows me to the front of the building where I check the register, Ruby trailing at his heel. I'd be an idiot to think he wouldn't bring Charlotte up, but I figured torture via text would be the way he'd go. I didn't expect him to show up at the store before we've even opened. He closed the bar last night. Shouldn't he be asleep?

"Well, I do want to discuss it. And I may or may not have spoken with our big brother last night, and I think he has some insights you may find interesting. Why don't we give Knox a ring? I'm sure this would be a call he'd be happy to wake up for."

"Why the hell would we call Knox to discuss something I already said I don't want to talk about?"

"Dude, it's clear she's the reason you went missing for three days in LA."

Angus picks up a candy bar from the front counter, and I smack it out of his hand.

"How exactly is that clear?"

He hops up onto the counter, casual as can be. The knots that took root in my stomach the moment I realized she wasn't still in bed with me twist. She's the last person I want to talk about.

Although, she's all I can think about, and there is too much to work out between the two of us. I'm not ready to share her with anyone, but I am ready to find her and set her straight on how things will go this time.

Leaning into my space, his face only a couple inches from mine. "Cal, we aren't stupid."

"Debatable," I say, averting my eyes so he can't see that he's got me.

"Brother, you came home messed up from that weekend, and we all know it was over a woman. Last night, when I asked her if she knew you, she said you were someone from her past. Sorry, dude, but you don't have a past that the rest of us don't know about."

He's such an asshole.

"Well, if it isn't Detective McKinnon. I didn't realize my life was under investigation."

"C'mon, you know it's not like that. I'm your brother, and I just want to know what's going on. Do we need to worry she's gonna hurt you again? Or is it a good thing she's here? I think you might want to talk to Knox because—"

"Gus, I don't want to talk to Knox or you about Charlotte. Just let it be. If I have something to talk to you about, I'll share."

He continues to sit on the counter, feet swinging, waiting for me to say more.

"Man, get out of here. I have to open the store and you know we have a strict no loitering policy."

"You act like you're the only one who can do anything around this place. You know you take too much on."

If only he knew how much I've taken on. He might not make comments like that so lightly. But it's not his fault he doesn't know the business is in trouble. I've kept it from him and everyone else.

"I'm hoping your blast from the past will loosen you up, and maybe you'll take a break here and there." He hops off the counter. "Call Knox. He's got some questions about how you and Charlotte met."

"You two are like a couple of teenage girls. Tell Knox not to hold his breath."

He looks at his watch, and instead of leaving through the back where he came from, he unlocks the front door and flips the closed sign to open as he pushes through it.

"Stop being an ass and call him."

Livvy slips in as the door closes and joins me behind the counter.

"Morning, Cal."

"Hey, Livvy."

"How'd you sleep last night, boss man?"

"Excuse me?"

"Heard you had quite a night and left with a new lady friend."

Fucking Owen.

Why did I ever think it would be a good idea to hire my

best friend's little sister? It's like working with Daisy every day.

"That brother of yours just doesn't know how to keep his mouth shut, does he?" I spit as I log into the computer behind the checkout counter.

"It's not like he's running around telling the whole town, although I'm sure word will spread quickly enough." She opens the register and counts her till as she talks. "I called him while he was at the bar, and he gave me a little play-by-play."

"I'm so glad my night could entertain the two of you. You're welcome."

"So, who is she? Owen said you two were being all secretive about how you knew each other."

"What is it with the people in this town? Don't you all have better things to do than worry about me and who I spend my time with?"

"Not really. This is the most exciting thing that's happened in Goose Hollow since the naked rodeo clown took that walk down Main Street in broad daylight. That was over a year ago. We're all desperate for something new to talk about."

Failing to hide her smile or the shake or her shoulders, it's clear she's enjoying this way too much for my liking. I really don't need everyone's bullshit right now. I've got too much going on. Like keeping everyone who works for us employed.

"You know what?" I storm off toward my office with Ruby trailing me. "How I spend my free time and who I spend it with is nobody's business."

"Here I was, thinking you might be in a good mood for

the first time in I don't know how long. Guess you didn't get laid after all."

Grabbing my phone off my desk, I lock up my office. "C'mon, girl. Let's go visit Mabel."

Excited, Ruby hops up just enough for her front feet to lift off the ground. She loves the ranch as much as I do.

"You're in charge. I'm taking the day," I say as I pass Livvy on my way out of the building.

"Hey! Where are you going?"

"Like I said, what I do is none of your business."

I'm outside, and the door is still closing when I hear her smart-ass reply. "You really need to get laid, Cal!"

"If only lack of sex was what had me in such a piss-poor mood," I mutter under my breath as I open the door to my truck and let Ruby jump in before me.

She takes her place in the passenger seat, and I start the engine and pull out of the parking lot, aiming the truck in the direction of anywhere but here.

Chapter Sixteen

Callen

"**G**ood girl, Mabel."

Keeping my voice calm, I lean against my chestnut quarter horse.

"You were a great distraction, sweetheart. Thank you." I gently glide my hand down her back leg and lift her foot to check her hoof. "Looks pretty clean. Only a couple of things to clear out on this one. We'll be done before you know it."

Like I have the two mornings before, I pick out the muck that gathered in her hoof during our two-hour ride, then pull the hoof pick from my back pocket to get rid of any additional dirt and debris. Releasing her leg, I put my tools down and pick up the brush and give her coat a good cleaning. She loves the attention, and she deserves it, too.

Working up a sweat and spending time away from the nosy people in my life has been a nice release. If only the objective of getting Charlotte out of my head had worked. Instead, I've spent the last two hours trying to figure out how I could have let her do it again. Why in the world did I let my damn heart and, let's be honest, my dick override what my brain was telling me?

But for now, I'm letting the calming task of brushing Mabel settle me. At least as much as the quiet of the barn and the slow, steady motion of brushing the horse can settle me.

Focusing on my breathing as I work, inhaling for a count of four and exhaling for another four counts just like Daisy taught me. She had learned the technique last year in some meditation or yoga class or something, and although I'll never admit it, her little breathing hack helps me fall asleep at night.

It would probably help now, if the sound of tires on gravel didn't interrupt my peaceful reprieve. Ruby takes off running to check out the situation. A car door closes, but when she doesn't bark, I figure it's someone she knows and loves.

"Which nosy bastard do you think it will be?" I say to Mabel as the footsteps get closer.

"How dare you talk about your mother like that?"

Oops.

Mom rounds the corner, looking better than she has in the past six months. Pleased she's caught me making a smart-ass comment has her smiling a smile we don't see nearly enough these days. It's a welcome sight. There are still bags under her eyes from sleepless nights, and she's thinner than I can remember her ever being, but there seems to be some light creeping back into them and it looks good on her.

"Sorry, I thought it was one of your interfering children or possibly Owen poking their nose in my business."

"No, son. It's just your interfering mother," she says as she reaches out a hand for Mabel to sniff, before rubbing her chestnut nose. She pulls a carrot out of her pocket, and Mabel happily accepts her snack.

"How're you doing, Mom?"

"I'm just fine. The question is, how are you?" she asks, leaning against the stall doorframe, studying me.

Careful not to give my mixed-up emotions away, I brush Roxie's flank. "I'm always good, you know that."

She chuckles. "You have always been the worst liar in the bunch."

She's always been able to see through me. I keep brushing, careful to keep the horse between us, blocking her view. "I don't know what you're talking about."

"You know, I met Charlotte outside the store a couple of weeks ago. Sweet girl. Beautiful."

My fucking siblings and their big mouths. Is anything sacred in this town?

"Okay."

"Your brother said you knew her before she got to Goose Hollow."

"Did he now?"

"And your sister said you seem to fancy her. Might have even left the bar with her the other night."

"Was there a family meeting nobody told me about?"

"They're just worried about you, Cal."

"Nothing to worry about."

"You really like her, don't you?"

"Doesn't matter if she doesn't feel the same. She's ghosted me. Not for the first time."

"I know I only met her once, but she doesn't seem like the type."

"She's good at making you think she's one thing when she's really the exact opposite."

"I'm sure there's more to the story. Have you tried calling her?"

"Hard to do when I don't have her number,"

"Well, this is a small town. Where's she staying?"

"I couldn't tell ya."

Why did it have to be mom that showed up today? She has a way of bringing emotions to the surface I can normally keep at bay. Right now, I am barely hanging on by a thread and if anybody can get me to break, it's her. Coming to the ranch is my way of decompressing. Escaping. Talking about my shitty love life with my mother is neither of those things.

"What about—"

"Mom, can we talk about something else, please?"

She hesitates, and I worry she's about to argue, but finally, her shoulders slump. "Sure, sweetie."

And... I feel like an asshole. Mom, and the whole family, for that matter, love me. Sure, they can be invasive and over-whelming, but they're nosey out of love. But this thing between me and Charlotte is something we have to work out for ourselves. No meddling family members necessary.

Finished with Mabel's grooming, I no longer have an excuse to hide behind her. I give her one last pet down her nose with one hand as the other pulls a small carrot out of my pocket. The soft fuzz of her lips tickles the palm of my hand when she takes it into her mouth.

Schooling my expression before facing mom, I fix my face

into a smile that I hope looks pleasant and not manic. "It's good to see you, but I have to put the tack away."

Silently, she follows me out of the stall as I clean up and put everything away.

"Walk with me," she says once I finish.

It isn't a request. Hooking her arm through mine, she guides me toward the barn door. Wordlessly, we stroll out into the late morning sunshine along the fence line. Ruby runs ahead of us toward the cows while a horse whinnies in the barn. The consistent wind we've been lucky to have all morning cools my skin and stirs up the glorious smell of dirt, manure, and alfalfa.

"You know, losing your father has been hard on all of us."

"I know."

"But you've had the added pressure of keeping the business going. Keeping his dream going."

"Happy to."

"I know you are, son. I also know that you've always felt the pressure to look after all of us. You're the one we all count on. Heck, the whole town counts on you. For your father to lay everything on you is a lot."

"It's fine."

She holds up her free hand to gesture for me to wait. "I want you to know how much I appreciate you, Cal. I'm not sure how I would have gotten through the past six months without you."

My eyes burn with emotion as I inhale and exhale for a count of four, not letting my emotions get the best of me. Losing Dad was hard on all of us, but mom lost her best friend and the love of her life in an instant. God, how I wish I could take her pain away. Her love is the greatest gift my siblings and I will ever know. Our mother would do anything for us. Hell, she fought cancer when we were kids, refusing to miss a practice, a school event or even kissing us every night when we went to bed. We were too young to notice the toll it took on her. To appreciate the magnitude of what she was going through. What we did know was that our family was the most important thing in her life. She made sure we knew we were loved and how important it was to give love. She would sell this place in a heartbeat if it was to help one of her kids. And I'm going to do everything in my power to make sure that never happens.

"Love you, Mom."

I'm not sure what else to say. We've stopped in front of the fence, where everyone's favorite highland cow, Bernadette, is waiting for us to give her the daily dose of love she's grown accustomed to.

"I love you too. But I'm worried about you." She slips her arm from mine so she can scratch Bernie on her head. "You haven't been yourself, and I don't mean since Charlotte came to town. I can't help but think there's more to it than just missing your father. If something's going on, you can tell me."

Not this, I can't.

"Nothing's going on that I can't handle."

"But you don't have to handle whatever it is on your own. You know that, right? Whenever you're ready I'll have a stack of pancakes waiting for you."

Sharon McKinnon and her pancakes. They are the healing salve that always make a crappy situation a bit better. Broken heart. Pancakes. Didn't get into the college of your choice. Pancakes. Break both of your arms and can't go to the high school dance. She'll feed you the pancakes. Day or night, a stack of pancakes will be there when you need them.

"Thanks, Mom."

"If you don't want to talk to me about it, then talk to Angus, Daisy, or Owen. And you know Knox is only a phone call away."

Knox could solve this with the snap of his fingers, but it's not his responsibility. It's mine.

"Yes, ma'am."

"Your father left the business to you to run, but this is your life. If it's not what you want, we'll figure something else out."

"I've worked there most of my life. It's a part of who I am. I have no intention of giving that up."

"As long as you remember that *you* are more than that store. The business doesn't define you. You are an exceptional man, and you have a lot to offer this world."

"I always knew I was your favorite," I joke.

"Shh... don't tell the others." She chuckles.

"My lips are sealed."

"Good. Keep it that way."

She rests her head on my shoulder and we're quiet for a few minutes. Bernadette's breathing and the distant noise of the other animals the only sounds. Mom puts up a good front, but losing Dad... well, it's like a part of her soul is gone and she's just floating through each day on autopilot.

"You doing, okay?"

"I'm managing, Cal."

"Do you need anything?"

"Oh, honey. I miss your dad something awful. I was

married to my best friend for forty-six years. There's no way to fix that kind of loss."

God, my heart breaks for her.

"Even if you just want me to come watch *Traitors* with you or have a meal. *You* are not a burden. I'm always here. No matter how big or small, there isn't anything I wouldn't do for you, Mom. *You* know that, right?"

"I know that, son. But don't you worry about me. I'll be fine."

I give her my best skeptical look. "Gee, I wonder where I get it?"

"Stop it." She leans her head back against my shoulder. "Now, what are you up to today? Playing hooky?"

"Nah, just needed to clear my head. Gotta run home and take a quick shower and then I'll head in."

"Did it work? Is your head clear?"

"Not even close."

We turn around and head back to the barn and my truck. We make small talk and leave the more serious conversation behind us.

When we get to the truck, I give her a hug and whisper, "Love you." The hug goes on for countless seconds. She's been through so much, and I can't imagine a worse pain than losing the love of your life.

Releasing her, she takes my face in her hands. "If she doesn't see all that you are, then she isn't worth your heart."

Chapter Seventeen

Charlotte

The water cascades down my face, mixing with my tears.

It took me two weeks, but here I am... crying in the shower.

Crying in the shower had been my norm for the month before I came to Goose Hollow. I've spent so many hours with shriveled fingertips from my time spent under the spray of my shower at home.

You never really know how you'll react when you lose the most important person in your life. For me, that person was my dad. He was my world. Dad raised me on his own and did a damn good job of it. He filled the roles of father and mother. Friend and mentor.

While building his firm and becoming a legend in entertainment law he didn't miss a tea-party or a track meet. He shared his love of music and woodworking with me, as well as how to be a well-respected lawyer. Dad was always fair and *always* professional.

It was important the staff and our clients saw me as strong and confident. To assure them that even with Dad gone they would be taken care of. Because of this, I bottled my pain and anger inside. Only letting it out when I was alone and only in the shower.

It was my refuge.

For weeks, I would sob endless tears under the spray. But as soon as I stepped out of the shower, those tears evaporated, and my emotions tucked themselves neatly away inside my heart. Compartmentalizing my feelings and stepping into Michael Carruthers' shoes and taking care of business.

My father's absence in the office was powerful. He was a special man. Everyone loved him and he loved every person who worked for him as though they were a member of our family, and they knew it. His favorite day of the year was Carruthers family day at Disneyland. He got a new pair of ears every year and couldn't get to his favorite ride fast enough, racing through the park to get in line for Space Mountain. There were multiple occasions when a coworker would burst into tears when I walked into a room because I reminded them of him. But not me. Somehow, my emotions would stay packed away and I would comfort them without shedding a tear.

Losing my dad hurts more than I could have ever imagined. It doesn't matter that he had been sick for a long time. You're never fully prepared for pain like this. I'm scared that taking the final steps to my new future, whatever that might be, will somehow distance me from him even more. That feeling is always tugging at my heart when I think about what comes next.

Yet with all of this on my mind, I have not shed a tear since I arrived here. Maybe it's the beautiful scenery or the change of pace and wonderful people. More than likely, the huckleberry soft serve and the bearded cowboy, who I had thought wanted more than one night with me, are the biggest distractions.

I've spent the last two days on virtual calls with clients and researching case law for one of the firm's upcoming trials, but Callen and his lack of communication is constantly on my mind. This morning when my alarm went off, and I saw that there were no messages from him I hit a breaking point and found myself in the shower. Crying.

It's as though the disappointment and rejection of Cal's cold shoulder brought up all the emotions I'd been able to keep at bay and they came flooding back. A rush of sadness, anger, and confusion brought me to my knees. The giddiness I felt as I left my note with my number on the bedside table while Callen slept the other morning is nowhere to be found as I sit on the shower floor holding my knees to my chest. That morning, my world felt like it was finding what it hadn't known it was looking for when I arrived in Oregon.

This morning, loneliness has taken hold of my heart. Memories of sitting at Dad's bedside his final weeks of hospice care. Holding his hand as he took his last breath the night he passed. All of it brought back to the surface because of a man.

This thought sends a surge of rage through my veins, and I pick myself up off the tile floor. This is bullshit. I will not spend another second feeling sorry for myself because of a man who has been nothing but rude to me since the day I got here.

I left him a note explaining I didn't want to wake him but that I had a virtual meeting with a client on the East Coast and had to leave. I left my phone number and told him to call me.

Yes, I disappeared on him two and a half years ago. I broke my promise and bailed before giving him my name or a goodbye. He's still angry about this and we need to talk about the reasons why I left, but that's hard to do when he's gone radio silent.

For someone who wanted to make it clear he was still the same man he was when we met in Los Angeles, he has a funny way of showing it. The same man who wanted more than one night. The same man who doesn't do casual and made sure this fact was crystal clear. He made me assure him we were on the same page before taking me to his bed.

Yet it's been three days and not a word.

Not a call.

Not a text.

Is this some sort of twisted revenge? Does he want me to feel some of what he might have felt the morning I left?

Sunday afternoon, when I hadn't heard from him, my instinct was to drive to his place to seek him out, but that seemed a little too needy. Desperate. It had only been eight hours since I left his place, and maybe he had plans? I went to bed with a pit in my stomach that night.

On Monday, I did my best to stay busy. I went for a swim, struggled through my afternoon meetings, and checked my phone a million times. Just like the night before, I went to bed sad and embarrassed, but last night my anger began to build, and my imagination ran rampant.

Has something happened to him?

Is this some sort of test?

Was everything he said Saturday a crock of shit?

He has my information. He can't seriously be mad that I left early because of work. I don't understand his silence. It doesn't align with everything he said three nights ago.

The more I think about it, the angrier I get. My tears change from tears of hurt and sadness to indignant frustration.

Enough.

As soon as I turn off this water, no more tears. I'm going to pull up my big girl panties and I'm going to find him and give him a piece of my mind.

He may be the same man he was before, but I'm not the same woman. I'm changing my life. Doing things that make me happy and taking charge of my destiny. And being treated like a doormat isn't a part of the new me.

Callen McKinnon can kiss my ass.

Chapter Eighteen

Callen

"Or do you like the blue better?"

The store has been open for three hours and I think Rebecca, my friend and local coffee shop owner, has been standing in our paint section for at least two of those hours. She's holding up what must be her twentieth paint swatch, the annoying headache I've been doing my best to ignore all morning is making its presence known.

"Rebecca." I sigh, unable to hide my annoyance. I've known her my entire life and consider her a friend, but I really don't give a shit what color she paints her guest bathroom. "Doesn't matter what I like. It's your bathroom. Green or blue. Your choice."

"Well, aren't you snippy today? What's crawled up your butt, Cal?"

"Sorry. I just have a lot of shit on my mind."

The fact that I haven't had a decent night's sleep in days doesn't help. Two more mornings have passed since I woke up to the smell of Charlotte on my sheets. Since then, she seems to have vanished into thin air. It's not like she doesn't know where to find me. Every time I think about it, I get pissed all over again. My temper getting harder and harder to rein in.

We may not have exchanged numbers, but she knows where I work. She knows where I live. Hell, she knows all my local haunts and most of my family. If she'd only ask, Angus would hand over my details in a heartbeat, but my brother hasn't seen her.

Yes, I asked.

And. That. Pisses. Me. Off.

My phone pings, giving me an excuse to walk away from Rebecca and the two paint samples she's been staring at for the past twenty minutes.

"Excuse me. It's Knox. Grab Loten if you need anything."

"Oh, of course. Please do."

What she really means is *anything for Knox.*

ROCK GOD

Hey, my friend Charlie is staying at the cabin for a long vacation. Will you pop in this morning and make sure there are fresh towels and sheets? Appreciate it.

CALLEN

Well, hello to you too. I haven't talked to you in two weeks, and you can't even say hello?

ROCK GOD

I said, hey. Call me after if you get a chance.
I'm in LA, so same time zone for a change

CALLEN

Sure. Anything else I can do for you?

ROCK GOD

Nope, just a pop-in on the cabin. Thanks,
bro.

Now, I'm Knox's cabin boy. Great. I would grumble about the new, unwanted task, but at least it gets me away from Rebecca, her paint selection or lack thereof, and the store for a bit. I could use the break.

"Hey, Loten!" I yell back to the battery aisle where he's stocking the shelves.

"Yep, boss?" he shouts back.

"I have to run to the cabin real quick, but I'll be back shortly. Watch the front for me?"

"Yes, sir. Be up there in just a sec."

"Thanks."

"C'mon, girl." Ruby wakes from her nap on her bed behind the counter and, after a quick shake, meets me at the door, just as excited as I am to get out for a while.

* * *

The cabin is only a ten-minute drive from the store, the last five minutes consist of a winding dirt road that leads to Goose Hollow Lake. A black SUV is parked in the driveway when the cabin comes into view. Great, I get to have personal contact with his renter. He could have warned me they were here already.

Lucky me.

Climbing out of the truck, I eye Ruby and say, "Stay here, girl. I'll be right back." It's not hot yet and the windows are down. As I cross in front of the truck, I notice the stickers on the SUV signifying it's a rental. Tourist. Even better.

I knock on the door and wait for a slow count of five before I knock again. I'm not in a rush, just bitter about being Knox's bitch boy. Regardless, there's probably more force than I really meant behind my second knock.

The lock on the other side of the door turns, and when it opens, I feel sick to my stomach. Charlotte stands in the doorway wearing only a towel.

You have got to be fucking kidding me.

"What the hell are you doing here?" I bark.

"Nice to see you, too."

Sass? Is she kidding me right now?

But her voice lacks its usual spunk. Instead, it sounds flat and lifeless. Something's off. Wet hair curtains her face, making it hard for me to get a read on her. But there's too much red in my vision to care. Not after what she's put me through yet again.

"Where's Charlie?" I demand, bulldozing my way into the house, not giving two fucks that she didn't invite me in.

"Excuse me?"

"You heard me. Where is he, Charlotte?"

She closes the front door and leans against it with her arms crossed. Silent.

"We were just together three nights ago, and you've

already moved on? What the actual fuck?" I march through the living room and into the kitchen, only to find it empty.

She pushes off the door and follows me, hands on her hips. "I didn't realize we were exclusive."

She could have slapped me across the face, and it wouldn't have hurt as much. Unable to look her in the eye, I storm down the hallway, searching for Charlie. If he's one of Knox's friends, he's likely a slimy Hollywood douche hiding out, too afraid to face a confrontation.

Possessiveness fuels my angry adrenaline rush when I yell over my shoulder, "I don't share, Charlotte. I made that abundantly clear. I haven't changed. You said you understood that."

I check the bathroom, still full of steam from her shower. But there aren't any douchebags hiding behind the shower curtain. Nothing here. Just the scent of Charlotte.

When I enter the hallway again, I can feel her watching me from the other end, but I don't dare look in her direction.

It's too much.

She looks too good.

Too naked.

I can't imagine her like that. With someone else.

That rage rips through me as I throw open the bedroom door so hard it bounces off the wall and back at me. I'll fix the damage, if there is any, another day. Holding the door back, I scan the space, but there's no sign of anyone else. I rip open the closet doors, but no cowards are hiding there either. The same with the second bedroom.

Steeling myself, I make my way back to the living room where she stands, arms crossed again, looking amused. She's blocking the way, forcing me to walk around her.

"Where is the coward? Outside?" I stomp through the small kitchen and throw open the back door, but only two steps outside, I see a picnic table that was never there before.

Everything slows down.

The fist around my heart releases its grip. Rage flees, leaving understanding in its wake. Relieved, I step back into the kitchen and find Charlotte leaning against the counter.

"You're Charlie."

"Charlotte, but my friends call me Charlie."

God, this woman. Her presence has my common sense vanishing and my need for her taking over. I run my hand through my hair and exhale. "Thank, Christ."

Fuck, if the way she's looking at me practically has me undone. She loves that she got a rise out of me. Yet, her eyes and nose are red. She was crying before I got here and that's a punch to the gut. I may be angry that she ghosted me, but I can't help but want to make whatever is wrong better for her.

"Why's that?" She bites her goddamn lower lip and twirls a piece of her wet hair around a finger.

Clearly something is wrong, and I can't help but wonder if she's coming on to me because she wants me to take away what's troubling her like I have before. Does she want me to take control?

"I think you know the answer to that question," I say, testing the waters to see where her mind might be.

"You don't share, I know." She rolls her eyes, then looks to the ground. As sassy as she sounds, there's a hollowness in her demeanor. She's hurting and I want nothing more than to be the salve that soothes her. When she lifts her gaze to mine her eyes are practically begging me to take away her worries.

And I know exactly how to do just that.

"Charlotte?"

"Callen?"

I easily pull open the front of her towel with a finger, and it falls to the floor. My dick is hard in an instant. She is magnificent, and I don't bother trying to hide my slow appraisal of her body. Sun-kissed olive skin with subtle tan lines, full breasts and hard nipples and an athletic build, with long legs topped with curvy hips. Her ass isn't in view, but it's an ass that men fantasize about. I know this firsthand. Her body has been my go-to spank bank material for two years now.

"I thought you were naked like this with someone else, Charlotte." My fingers itch to touch her, but not yet. I want to see where she takes this.

"So, what if I was? Who says you get a say in what I do or who I do it with?"

Is she really back to this again?

"I do."

Her eyes flicker with life when she hears my honest reply. If she needs to hear more honesty, I'll give it to her. Whatever keeps the light in her eyes.

As if being naked in front of me doesn't faze her in the least, she walks to the refrigerator and opens the door. The ambient light softly spotlights her perfect skin, highlighting her best attributes.

"Do you really think you can sleep with me, never call, then show up where I'm staying and demand to have a say in how I live my life?"

"How am I supposed to call you when I don't have your number, Charlotte?"

She opens a bottle of water, taking several long drinks,

her throat moving as she does. She knows what she's doing. Nonchalantly, she places the bottle back in the fridge and closes the door, then walks in my direction.

This woman is something else in all the most infuriating ways.

"First things first. I left a note with my number on the bedside table."

She what?

There was no note.

I searched the house.

"Second, my friends call me Charlie. Are we not friends?"

She saunters past me, stopping between me and the large oak table that takes up the entire dining space as my heartbeat gallops in my chest with the sight of her and the knowledge that she did leave a note. She did want more.

And right now I want to give her a hell of a lot more.

"I'm not your friend, and you know it." I walk past her, pulling out the matching wood chair at the end of the table. "Now, get over here and set that fine ass of yours on this table and spread your legs."

"And, why would I do that?"

"Because I'm going to leave you with a reminder of why you and I will never be friends."

Chapter Nineteen

Charlotte

There's something about this man that I can't resist. Something that has me submitting to him without a fight.

His perusal of my body when he stripped off my towel was animalistic, and I know he'll find me dripping for him. He couldn't hide the hard-on in his jeans and knowing the feeling was mutual, did nothing but egg me on. As does knowing that he never found my note. He wasn't out for revenge. He wasn't ghosting me. Callen thought I was ghosting him.

This is why my butt is now perched on the edge of the big table where I eat alone every night. At his command, I slowly open my legs. He takes in the view, and when his eyes go to my pussy, he looks even angrier than he did when he thought there was another man here. And it's sexy as hell.

"Lie down."

I do as ordered because he was not asking, and I want nothing more than for him to take control.

Standing over me, he places his hand above my heart and then leisurely drags his index finger between my breasts. Instinctually, I arch my back. Wanting more. Tracing a path over my stomach and belly button, he slows as he approaches the spot I'm desperate for him to touch. Centimeter by centimeter, he gets closer and closer until he finally reaches my clit. His index finger lightly brushes the sensitive nub on his way to run his finger through my wetness. Then he drags his finger back to my clit circling around the overheated area but never touching it. Gently and oh, so intentionally teasing me until I'm writhing on the table.

"Do I have your attention now?"

All I can do is nod. Holding my breath, as I wait for more. Pray for more.

Loving every excruciating moment of anticipation.

But then the torturous pressure of his hand disappears completely.

"Charlotte, our time together was more than a weekend fuck, and we both know it. You knew it just as well as I did."

I meet his gaze, staring into eyes so intense I can't look away. My body is on fire, wishing he would touch me again. Wanting more of his words to fill the place in my heart I've saved for him all this time.

"Yes, the sex was out of this world, but we also talked for two days straight. We shared nearly everything except our names." He leans over me, his left hand on the table next to my head as he inserts two fingers into my needy core with his other hand. "How else would I know you were a daddy's girl who followed him into the family business, but your dream job would be to flip houses?"

His fingers pick up their pace, and he takes my nipple into his mouth. His tongue circles the tight tip as my heart beats faster from his confession while the growing need to come on his hand intensifies. He moves to the other nipple, his fingers relentless in their rhythm. The warmth of his body so close to mine tingles against my bare skin.

He releases my breast, but his fingers keep moving. His face is so close that his breath tickles my cheek when he says, "Or that you did a little more than kiss a girl in college, and as nice as it was, it wasn't your thing. Or there's the fact that you love Hall & Oates because you grew up singing along to them with your dad. You hate high heels, but admit they make you feel powerful at times."

"Callen," I breathe. My body is overwhelmed by his actions, my heart by his words.

I'm disappointed when he stands, removing his proximity and his fingers. Wanting to beg for him to touch me again, but the sound of him dragging a chair across the floor silences me.

I push up on my elbows just in time to watch him sit before me, admiring my body for a beat before his eyes meet mine as he leans forward. His tongue flattens against me, and he licks until he reaches my clit, sucking it into his mouth.

The sight of him watching me watch him is fucking hot.

The friction of his beard against my most sensitive area has me nearly feral. But as much as I want to rip his clothes off and mount him, there is no way I would miss out on this moment because it's so much better than any quick fuck. One thing I know for sure is that this man knows how to make me feel good.

He continues to lick at his own pace. He knows I want him to go faster, and he knows I'm aching to come. Needless to say, I'm more than disappointed when he stops to press his lips against my center as if giving me a good night kiss. Slowly, he runs a finger through the mess he's made of me, and two fingers press inside me once again.

Thank God!

"You are a firm believer that tacos are not just meant for Tuesdays. You love peanut butter but hate coffee. Your favorite dog growing up was a pit bull named Steve."

How is this my life?

Who gets a second chance with a man like this? A man who remembers every word I've ever told him and sets my body on fire with every touch.

"But Charlotte, more importantly, I know how to make you come until you forget your own name." With his beard tickling my thighs, he settles back between my legs, and licks from my opening to my sensitive bundle of nerves. Before he demands, "Now fucking come for me, Charlotte."

And I do.

His mouth and his fingers give me exactly what I want.

What I need.

And I come undone, and his reminder is loud and clear.

He doesn't share, and I wouldn't want him to.

Once I float back to earth, he stands, licking his fingers clean.

"I'll see you soon, and in the meantime, don't forget our little discussion."

He walks away and out the front door without looking back as I lay spread-eagle on the table, wondering what in the world just happened.

Chapter Twenty

Callen

Walking the two blocks from my place to the pub, I'm trying to think of baseball, kittens, anything but Charlotte writhing on that table this morning. The table I've eaten many meals at. But no meal has ever been as sweet as the taste of her. Hence the rock-hard disturbance in my jeans all day.

The relief I felt when I found her note under my bed surprised me. It shouldn't have, considering the flame between us that's stayed lit all this time, but it still took me out at the knees.

I lay on my bedroom floor with Ruby cuddled up next to me while I read her note over and over again.

Chip,

I'm glad you haven't changed, and I'm glad you finally know my name.

I have an early conference call with a client on the East Coast and didn't want to wake you. Call me later.

My number is 310-555-0100.

Love, C

She hadn't ghosted me.
She wasn't avoiding me.
Not wanting to give her a chance to get me out of her head, I texted her from my spot on the floor.

CALLEN

Dinner at The House around 6pm?

CHARLOTTE

I see you found my note.

CALLEN

It was under the bed.

CHARLOTTE

You asking me out, Cal?

CALLEN

Only my friends call me Cal, and we will never be friends.

CHARLOTTE

Then what will we be?

ME

A hell of a lot more than friends.

CHARLOTTE

See you at 6.

She brings out a side of me I never knew existed... a beast that sees and wants only her.

Nothing and no one else matters.

So, when I catch sight of her wearing tight jeans and bright pink heels at the same high-top table surrounded by several locals once again, that beast that belongs to only her takes over, and I want to rip all the other males in a five-mile radius to shreds.

"Evening, gentlemen. Thanks for keeping Charlotte company, but she's here with me tonight. Actually, anytime you see her, consider her with me, even if I'm not here. Are we clear?"

My lifelong neighbors look at me like they've never met me before.

"Uh, sure, Cal. We get it. Had no idea she was your girl," Mark says, elbowing Owen, who's holding his hands up.

"I am nobody's *girl*," Charlotte interjects, but the guys ignore her.

"Yeah, man. Had no idea."

Greyson reaches out to her, offering his hand. "Nice to meet you. Welcome to Goose Hollow."

"Call me Charlie, and it's nice to meet you, too."

All the guys but Owen walk away, and the testosterone-filled monster inside me calms. But Charlotte pretends to be pissed.

"What exactly was that? I am not some fire hydrant you can pee on to claim as your own."

"We discussed this earlier."

"A discussion involves two people. You did all the... the talking."

"I didn't hear you complaining."

She blushes and turns away from Owen, embarrassed. "That may be true, but did you hear me agree to anything?"

"Semantics."

Behind her, I see Angus strolling our way with a shit-eating grin. I subtly shake my head, telling him now is not the time, but he doesn't change course.

Charlotte's hands rest on her hips. She's got that fire in her eyes that says she's not going to make this easy on me. It's sexy as all get out. "Whether you like it or not, there's a lot more to discuss before you go scaring people away—"

"Hey, big bro, what brings you in tonight?" Angus sets beers down in front of Charlotte and Owen.

I hold up a hand to silence him. "Not now."

"C'mon. The least I can do for the woman who made Knox's *incident* in Amsterdam disappear is buy her a beer."

"Wait. What?"

She pulls out the chair pushed under the table in front of her, then takes a seat and a sip of her beer. "Thanks, Gus."

"No problem, *Charlie*." Barely containing his smile, he's clearly loving every awkward moment.

"How do you know Knox?" I ask Charlotte. Only Angus answers for her.

"Dude, she's his attorney. She's the one who gets him and the rest of the heathens in the band out of trouble for their stupid shenanigans."

I feel sick.

She was mine. But apparently, she was his first.

Knox has slept his way around the globe and back again. The odds he's been with her are higher than those that would say he hasn't been.

I can barely breathe.

The look on her face says she's confused by my reaction.

"It looks like you two need to have a little chat, so we're gonna leave you to it."

Owen and Gus leave, and she watches me carefully, waiting for me to speak first.

"Please tell me you haven't slept with my brother."

Her face flushes with anger. "What did you just say?"

"Listen, he's a rock star, and few women in his life are just his *friends*. He's had more one-night stands than the entire population of Goose Hollow."

"He's my client, you asshole!"

"I had to ask."

She stands so fast and furiously her high-top chair falls to the ground. She's a little taller tonight with her heels on and almost in my face when she steps in close enough for only me to hear her. "Turns out *you* don't remember *me* as well as you think you do. Besides college, you were the only man I've ever been casual with. You better be careful what you're implying about me if you think you're ever going to touch me again."

I'm frozen to the spot, unable to reply. She's right. I am an asshole. I was out of line, and I know it, but I can't seem to help myself when Charlotte Carruthers is involved.

As soon as she's out the door, Angus is in my face. "What the hell did you say to her?"

Panic and dread hit me like a punch to the gut because this is my fault. I didn't take the time to ask her how she knew my brother when she turned out to be Knox's friend at the cabin. Her naked body spread out on that fucking table more than distracted me.

"I fucked up, Gus."

"Well, you better figure out a way to fix it. She's not the kind of woman you let get away twice."

He has no clue how right he is.

I'm such an asshole.

Chapter Twenty-One

Charlotte

"And then he asked me if I had slept with his brother! Every time I catch a glimpse of the man I met that weekend; he disappears as quickly. He was such an asshole!" I fume on the phone to my best friend.

Karissa McGovern and I went to elementary school together. When my dad's firm took off, I moved to a private school, but we stayed thick as thieves. I went into law, and she became a high school counselor. Our careers seem night and day different from one another, but over the years we've found they're quite similar. Many of my clients are not used to being told no and still behave like spoiled teenagers who can't seem to make the right decision to save their lives.

"Oh, Char. I think he just sounds confused. You ghosted him once, and he thought you had done it a second time. Then he finds out you work for his brother, which he didn't hear directly from you. The poor man doesn't know which way is up."

Karissa has always been my voice of reason. She's the only person I've trusted with the details of my weekend with Callen and the events of the past month. She knows me better than I know myself.

Regardless, Callen didn't seem confused when he bossed me around this morning, but I haven't shared that part with her. There are some things I don't need to tell Karissa.

"That may be true, but it doesn't give him the right to speak to me like that. In public, no less. Since when do we let men tell us who we can and can't talk to?"

"Charlie?" There's laughter in her voice.

"Karissa?" I bite back, not appreciating that she's finding humor in my situation.

"You sure a small part of you doesn't love it?"

"Oh, shut up! I'm never telling you anything ever again!"

She's referring to my confession after our nameless weekend. I foolishly admitted how much I liked it when he took control, so I could let go for once. Like I did this morning.

"I know this is different and agree he needs to watch how he speaks to you in public but remember how you felt that weekend. Letting go helped you take back your power. It was what you needed to get your head straight."

"That was then. I'm not in the same place I was—"

A knock on the door interrupts my thought.

"Crap. Someone's here. I have to go."

"Okay, call me later."

I peek out the front window, and the same black Dodge I watched Callen drive away in is parked in front of the house.

"Wait! It's him. Shit! What do I do?"

"You let him in, and you *talk*. Your clothes stay on, and you use your words. And *then,* you call me and tell me all the juicy details. Bye."

She hangs up, and I slide my phone into my back pocket, taking a moment to gather my thoughts. I'm still pissed, but I would be lying if I said my body wasn't already reacting to his presence. And he's still on the other side of the door. But Karissa is right. My clothes need to stay on until he apologizes and we set a few things straight.

He knocks a second time, and I brace myself for his bossiness when I turn the knob and open the door.

God, he is something else. All six feet and then some of him stands sheepishly with his hands in his pockets and a look that says he knows he messed up.

"Can we talk?"

Can we? I'm not sure either of us is capable of just talking when we're unsupervised in the same room.

"I'd like to apologize," he says when I don't answer.

Curious to see which part of tonight he deems worthy of an apology, I step back and gesture for him to enter. He passes by me and immediately begins to pace in the space between the small living room and dining area as his hand rakes through his hair.

I close the door and lean against it, waiting for him to work out what he wants to say.

Finally, he spins to face me. "How about we try something different for us? No sex. Just a simple two-sided conversation where we talk."

I'm not sure if I'm relieved or disappointed that he too thinks it's best if we left our clothes on. I know we need to talk, but I sure do like him naked.

"I can do that," I acquiesce.

Walking past him, I take a seat at the dining room table in the chair at the far end. He sits at the other end, where earlier today he reminded me how much I like it when he takes control. Having the table between us seemed wiser than sharing the small couch together, but as visions of this morning run through my head, I regret my decision.

His hand is flat on the table where my ass had been only hours before, and he rubs it in a slow circle before he opens his mouth. "I'm sorry, Charlotte."

"Thank you." Those two words are all I'm ready to give him.

"I was irrational. I took my insecurities out on you."

Callen McKinnon admitting he was insecure is not something I expected to hear.

"Our time together was one of the few things I never had to share with anyone else. It was just you and me. To find out my big brother was a part of your life enraged me. I know he's your client, and... my behavior was unacceptable. Deep down, I knew when the words came out of my mouth that it never happened. I just want you all to myself. Even if it's completely professional, it sucks that Knox is a part of your life, too. That he knew you first."

His sincerity is on his sleeve, and if the table weren't between us, I would likely have crawled into his lap and held him. Because despite my earlier anger, I still want to comfort him.

"You really meant it when you said you don't share."

Even though I'm smiling, his furrowed brow says this isn't a joke to him. He doesn't reply but carries on.

"So, what do you say we start over? Try the friend thing and see where it goes?"

The *friend* word hits me square in the chest, and the balloon of excitement expanding in my lungs at our proximity deflates.

"Um, sure. But, earlier in your text, you said we could never be friends."

"I said we would try the friend thing and see where it goes. Because I would really like this to go somewhere, but I think we need to slow things down."

"Okay," I agree.

"Good." His stiff posture slackens a bit, relieved I've accepted his proposal.

"Friends who drink wine while they chat?" I ask.

"That would be nice."

We both stand and move to the kitchen. "All I have is Riesling. Is that okay?"

"Sounds good."

"Will you grab a couple of glasses from the cupboard?"

He grabs the wineglasses, and I open the bottle, feeling his gaze on me the entire time. Already hot and bothered, I'm wondering how foolish we must be to think we could pull off being friends. Two minutes in and I'm already failing.

"Outside?" I suggest. Hoping there's a breeze to cool me down.

He opens the back door and walks toward the picnic table. He makes a show of critiquing my craftsmanship, checking out the underside and setting the glasses on top. Then he shakes the table to check for stability.

I know it's well made and don't need his validation. I'm

confident in my work, but I'd be lying if I said what he thinks doesn't matter. Oddly nervous, I wait for his appraisal.

"It's good, Charlotte. Really good."

Feeling taller than I did earlier in my three-inch heels, I smile a knowing smile, because I knew it was good, but pride swells in my chest with his approval. "Why, thank you. I had fun working on it. It was a nice escape."

"Yeah?"

"I'm not only here for a vacation. I needed to step away from my day-to-day life for a minute and figure some things out. Life has been a lot, and I really needed a break from reality."

"And building things is how you do that. I remember you telling me you couldn't park in your garage at home because it was full of projects."

"You know, your memory is kinda scary."

He shrugs and takes the bottle from me, pouring each of us a glass. Without speaking, he walks to the back porch swing, where we sit facing the lake. The changing colors of the sky serve as the perfect background to the light shining off the lake's surface.

We're quiet for several minutes. The natural rhythm of the swing rocks us gently as we enjoy our wine and the view. I know I've hurt him, and he deserves answers. He found the humility to say he was sorry. It's my turn now.

"When we met, I was going through something pretty heavy. And this was on top of the burnout from working an all-consuming job I don't particularly like."

"Right, you didn't love your job, but you love working side by side with your dad doing something *he* loves."

His ability to recall everything I've ever told him brings a smile to my face. Keeping my attention on the lake, I carry on.

"Earlier that week, my stalker—yes, I had a stalker—was sentenced to five years in prison. The court case took its toll on me. Callen, I was exhausted."

The swing stops swinging back and forth, and I realize it was him setting the easy pace.

"What do you mean, stalker?" His voice is low and hard.

"Well, you know... your typical movie of the week bad guy. I first noticed something was off when I saw a man going through my garbage on my home security camera. I thought it was a strange one-off. Then the same man started showing up on the street in front of my house. He would just stand there in plain sight, staring up at my place. I took pictures and called the police, but at that point he hadn't approached me or threatened me. There wasn't anything they could do."

"Fuck," he says, on a hushed voice, more to himself than me.

"But then the threatening emails and texts started. Calls from unknown phone numbers rang all night and day. I changed my number multiple times, but the calls and messages never ended. Turns out he's some kind of IT hacker extraordinaire."

"Shit, Charlotte."

"Oh, it gets worse."

"Worse?"

I nod, taking a deep breath. "One night, I came home late and found pictures of myself sleeping spread across my bed. There was a note with words cut out of a magazine. It said he was watching me and some other sick and twisted stuff that I don't even want to think about. Callen, he was in my house while I slept in my bed. Alone."

The memory of that night unsettles my stomach.

"What the actual fuck?"

"I know. Right?"

"Charlotte, I'm... I..."

His entire demeanor shifts. His jaw muscle twitches, and his nostrils flare.

I take his hand in mine. Maybe it's not something all friends do, but it feels like a natural reaction to his rage, and I've had time to get over it.

"How did they get the bastard?" Callen asks.

"Well. It took some time, but I have a great lawyer who has friends in high places. The police ran his license plate from the footage they found on a traffic light camera near my house. We got an ID and I filed a restraining order. But he didn't seem to care. If anything, it pushed him further. That's when he turned up at the firm and locked himself in my office. With me inside it. Not only did he break the restraining order, but he held me hostage."

Turning toward me, he exhales a big breath before he asks, "Did he touch you?"

"No, he didn't. It was strange. Almost like he knew by showing up that day he would be caught."

He lifts our hands and kisses the back of mine. "I'm glad they caught him."

I squeeze his hand. "Me too. I met you the week they sentenced him to five years in prison."

"That isn't anywhere near long enough."

"Well, it was something, and for now, I'm enjoying the peace of mind, knowing he's behind bars."

"Charlotte…"

This time, *I* use *my* toes to bring the swing back to its gentle rocking. I need it to soothe me while I relive one of the hardest times in my life. There's more to say, and I need to get it all out before I lose my nerve.

"Two days after the sentencing, my dad was diagnosed with terminal cancer, giving him six months to a year to live. When I met you, I needed a release, but after everything I had been through, I wasn't ready for more. I didn't have the emotional capacity for more. You were a stranger who didn't know me, my family, what I did for a living, or what I had just been through. You didn't pity me or feel sorry for me. For one blissful weekend, I got to be the old me. I could pretend my dad wasn't dying and that some psycho wasn't in jail for what he had put though. The time we spent together was magical. There was power in our anonymity. Giving you my name…." I shake my head. "That would have been giving you… a man… the power I desperately needed to recapture."

"Fuck, that's a lot, Charlotte, and I'm so sorry to hear about your dad." He lets out another heavy sigh. "To be honest, I'm doing my best not to lose it right now. The thought of someone doing that to you…. Knowing you were afraid in your own home. That he invaded your personal space. Well, it makes me sick."

His grip on my hand tightens, but not to the point of pain. The hand not holding mine is clenched in a fist, his knuckles white from the tightness. He tilts his head back, and just as I'm about to speak, he takes a fortifying breath and looks at me—not with pity, but with sadness.

"I get it. I do. Now that I know the reasons behind your decision, it's completely understandable you wouldn't have wanted to share all of this with a nameless stranger. But, God, did I want more of you."

"I did too, but Callen, it wouldn't have worked. I wasn't ready. You'll never know how glad I am to have the chance to say thank you."

"Thank you?"

"For helping me remember how to be happy."

He lifts our hands to kiss the back of mine again. Doing all he can to show restraint in our new *just friends* era.

"You gave me so much in those forty-eight hours. I'm not sure if it makes sense or if I can explain it the way I want to, but I took back my power by withholding part of me from you. But I also did something I've never done before."

"Oh yeah? What was that?" His voice is soft. Caring.

Ignoring the heat rushing to my cheeks, I keep going. I've had so many things I've wanted to say to him for so long, and I need this to come out right.

"I let you take control in other ways. I had never been that free before. Had never let pure pleasure take the lead and let myself indulge in it. In you."

I finally brave a look in his direction so he can see the sincerity in my eyes.

"By letting you show me what I liked and what would make me feel good, you gave me a piece of myself that was missing. I don't even want to know how you know how to make me feel the way you do, but I'll never be able to thank you enough for our time together."

Letting go of my hand, he pulls me closer, wrapping his arm around my shoulder and squeezing me tight to his side. The swing rocks again at his pace, and my head rests on his shoulder as we take in the setting sun and its reflection on the water.

"My dad died last month."

He kisses the top of my head. "I'm so sorry."

"That's why I'm here. To clear my head. Knox knew everything I was going through. He said the cabin was free for the foreseeable future since he's on tour for the next year and a half, and as you know, the security system is top-notch. He told me to take my time and stay as long as I needed."

"I'm glad he did. In fact, I've never appreciated my brother more."

"Me too."

We cuddle tighter into one another, but don't take things further.

"How are you dealing with the loss of your dad? I know how important he was to you."

"It's hard, but we had a long time to come to terms with things. When his health declined, it went fast, but I was fortunate to have had the warning we did. We talked about everything. There wasn't anything left unsaid. For him. Or for me. We were really lucky to have that."

He stiffens underneath me and clears his throat. "What kind of talks? Were you able to tell him that you might want to make a career change before he passed?"

"I did finally admit that as much as I wanted to love my job, I hated being an entertainment lawyer. Once I spilled my guts and he realized I had chosen my career path to make him happy, he insisted I figure out what would bring me joy and to do just that. In the end, that's all he ever wanted for me. Happiness."

"That must have been a tough conversation to have. I'm proud of you."

I smile up at him. We may have been naked and screwing like rabbits 50 percent of the time, but I shared more with him that weekend than I have with anyone else and it feels could to have my confidence back. He may not have known exactly what I did for a living, but he recognizes that telling my dad was one of the hardest things I've ever done.

"He wants me to sell the business to a good friend of his. He already set it up for an easy transition to his friend Richard's firm. Our current clients will be able to work with the new firm at their current rates should they choose to. My dad trusts Richard implicitly. All I have to do is make the call, and it's done."

"But it's not as simple as that, is it? Not when the memory of your dad is involved."

How does he see right into my heart and know exactly what I'm feeling? We barely know each other.

Still, he sees me.

He knows me.

I don't mean to cry, but tears fill my eyes and roll down my cheeks before I can stop them. It's like he has a direct line to my emotions. He opens up a piece of my heart nobody has before. A piece of my heart I had unknowingly been saving for him.

We don't talk anymore. Instead, he holds me while I cry, and I let him.

Once the sky has faded to black, he carries the wine bottle and our glasses back into the house, locking the back door behind us. He's getting ready to leave when all I want is for him to stay. Where he only wants to be friends, I'd give anything to sleep in his arms tonight. But he's right. We need to get to know each other with our clothes on if we want to see where things might go.

I follow him as he walks out the front door, turning and shoving his hands in the front pockets of his jeans, he clears his throat. "Can I take you to lunch tomorrow?"

"That would be nice."

"Cool. I'll text you in the morning with the details."

"Sounds good."

I swear him not kissing me goodbye is more awkward than any first kiss I've ever had.

"Lock up and make sure you set the alarm, and I'll talk to you tomorrow."

"See you tomorrow."

I lock the door and am setting the alarm when my phone pings. I'm surprised to see it's a text from Callen. He hasn't even made it to his truck yet.

CALLEN

I'm really glad Knox sent you to Goose Hollow.

CALLEN

Sleep well, Charlotte.

Chapter Twenty-Two

Callen

There's something to be said for shutting the hell up and listening.

In my case, giving Charlotte a chance to talk while I kept my mouth closed was the smartest thing I've ever done.

Knowing what I now know helps to make sense of why she left me the way she did. But the rage I felt when she told me about her stalker has stayed with me. I can't help but think if she had been mine, I could have protected her. That bastard never would have gotten anywhere near her.

The things I wanted to do to the man who made her life a living hell....

When I woke from the couple hours of sleep I managed to get after scenarios of what could have happened to her ran rampant through my head, the first thing I did was send her a good morning text. I didn't expect a reply that early in the morning, so it was a pleasant surprise when she texted right back, and we made our lunch plans.

Ruby and I are waiting for her at an outside table in front of Gracie's Crooked River Café when Charlotte rounds the corner and heads in our direction. Repeating *just friends* over and over in my head, I try to reel in my carnal need for her. Try to ignore her bare tan shoulders only covered by the spaghetti straps of her long flowing summer dress. The form-fitting torso loosens into an ankle-length flowy skirt. Her ponytail bounces as she walks, and there is a big, beautiful smile on her face.

Damn, I think she's happy to see me.

Taking a deep, calming breath, I pat Ruby. "There she is, girl. We have to be on our best behavior so we don't scare her away."

I stand when she nears, but all of her attention is on Ruby, who pulls on her leash to get to Charlotte. The leash I only put on her today because of our previous run in at the park.

"Well, hello sweet girl. It's nice to see you again." She lifts her sunglasses to the top of her head, and her bright eyes meet mine. "Is it okay if I pet her?"

"She would be heartbroken if you didn't."

She squats in front of Ruby and rubs behind her ears. "Aren't you pretty? What a good girl."

After giving my dog the attention I wish she'd give me, she stands and says, "Hi," as she opens her arms, stepping in to give me a hug.

"Hi." I hug her maybe a second longer than I should, but

it feels too right to have her in my arms. And she smells... so... damn... good.

She steps away, and for a beat, we just look at each other with stupid smiles on our faces.

Clearing my throat as I snap out of it, I pull out her chair. "I hope you don't mind sitting outside? I like to take Ruby with me when I can."

"No, not at all. This is perfect."

She takes her seat, and I do too, rubbing my clammy palms against my jeans. My nervousness makes no sense whatsoever, considering I had her naked with my head between her legs a little over twenty-four hours ago. It could be the relief that the reason she didn't want to give me her name went much deeper than I could have imagined.

Maybe it's the knowledge that she's thinking of making big life changes, and I desperately want to be involved in those changes.

Regardless of the reason, sitting across from her smiling like an idiot won't get us anywhere.

Daisy's best friend Mia comes and takes our drink orders, and after she leaves I clear my throat awkwardly once again.

With no idea what else to do, I try for easy, generic conversation. "So how are you liking Goose Hollow?"

"I love it here. I've spent some time in Bend and Redmond as well, and the entire area is beautiful."

"Do you know how long you'll be staying?"

Please say you love it so much you're never leaving.

"Well, as long as life will let me. At some point, I'll have to go home and face reality."

I want to push and ask for more details, but I swear I can

still feel last night's tears on my shoulder. We need to keep today's vibe light and breezy.

No more tears.

I'm glad she trusted me enough to open up, but it hurt my soul to know she was in pain and had suffered so much.

"What about your mom?" It's a hail Mary, but it was the first thing I could come up with. "I don't think you've ever mentioned her."

"Well, she isn't much of a presence in my life. When I was small and my dad was just starting his career, she left him for another man with more money. Then she left that man for another man with even more money and is currently on her third husband."

Shit. Way to go, McKinnon.

"I'm sorry to hear that. Makes sense why you and your dad were so tight."

"It's all good. I learned a lot from her. Most importantly, I didn't ever want to *be* her. I know my worth, whereas her self-worth equates to the depth of the bank account of the man she's with. I can take care of myself. Having someone to share life with would be a wonderful bonus, but not a necessity."

With every layer she peels back for me, I see her clearer.

My respect and attraction for her grow stronger and stronger.

"Your dad never remarried?"

"Nope. He said he was too busy, but I think she broke his heart, and he never fully trusted women again."

"That's a shame."

"I guess you could say he was married to his work. And he made it clear he didn't want that for me. I think he would be happy to know I was here. Taking this time."

"Well, while you're here—" I'm distracted when I see Mr. Jameson across the street looking lost. This is the second time this week he's wandered around downtown. He hasn't been the same since Mrs. Jameson passed last fall. "Excuse me, I'll be right back. Do you mind watching Ruby?"

She looks confused but takes the leash.

It will be ninety degrees today, and Mr. Jameson has on a sweater over a collared shirt. I jog across the street to catch up to him as he shuffles along the sidewalk, looking into the shop windows. He's most likely trying to find his daughter's coffee shop.

He doesn't hear me when I approach and he startles when I say, "Hey, Mr. Jameson, how are you doing?"

"Oh, McKinnon, it's you. I'm good. How are you, son?"

He has taken to calling all of us in the family by our last name. I'm pretty sure our first names have escaped him.

"You headed to Becca's place?"

"Oh, yes. Rebecca. She's got the best coffee in town."

"She does, but she's on the other side of the street. Why don't we walk over there together?"

It's heartbreaking to witness the slow decline of one of the pillars of the community. The Jameson family has lived in this town for generations and helped make it what it is today. Before she passed away, his wife organized the Fourth of July parade every summer and the Christmas festival every winter. Their oldest son lives in Arizona, but their daughter still lives here and works at our local credit union. One granddaughter is a journalist based in New York, and the other, Rebecca, really does make the best coffee in town.

Rebecca runs her shop and helps her mother take care of

her grandpa and I've never seen her without a smile on her face.

We chat as I carefully guide him across the street, doing my best to help without him noticing. It's a slow walk, but we get there, and when we do, Rebecca is waiting for us on the sidewalk in front of her cafe.

"Hey, Pops, whatcha doin' out here in this heat with a sweater on?"

"It's not too hot for me, Gloria. Now, how about some coffee?"

Her eyes water, but she doesn't let any tears fall when he calls her by her mother's name.

"Thanks, Cal," she mouths, taking her grandfather's arm to usher him inside.

"Sure thing, Becca. Anytime."

She smiles weakly and her attention returns to her grandfather. The sorrow in her eyes makes it clear she knows tough decisions will need to be made, and soon. With everything going on in my life right now, I still don't envy the Jameson family and the road ahead for them.

Picking up my pace, I jog back to the café and find Charlotte watching me while her hand leisurely pets Ruby's head. What a sight they are. I'm damn lucky my feet don't skip the same beat my heart does, or I would be assed out on the sidewalk.

Ruby's tail wags, but she makes no move to greet me when I approach the table.

I'd call her a traitor, but I get it. I'd choose Charlotte, too.

"Sorry about that. Now, where were we?"

"Is he okay?"

"He is now. Thanks for watching my girl."

"No thanks needed. She's the sweetest. If she comes up missing, you know where to look."

"You thinking about stealing my dog?"

You've already stolen my heart. Then stomped it into the ground and destroyed it. You might as well steal my dog, too.

"Do I have a master plan yet? No." She winks. "But I'm working on it."

From there, we make light surface-level conversation and eat lunch. Neither of us brings up last night's discussion.

My phone rings, and Daisy's face lights up the screen.

"Sorry, do you mind?" I ask, holding the phone up for her to see.

"Go ahead."

I accept the video call. "What's up, sis?"

"Did you ask her yet?" Daisy's excitement practically vibrates my phone.

It takes me a moment to remember what she's referring to. "Shit. I'll do it right now."

"You still at lunch?"

"Yep."

"She right there?"

"Yup."

"Tell her I said hi and pretty please!"

"Daisy says hi." I hold the phone up for Charlotte again.

Charlotte lifts her hand in a wave. "Hi, Daisy."

I turn the phone back around. "Listen, I'll ask her right now and let you know."

"Thanks. Enjoy your lunch. Both of you keep your hands above the table."

I hang up without saying goodbye.

Siblings can be so stupid.

"So, what are you supposed to ask me?"

"First things first... you are free to say no. I know you're on vacation, but one of our cousins is having a wedding at the end of the summer and needs tables. I may or may not have told her about your table, and she wants you to make some for the wedding."

She's beaming. "Some?"

"Ten, to be exact."

You would have thought I'd told her she could take Ruby home with her she is smiling so big. But she hasn't answered.

"Simple tables," I clarify. "Nothing as time-consuming as your picnic table. I know you're not sure how long you'll be here, but if it's something you're interested in, you can use the shop at the store if it makes it easier. You'd have everything you need on hand. Take your time and let—"

"Yes! Yes! Yes! I would love to!"

I chuckle at her enthusiasm. "Great, I'll send you Daisy's details, and she can give you the info you'll need."

"Thank you, Cal."

"Callen."

"What?" she asks, confused.

"Cal...len," I say, slowly sounding out my name.

The shy smile and sudden blush on her cheeks tell me she understands my meaning. We're trying the friends thing to see where it goes, but we will never just be friends. We both know that.

"Well, thank you, *Callen*."

"Let me run in and pay, then I can take you over to the shop and show you around."

"Here. Let me pay for mine." She pulls her wallet from her purse, but her hand catches on the dog leash, and her wallet and everything inside it scatters under the table. "Shit."

"Here, I got you."

I bend down to help her pick things up, and fuck all, if my stomach doesn't somersault all over itself when I see Bob Dylan staring up at me.

Our hotel key.

She kept her key all these years.

Not only did she keep it, but she also carries it around with her.

She snatches it up and Bob's gone in a flash. Doesn't matter because she kept him, and that's enough.

I gather insurance cards and a credit card and hand them to her without mentioning the key. I'll save that for another day and let it fuel me. Let it give me the patience I'll need as we spend time together, but keep our hands off each other.

To do this right.

To make sure she doesn't want to walk away again.

Chapter Twenty-Three

Charlotte

After lunch, I followed Callen to the store, and he showed me around the shop. The smell of wood and the feel of tools in my hands combined with his proximity was exhilarating.

Overwhelming.

Everything about Goose Hollow and Callen is overwhelming in the best possible way. Opening my world up to new dreams and maybe even new possibilities.

His support of my passion and complete faith in my abilities is incredibly sexy. Working in a male-dominated industry with mostly male clients, I've had my fair share of men thinking there's no way I'm up to the task. At least, until I prove them wrong.

And I always prove them wrong.

Sexy or not, he stayed true to his word, and even though

the sexual connection between us is always tingling just under the surface, we didn't act on it.

He didn't bring up our past or even last night's conversation, and when I left the shop, he leaned in and placed a friendly kiss on my cheek.

On my way back to the cabin, thoughts of Callen helping Mr. Jameson to the coffee shop and of Ruby following Callen everywhere floated around my mind. She loves her daddy a whole heck of a lot, and dogs know what's up. Also, I couldn't help but notice the way his disposition changed ever so slightly when we got to the store. It was subtle enough that I almost missed it, but the tension in his shoulders as he walked me around caught my attention.

But what I really can't stop thinking about is the panic that consumed me when the hotel key fell out of my wallet.

The same hotel key I couldn't part with after I walked out of the Sunset Marquis, knowing I was depriving us both of something beautiful. A constant reminder of his brown eyes, soft touch, and his desire for more. In some ways, keeping the souvenir was a form of masochism, but it has become a good luck token. Anytime I change purses, I make sure to slide it into my wallet or zipper pocket of my bag.

Always bringing it with me.

Bringing *him* with me.

He didn't mention the key, so I think I'm in the clear, but I've been sweating bullets all day. And not because of the ninety-degree weather. I'm sure he would have said something if he had seen it. He wouldn't miss the opportunity to tease me, would he?

Now, I'm sitting in Daisy's living room drinking a glass of rosé. We've gone over the details of what's needed for the tables, talked about her job as an interior designer and occasional contractor, and she's shared lots of town gossip.

Her place is small but perfect, a quaint bungalow transformed into a chic yet comfortable oasis. Being child and pet-free affords her the luxury of various shades of white, beige, and light gray. Such a stark contrast to the dark rustic cabin I'm staying in.

When I first arrived, putting my best foot forward around his sister had me shaking in my flip-flops. Whatever Callen and I are is important to me, which means what Daisy thinks of me is important. We may have hung out at the bar the other night, but one-on-one time with her in the quiet of her home is a whole other thing. Yet within minutes of my arrival, all thoughts of impressing her had vanished. She is so sweet and fun, and hearing how badass she is with running her business in the world of contracting was awe-inspiring. I might even say we're kindred spirits.

"Daisy, I am so envious of you and your career. What I wouldn't give to feel the way you obviously do about your work." I take a sip of my wine. "I'm at this crossroads of finally having the chance to do what I want or continuing to do what I've always done and know I'm good at. And the truth is, I'm scared shitless."

Her reply is to top off my glass before scooting back into her couch to get comfortable, and looking at me as if to say, "tell me everything," so I do just that.

By the time I reach the bottom of my first glass of wine, I've filled Daisy in about my dad's passing and my decision to come to Goose Hollow to think about what to do with my life. And even the lack of relationship I have with my mother.

I don't tell her every sordid detail of my past or mention her brother, but I share enough to reveal why I'm here.

"If your dad has it all set up, what is there to think about? Sounds like you already know what you want to do."

She's right. I know she is. But what if...? I don't even know if I can speak the words out loud, but something about her makes me trust her as if I'd known her my entire life.

"What if I fail?"

"Oh, sweetie." She waves her hand in front of me. "I don't really get the failure kind of vibe from you."

"Well, I may not have a history of failing, but I certainly have the potential for it."

"So what?"

"What do you mean?"

"So what if you fail?"

"When it comes to my professional life, I've never failed. What if I give up the business my dad spent his life building, and I'm total crap at doing whatever it is I decide to do? I may not love my job, but I'm great at it."

"Charlie, failure is a part of life. We've all done it. It sucks, but it isn't fatal."

We've all done it, but it isn't fatal. I think I want to be Daisy McKinnon when I grow up.

"You'll get some things right and learn from what might have gone wrong, and you'll adjust. Maybe building furniture and flipping houses isn't what you thought it would be. That's okay too. You may not love it as much as you hoped you would, but you'll always regret not giving it a chance."

"You sound a lot like my friend Karissa. In fact, she's given me a version of this talk more than once in the past month. Is there some best friend tutorial that I missed out on while I was in law school? You two would get along so well."

"Karissa sounds fantastic." She winks, pushing her brown bob behind her ear.

"She is. Besides my dad, she's always been the person in my life I can count on, no matter what."

"Well, you need to invite her here. We can show her around Central Oregon, and I promise we'll have a good time."

"I just might do that. Seriously, though. Thanks for the advice. I appreciate it."

"Well, while you're in the mood for advice, shall we talk about my brother?"

"Knox?"

I knew we'd get here eventually, but I have no idea what Callen has told her and don't know how much he'd want me to say.

"Nice try. And I don't mean Angus either."

I take a sip of wine. "This sure is good," I say, stalling for time.

"Listen, I don't know much about what went down with you two, but I know he was never the same after he came home from California. I can't believe I'm going to ask this, but he's my brother, and I love him so..."

Pouring myself more wine, I gulp down liquid courage and brace myself for whatever she's about to ask.

"What are your intentions with my brother?"

Not what I was expecting. I choke and do my best not to spit my rose all over her. "Excuse me?" Grabbing a napkin, I mop off my chin.

"You heard me. I like you, and my brother, well, I think

you know he likes you, too. He's under a lot of stress right now and doesn't need to add heartbreak into the mix."

I don't know what my intentions are but have no intention of breaking his heart. "We're... friends. Keeping things platonic."

She chuckles into her wineglass before taking a sip. "Yeah, like that's gonna last."

She has a point, but I don't concede. "Daisy, the last thing I want to do is his hurt your brother. I didn't come to Goose Hollow knowing I would find him again. All of this is as big of a surprise to me as it is to him."

"I know," she beams. "It's kind of magical, don't ya think?"

I shrug and smile. "It is a pretty crazy coincidence."

"Sounds meant to be, if you ask me."

"Well, we're taking it slow." As long as you don't count sex at his place and then whatever that was yesterday on the table. I wonder if Knox would let me take the table with me when I leave. I'm not sure I'll ever be able to part with it now.

"I get it. And that's smart. What's not smart is my big brother keeping his problems with the business to himself. It's a family business and belongs to Mom and all four of us kids, but he thinks he needs to deal with whatever it is on his own."

"What do you mean?"

"Well, Callen hasn't been the same since our dad died."

"Wait, your dad died?"

"Six months ago. He didn't say anything?"

"Shit, I'm so sorry, Daisy. I had no idea. Why did you let me ramble on about my dad? You should have said something."

My heart breaks for Callen, Daisy, and their whole family. I know better than anyone how hard it is to lose your father. I can't believe he let me go on about my dad and didn't mention a thing about losing his, too.

Why does it hurt so much that he didn't tell me?

And why didn't Knox ever say anything? These McKinnon men are infuriating.

"Thanks. It was sudden. He had a heart attack."

"Oh, Daisy."

"It's Callen you need to worry about. Like I said, he hasn't been the same since we lost Dad. I know something is going on with the business, yet he acts like everything is fine. He won't tell us anything."

My heart hurts knowing he let me lay all my burdens on him last night, and he never mentioned what he was going through. "Have Knox and Angus tried to talk to him?"

"Yep, and he lies through his teeth and pretends everything is cool. We haven't said anything to Mom. She's barely surviving day by day as it is. She acts like she's fine, but I can see that the light in her eyes has dimmed." She slams the rest of her wine and holds her glass out for me to fill. "Thank you. Hey, tomorrow's the Fourth. You got any plans?"

"Can't say that I do."

"Well, you do now. My friend Mia and her family have a big blowout at their lake house every year. There will be barbecue and fireworks over the lake, and you're coming."

Will Callen be there? I want to ask but don't.

"Sure, I'd love to."

"It's a date!"

Chapter Twenty-Four

Callen

What a day.

The store may be closed for the holiday, but I never seem to get a day off.

It started with a frantic call from Stan at the rec center. A pipe had burst, and the kitchen was flooding. Not only was I his only option, but I can't say no when someone is in need, so I spent five hours fixing the burst pipe and helping Stan clean up the aftermath. The last place I want to be is a social event where everyone I know will be in attendance. So why am I trying to find an open parking spot along the long car-packed road that leads to the Powells?

Because Charlotte texted to say Daisy invited her to tonight's festivities and wanted to know if I would be there.

Had she asked me that question before telling me she was attending, the answer would have been a steadfast no.

Followed by me inviting myself to the cabin where we could watch the Powell's fireworks from her porch swing. On the other side of the lake, we'd have a perfect view all to ourselves.

But no such luck.

She's going to the barbecue tonight.

So dammit. I'm going too.

As I walk toward the house, my nerves ignite. Too many voices, bottle rockets being shot into the air, and loud music confirms what I already know. My idea would have been a whole hell of a lot more fun, but life isn't always fair. And don't I know that to be true?

Daisy and Angus will be here, and I know it's not fair of me to hold resentment toward my siblings, but lately, I can't shake the feeling. Even though I've kept them in the dark about the clusterfuck of a shambles Dad left the family business in, I'm irritated every time I'm around them lately. Who am I kidding? I'm annoyed in general these days. I still can't believe our beloved father hadn't paid taxes in years and now I somehow have to come up with $1,374,512.03 in back taxes, or we lose the business.

Even though it belongs to the family, Dad left me in charge and as the executor of his will. I haven't had the heart to tell my mom or my brothers and sister that Dad wasn't the superhero we all thought he was. He was a great man, but clearly, he had flaws none of us ever knew about.

Between the back taxes, my recent decision to sell the property where I intended to build my dream house to help pay said back taxes, and my day spent at the rec center, I'm not exactly in the mood for a party.

But if Charlotte's here, I'm here. She's the only thing that seems to dull my irritation with the world these days, yet she is her own source of aggravation.

I want her.

Only her.

As glad as I am that she's here, in Goose Hollow, this is only a break in her reality. Eventually, she'll go back to California. Therefore, even when I'm with her, I'm irritated.

Irritated by the pain I know is inevitable.

I've never been one to live in the moment, always armed with a plan and working toward a goal. But with Charlotte, it's all out of my hands.

She's the one in control.

As much as she may like it when I take over behind closed doors, she has all the real power.

She has since the first moment I heard her voice.

I walk around the side of the house to avoid as many people as possible for as long as I can. But when I round the corner the gathering comes into view, and even I can't deny the Powells know how to throw a party.

Outdoor lights line the half acre of perfectly kept grass, which is no easy feat in this part of the state. People scatter from the back deck down to the water's edge. The event is catered, and still several large tables are filled with food brought by those in attendance. Potluck dishes are to the right, close to the deck and picnic tables. Adirondack chairs are scattered over the lawn. I pass the drink table stacked with the obligatory red cups and punch bowls and head toward the beer tap and coolers at the end.

I don't make it two steps toward the beer before her laughter redirects my steps, guiding me toward the sound like some sort of beacon. When Bobby Randall moves to the left, I see her standing with Daisy and a group of my sister's friends. She's shaking Murphy's hand, and the vise she has around my heart tightens as my body moves toward them with purpose.

It's not jealousy. It's a primal need that takes over whenever I see her near another man.

What it is... is new.

I was never territorial over my ex. Never had this overwhelming need to be near her, touching her. Making it clear to everyone in a five-mile radius that she's mine.

I know as well as I know my own name that Charlotte Carruthers is *the one* I'm meant to be with.

She's my endgame.

Why else would she be here? In my hometown.

Fate isn't something I've ever believed in, but even a fool can see something is at play here. I'm not sure what it is, but I intend to let this thing between us progress. Because she may be my endgame, but I'm clueless how that becomes a reality when we live two completely different lives.

Not to mention my brilliant idea of playing the *get to know you* and *let's just be friends* game. I know it's the right thing to do, no matter how drawn to her I am. We know we're explosive between the sheets, but a real relationship requires so much more. Keeping things platonic is the only way to see if we share more than incredible sexual compatibility. And I'll wait as long as it takes to get there. It's important we do this the right way.

I'm reminding myself of this as I approach the group, fighting the urge to shove the other men out of the way to get to her. When she spots me, her eyes go wide, and try as she might, there's no hiding the smile crossing her features at the sight of me. And doesn't that make my dick hard and my heart want to beat out of its damn chest?

I'm so fucked when it comes to this woman.

Her hand comes up to her chest to play with her necklace as she moves the chain from side to side. Her long blond locks are down, and she's in a light blue summer dress that exposes her arms and ends a little below her knees. A cream sweater is wrapped around her waist, and the look ends with white sneakers. Casual but beautiful.

My eyes stay locked on hers as I insert myself into the circle of friends she's chatting with and take my place by her side. Right where I'm meant to be.

"Hi," she says for only me to hear.

"Happy Fourth," I reply, leaning down to kiss her cheek.

When I pull back, the blush on her face does nothing to calm the hardness continuing to grow against the zipper of my jeans.

C'mon, Callen. This isn't the seventh grade. Get your shit together before you embarrass yourself.

My kiss was innocent enough, but the group stares at me as though I have three heads, confused by the gesture. Charlotte takes a step to the side, putting space between us, and I don't like that at all.

The last thing I want is space, but this whole damn friend game was my idea.

What the hell was I thinking?

"Thought you weren't coming, big bro," my little sister asks, reminding me Charlotte isn't the only person here and engaging the group would be the polite thing to do. But I'm still not in the mood.

"I changed my mind."

"Hey, Cal. How's it going?" Daisy's best friend, Mia, asks, bouncing her little boy on her hip.

Mia is family. She's beautiful, with long black hair and brilliant blue eyes, but I look at her the same way I do my sister. And her little boy, well, I consider him my nephew. We all do. But Mia has her secrets—one of which being the identity of Sawyer's father.

"Good, Mia, how are you?" I lean in for a hug, and when I do, Sawyer reaches out for me, and I take him out of her arms. "Look at this handsome little man. He's growing like a weed! Aren't you, buddy?"

There's something about Sawyer. Since he was born, I've felt a connection with the little guy. It feels like I know him. Sounds crazy, but there it is.

"Can you believe he's officially a year and a half? It's crazy how fast time is going. It's been exhausting, but he's more than worth it."

"You doing okay?" I hold Sawyer above me, making airplane noises and flying him in the air like he likes. "You need anything?"

"Thanks for asking, but we're okay. My parents are an enormous help, and Aunt Daisy spoils him rotten."

"I'm sure he deserves it all." I bring his chubby little body to my face and gently press a raspberry on his cheek, making sure my beard doesn't irritate his skin. He laughs that addictive baby laugh, so I give him another one on the other cheek.

"Charlotte, have you met Sawyer?"

I prop my favorite little man on my hip and turn to her, holding his hand up and encouraging him to wave. He takes over on his own, waving at her as he kicks his legs, bouncing himself on my hip.

"Yes, I have. He's been charming me with those beautiful blue eyes of his."

Seriously, I can't even trust the baby with her. I whisper in his ear. "Hey, man. Bro code. She's mine. Hands off."

Her eyes sparkle with delight, and her blush is back, but she doesn't protest. However, Sawyer throws the bro code into the lake when he reaches for her, and she takes him in her arms.

"Looks like you've got some competition, Cal." Murphy chuckles.

"Et tu, Sawyer?" I say, my hand over my heart.

Murphy was at The House the night I danced with Charlotte. He knows Sawyer is the only one who gets to touch her.

"Hey, Murph."

"What's up, man? Good to see you." He holds his beer cup up toward me in salutation.

Murphy's a good guy, and I've known him all his life. That doesn't mean I didn't want to rip his throat out when I saw him shaking hands with Charlotte.

"You too."

My side of the conversation comes out stunted because I'm distracted watching the twosome next to me. Charlotte rubs noses with Sawyer, and he grabs her hair to pull her face closer. She gently pries open his little fists to free her hair and throws it behind her shoulders, out of his reach.

I feel my sister staring and glance in her direction. She gives me a knowing smile and wrinkles her nose at me.

She's happy for me.

However, I don't want her to get too excited. Things are just beginning, but if I have my way, they won't end in pain this time. Hell, they won't ever end.

Daisy looks over my shoulder, and her happy demeanor fades. I turn to see who has changed her mood, and my stomach knots when my ex-wife comes into view. She looks at me with a hopeful smile, and I turn my back on her, directing my attention toward Daisy.

"Why is she here?" I ask, trying to hide the disgust in my question.

"She and Wyatt broke up, and she moved back to town last week. I would have warned you, but I didn't know you were coming."

Wyatt.

My cousin.

That's right. My wife cheated on me with my cousin. Nothing like keeping it in the family. Kacey and I had been together since high school. Ours may not have been the passionate kind of love, but I was still faithful. I never would have stepped out on her. Apparently, she didn't feel the same level of loyalty.

I was relieved when she and Wyatt moved to Portland. When you end a relationship in a small town, there's no escaping your ex. With one grocery store, two taverns, my brother's bar, and only a couple of restaurants, there is no way around it. You will have to deal with them on the regular. So, when they moved out of town, I couldn't have been happier.

Hearing she's back is just the cherry on top of the shit show that is my life.

"Who is that?" Charlotte asks Daisy in a whisper, still bouncing Sawyer on her hip.

My sister silently mouths back, "Cal's ex."

Eyes wide, her grip on the baby tightens a bit as she

focuses on Kacey. She rubs Sawyer on the back and gives his chubby cheek a kiss. Soothing him in an effort to soothe herself.

All of my attention is on the woman with the baby in her arms. She is beautiful, and her natural way with the toddler is absolutely gorgeous. The way she seamlessly fits in with Daisy and her friends is easy. Seeing her here, at the Powell's annual party, isn't strange. She looks like she's meant to be in Goose Hollow around everyone I care about.

Like the key in her wallet, she fits.

For me, she is the only key that fits.

Chapter Twenty-Five

Charlotte

I know too much. I know what she did to him, and I have no desire to meet the woman who cheated on Callen with his cousin. It may have been years ago, but his reaction to her presence seems like a prequel to an uncomfortable moment about to commence.

"Hey, Mia, is it okay if Sawyer and I go look at the lights?" I ask.

"Sure. As long as you don't mind taking him."

"Not at all. He's a doll."

Callen looks at me with a blank expression, as though he's already ready for Kacey to join the group, and he's trying not to react. The joyful man who was playing with Sawyer is gone.

I give his arm a light touch. "We'll be back."

I'm only two steps away when I hear her speak. "Hey, Mia. Hey, Daisy. Happy Fourth."

As much as I would like to stay nearby and listen, her lighthearted tone makes me want to puke. Like she can just breeze on in like nothing ever happened. I force myself to keep walking to the edge of the property behind the food tables where the lights are strung. Connected by tall stakes in the ground, they're right above our heads, and Sawyer lifts his hand to touch them, but they're out of his reach.

Turning us so we're facing what seems like must be most of the town's population. My heart skips a beat when I spot Callen still standing with the group, turned away and watching us. When I say turned away, I don't mean he's angled his body so he could see us. I mean, he has turned his back on everyone and is watching me.

If I weren't holding this baby, I'd be showing him exactly what I think of this *just friends* farce. It's obvious we're both going through the motions. Pretending. Because Callen watching me, watch him, watching me is one of the hottest moments of my life. Almost as hot as him ordering me to spread my thighs on the cabin table.

There is something about his intent focus on me that gets me going.

He certainly isn't hiding what we both know is true. We will always be much more than friends.

Kacey walks away from the group, heading for the keg, and as Sawyer and I start back toward his mom and Callen, I can't help but watch her. She's tall and thin with a pale complexion and long black hair. Wearing a tight white tank, jeans, and cowboy boots, she looks like she belongs here.

Callen meets me halfway, standing close and rubbing the

back of the little man in my arms. "Hey, big guy. How were the lights?"

Watching his natural disposition with the baby penetrates a maternal corner of my heart that I never realized existed until tonight. This man surprises me every day. His carefree honesty and bossiness in the bedroom had me at hello during our lost weekend, but since I've been here, I've discovered new pieces of him that only make me want him more.

"He's such a sweetie."

"He really is. Something about this kid just does me in. I can't get enough of him."

And I can't get enough of you.

"Where's his daddy?"

"Good question. None of us know."

"Did he abandon them?"

"Not sure. Mia won't tell us who the father is. He could be here right now, and none of us would be the wiser. Not to mention, she's doing all of it on her own. I'm not even sure the father knows he has a kid."

"Whoa."

"Right?" Sawyer has trapped Callen's finger in his pudgy fist. "She's pretty tight-lipped about the whole thing. I just hope nothing bad happened to her, and that's why she's not saying anything."

"It's pretty cool she has all of you to support her."

"She and Daisy have been friends their entire lives. She's basically family. Besides, that's what we do here in our little town. We take care of our own."

He's close.

So close.

I tilt my head back to look him in the eyes. "I like that about this place."

His eyes, intense as always, have a new sparkle in them and one corner of his mouth lifts.

"Nice change from the people in LA?"

"You could say that."

He begins to say something but falls silent when his gaze moves to my lips, setting me ablaze before his chocolate eyes meet mine again, reflecting back the same passion burning inside me.

Sawyer screeches and bounces restlessly on my hip.

"Oh, my. You want your mommy, little one?" I ask, but he reaches for Callen.

"Buddy, I'll be right back. I'm just gonna go get Charlotte and me some drinks." He rubs the baby's head and plants a kiss on the top of it.

When Callen lifts his head, he's close enough to kiss me, too. Instead, with his eyes on my lips, he asks, "What can I get you?"

Flashes of a future with him and of a baby of our own temporarily render me speechless, but I recover quickly. "Whatever's on tap works for me."

"Okay, be right back."

Sawyer and I are crossing the large yard when I catch Daisy, Mia, Angus, who's joined the group, and Murphy, all watching us, smiling from ear to ear. I approach cautiously, wondering what they're up to.

When I reach them, Mia puts her hands out for her son. "Give me my child and go deal with whatever that was."

"What are you talking about?"

"Girl," Murphy butts in. "You have got Cal McKinnon all wrapped up."

"I don't know what you're talking about. We're just friends."

The four of them look at each other and then burst out in laughter. As ridiculous as they are, I'm glad it's obvious that he's into me. Maybe that means everyone here, including Kacey, gets the drift too.

"Charlie, c'mon," Mia says. "Did you see him kiss any of us on the cheek when he got here?"

"I wasn't really paying attention," I lie through my teeth.

The moment he walked onto the property, I knew he was here. Even now, I can feel the electric current that hums to life whenever he's nearby. Of course, I noticed his kiss. I noticed it with every fiber of my being.

"Well, we were. I thought my child was going to end up in the middle of a make-out session over there." Mia gestures behind me.

Instinctually following her hand, I observe Kacey walking across the yard, heading toward the keg. Toward Callen.

Oh, hell no!

"I'll be right back," I say to no one in particular.

I wouldn't call the emotion flooding my veins with adrenaline jealousy because this possessiveness, or possibly protectiveness, is more powerful than any green-eyed monster I've ever felt. Callen has just grabbed our beer cups and is next in line for the keg when she reaches him.

She taps him on the shoulder, and he looks her way but doesn't turn his body to face her, clearly uninterested. I'm only a few feet away when she says, "I'm really sorry to hear about your dad, Cal."

Nope. Nope. Nope.

She will not use his sorrow to prey on him and work her way back into his life. Not on my watch. My heart takes full control of my body and mind. I slide my hand into his not holding our empty cups, interlacing our fingers. "Hey, babe."

His fingers tighten around mine, accepting my lifeline. "Hey, babe." He gives my hand a squeeze when he says, *babe.*

Kacey looks from me to Callen, back to me, and then our linked hands.

I smile my brightest smile and extend my free hand. "Hi, I'm Charlie."

He lets out a low chuckle when I use the name only my friends call me. It's at this very moment that the possessive knots in my stomach untie, replaced by a rush of dancing butterflies. Because if I had my way, Callen would be the only person to call me Charlotte from here until the end of time.

It takes her a few seconds to take my outstretched hand, and when she does, her handshake is limp. Weak.

"Hi, I'm Kacey."

"I've heard so much about you. Nice to put a face to the name."

My words are sugary sweet, but my implication that I know what a cheating bitch she is floats on the air between us.

"Oh, um. Nice to meet you, too."

The person at the keg finishes, leaving the tap open. "Looks like it's our turn," I chirp through my smile.

Inside, I'm screaming, *walk away, bitch!*

"Well, it was good to see you, Cal. Nice to meet you, Charlie."

"You too. Have a fantastic night."

I wiggle my fingers in goodbye and turn my back on her to join Callen next to the ice-filled garbage can holding the keg.

"Hey, *babe*." He pours and hands me my beer with a satisfied grin on his face.

Taking my free hand in his, he angles me away from the crowd of people hovering around the food tables. We're both quiet as we stand off to the side of the party, watching everyone.

His thumb moves in a circle over the back of my hand, and I chance a glance at his face. His smile is gone, replaced by a furrowed brow. I look away, pretending to watch the crowd while a battle of emotions takes place behind my rib cage. My thundering heart yearns to keep her control over me.

Is this it?

Is this the moment I take my life into my own hands and do what I want?

What makes *me* happy?

What does it mean if I let my heart lead instead of my head? I live over eight hundred miles away. Does letting my heart win mean I've made my decision about what I'm doing with the business?

What I'm doing with my life?

"What was that about, Charlotte?" His voice doesn't hide the conflicting emotions he seems to be fighting as well.

"I don't share, Callen."

Yep, my damn heart won this battle.

His thumb freezes, ending the gentle caress from a moment ago.

"Don't say it unless you're crystal clear on what that means."

My heart continues its thundering cadence in my chest, and funnily enough, my brain says this is the smartest thing I've ever done.

"The friend thing was nice, and I do want to get to know you. To be your friend. But I want a lot more than friendship from you. And I'd like to make it clear to Kacey and everyone else here tonight that you are far from available."

Holy shit. Did I just say that?

"Charlotte..."

A sliver of insecurity penetrates its way under my skin, and I can't bring myself to look at him just yet.

"If it's not what you want, tell me now, Callen."

He lets go of my hand and steps in front of me, taking my face in one of his large hands, his thumb brushing across my bottom lip. No longer letting me hide from him or the implications of my admission.

"I was trying to do the right thing. To give you a chance to catch up to me."

"And I appreciate that. Trust me, your friendship is incredibly important to me, too, but I don't think just friends will work for us."

"I don't either, baby." He rests his forehead against mine. "But what about when you leave again?"

"We'll figure it out."

"I can't go through you walking away again."

"We can deal with logistics later. Let's just live in the moment."

"Charlotte, I can't—"

I grab his beer and leave our cups on the table next to us, then his hand in mine and I lead him toward the house. This time, my body and its lustful needs take the lead. I have no clue where it's taking us, but I sure am excited to get there.

"Where are we going?"

We pass through the open French doors that lead into the house, and I follow my instincts. Head on a swivel for somewhere private to finish our conversation. I see stairs that lead to an upper floor and take them, pulling Callen behind me. I open the first closed door on the left and flip on the light switch. It's a large laundry room with a long counter ending with a washer and dryer at the far end. It's perfect. Nobody should bother us here.

Locking the door once we're inside, it's my turn to take charge.

"Charlotte, what are we doing in here?"

"There." I point at the counter.

"What?"

"Stand there." I gently push him where I want him to go.

Once he's where I need him, I unbutton his jeans, and pull down his pants and underwear, taking him in my hand. "Do I have your attention?"

"Yes. Fuck yes."

I can't help but grin. "Good."

Stroking his hard length with my hand, I lift on my toes to kiss him like I've wanted to all night. Forgoing caution, we tangle our tongues in a messy, hot dance we have no control over. Hands exploring in a frenzy, need radiating from both of us.

Pulling away, I lift his shirt over his head and drop it to

the surface behind him. My lips find his again, but I don't let them linger. Dipping down, I place a kiss over his heart before dragging my tongue up his neck to the shell of his ear. His cock flexes in my hand even harder now.

I whisper in his ear, "I remember everything about you, Callen."

"Charlotte—"

"Shh... It's my turn. I don't have a table at my disposal, so a laundry room will have to do."

A folded-up blanket on the counter catches my eye, and I reach to grab it with my free hand, never releasing him from my grip. I drop it at our feet and flick my tongue over one of his nipples.

"You like your coffee black and strong." I move my attention to his other nipple. "And you think brushing your teeth when you wake up is stupid because coffee breath is just as bad as morning breath, so why waste time brushing your teeth twice?"

As I release him to make a path down the muscles of his stomach, I feel him chuckle against my lips on his abs. No doubt he's recalling the conversation we had, drinking coffee in our hotel bed. I smile against his skin but keep going.

"You grew up in a Chevy family, but you drive a Dodge, and the rest of your family gives you shit about it."

My mouth kisses his pelvic bone, and his cock jumps again. I brush my lips against the other side, and my knees hit the blanket. His hands grip the counter as he relinquishes control to me.

"You love your siblings, but hate being the middle boy." I lick the thick vein running the length of him. "You think you don't compare to your brothers, but Callen, that couldn't be further from the truth."

My tongue teases his tip, and he hisses through his teeth.

"You. Are. Everything."

I take him in my mouth, and the memories of exactly how he likes to be sucked race through my mind. My hands grab his ass cheeks, pushing him even deeper into my mouth so I can do that thing with my tongue that I know makes him crazy.

"Fuck, Charlotte." He pulls me off him and tilts my face to look at him. "You don't need to do this."

Not taking my eyes off his, I lick pre-cum off the head of his shaft and then suck it into my mouth. When I release the head like a lollipop; the sound bounces off the walls of the small room.

"You were the star tight end on your high school and college football teams." I cup his balls in my hand and take him in my mouth again, but release him quickly, grinning up at him. "Don't think I forgot you were prom king because I didn't. I also know you didn't get to go to prom because you broke both your arms when you crashed on your four-wheeler."

My free hand takes the base of his shaft, working it up and down his length for a moment as our eyes stay locked on each other.

"Callen?"

"Yeah," he barely breathes out.

"It's time for you to fucking come for me."

It's not word for word what he said to me the other day in the cabin, but he gets my drift and doesn't protest when I take him so deep he hits the back of my throat, causing me to gag. I recover quickly and take him long... deep... over and over until he shouts my name and gently tugs on my hair to pull me off him, but I refuse. I know what he's doing.

"Charlotte, I'm going to... Charlotte..."

I'm relentless, not backing off. His grip on my head tightens, but it isn't painful. He doesn't try to set the pace because I know what he likes, and I'm already working him at the rhythm that takes him over the edge.

"Fuck. Charlotte. What. Are. You. Doing. To. Me?"

He spills down my throat, and I don't stop until he's done.

His grip on my head relaxes, and he runs his fingers through my hair, brushing it back so he can see my face.

"Thank you." His thumb slides over my bottom lip.

"I'd say we're even now."

He helps me up and lightly kisses me. "Baby, we'll never be even."

"No?"

"If it means we keep trying to one-up each other like this, I sure hope we never are."

I shake my head, bending to pick up the blanket while he pulls his pants up. I put the blanket back where I found it and hand him his shirt as I drag my freshly manicured red nails down his abs. "Don't forget this."

He takes his shirt from my hand and kisses me long and hard. Then he pulls it on and opens the door.

"We're really doing this?" he asks at the bottom of the stairs as he guides us through the house.

"I think we are."

He stops us just before we reach the doors to the backyard.

"Charlotte, we either are or we aren't. No thinking, no maybes, no just friends."

Oh, this man.

I reach up and touch his cheek. "We. Are. Doing. This."

"Good." He throws his arm over my shoulders, and I take his fingers in mine as we walk outside, not hiding from the world that we are now most definitely an *us*. "There's someone I would like you to meet. Officially, that is."

"Oh yeah? Who?"

"My mom."

Chapter Twenty-Six

Charlotte

The truck bounces side to side as Callen drives us down the dirt road we took off the highway leading us to his family's ranch. The ranch where he grew up and once lived with his ex-wife.

With the truck windows down, Ruby runs from window to window in the back of the cab as crops of alfalfa breeze by on both sides of the Dodge.

"This is her happy place." He looks at Ruby in the rearview mirror, his expression is unreadable. "She misses it."

"How about you? Do you miss it?"

"Parts of it. I miss the quiet. The trees. The work."

"The work?"

"Cleaning out a horse stall or harvesting crops can be very therapeutic. I miss the time to myself. The time to think. But my parents have hired help for all of that now. Hopefully, I can keep things running at the store so we can afford to keep them on." His voice trails off as if his last comment wasn't meant to have been said out loud.

Daisy was right. He seems to have the weight of the world on his shoulders. I'd love for him to confide in me, but only if he's ready. "What do you mean?" I say, testing the waters. "Are things not going well at the store?"

He stiffens. "Things are fine. I'm figuring it all out, but it will be fine." His entire demeanor changes every time the store is mentioned.

And I know him well enough to know that's the most I'll get out of him on the topic. Not wanting him to shut down, I attempt to shift the conversation in a different direction. Reaching across the center console, I playfully brush my fingertips down his forearm and link my fingers with his.

"Do you ever come out and ride?"

"When I lived here, I would get up with the sun every day to help with the morning chores and then go for a ride to check on the livestock before heading into town."

"Livestock? I thought you grew crops?"

He chuckles. "Yes, livestock. We have more chickens than I can count. Goats, horses, and we usually have a small herd of cattle roaming the back acreage, but you can't see them from the road. I'm sure you'll meet Bernadette at some point."

"Bernadette?"

"You'll love her. Anyway, the crops bring in the income. The cattle provide a nice little tax write-off." His brow hardens. "Dad always found ways to cut corners."

This ranch, the family business, it's been his world his entire life. His dad sounds amazing, but it's clear he left

Callen some sort of mess. I'd really like to wring Aidan McKinnon's neck right about now.

I squeeze his hand in reply. Not sure what else to say.

Up ahead of us, the fields end, and tall trees surround a dark brown log-cabin-looking two-story home. The closer we get, I realize it's not actually a log cabin, though it has the feel of one made of dark wood and magnificent stonework. It's beautiful, and I can picture the four McKinnon siblings growing up here. The property is such a stark contrast to my upbringing in a big city.

It's beautiful. Peaceful.

"That's my parents' house," he says as he drives past the gravel drive. Pointing to the left, he says, "Over there is the horse barn, another barn with a bunch of shit in it that cleans up real nice for parties. The smaller building is for the goats, and the chicken coops are behind it. The cattle are in the field on the other side. We'll head over there in a bit."

Who would have thought this was where Knox McKinnon grew up? Callen's big brother is the epitome of a rock star who lives the life fame and fortune have provided him. But he started life running through these fields and shoveling horse shit.

As we round the house, the road forks into two well-worn dirt roads. Callen points to the left and says, "That way will take you to Angus's place. These days, he stays at the loft above the bar half the time."

He takes the other road, and we drive about a half mile before another house comes into view. It's similar to his parents' house but smaller. He pulls up and cuts the engine in front of a beautiful house with a dreamy front porch that has a covered swing that matches the one at the cabin.

"This is my place. C'mon, I'll show you around."

When I meet him in front of the truck, he takes my face in his hands and kisses me gently. His lips soft on mine. We take our time indulging in each other. These long, tender kisses are our thing.

We do a lot of this.

The world stops, and it's only the two of us.

No life-changes.

No worries.

As we pull away, he takes me by the hand and leads me up two wooden steps to my dream porch that looks like it wraps around the house. There's a porch swing on the left and to the right is a wicker chair and table set all framed by a perfect white railing. But on closer inspection, I notice it's covered in pine needles and needs a good sweep. Doesn't look like anyone's been to the house in quite some time.

He opens the door without a key and walks inside. I follow him in, and a mixture of emotions swirls in my belly as I take in the rustic charm and comfortable surroundings. It's so him. But Kacey lived here too. They lived here as husband and wife, and I don't know how to feel about that.

The large, open living space has an oversized brown leather couch facing an enormous stone fireplace. Two side tables flank the matching loveseat, and a large oak coffee table sits in front of the couch. With dark hardwood floors and the dark furniture, the home has a manly vibe.

It feels like Callen.

There's no sign that a woman ever lived here at all. Most of the walls are bare, except for two black and white framed pictures on either side of the fireplace. One of the McKinnon

Hardware storefront and the other an aerial view of the ranch.

"Callen, I love it," I gush. Because I do. It's perfect.

"Thanks. I built it with my dad and some of the guys down at the store. It was a labor of love. Until it wasn't."

"You don't think you'll ever move back here?"

"Nah, this house only reminds me of my failures. A time in my life I'd rather forget."

"But you created a thing of beauty with your bare hands. How can you consider this a failure?"

"Well, when you find your wife in bed with your cousin in the house you built with your bare hands, it can sour things."

"God, they're both such assholes."

He steps up behind me and wraps his arms around my waist. "I can't put it all on her. We should have never gotten married. We had just been together for so long that we didn't know anything else. Getting married was simply the next step."

"But you loved her."

"I did. But I knew the day I watched her walk down the aisle that I loved her because she was my best friend. I wasn't *in* love with her. It was never what it should have been. I was faithful, and she wasn't, but I should have never asked her to marry me. I trapped us both, and then it all went to shit. What happened in this house was my biggest failure."

I turn in his arms so I can look at his handsome face. "Well, as sorry as I am that you went through the pain of a failed marriage, I have to say it's a win for me. I can't imagine my life without you in it."

"Same here, sugar. I just wish I'd met you sooner."

"I wouldn't have been ready for you."

His eyes shine with delight. "You sayin' you're ready for me now?"

"I believe I am, Mr. McKinnon."

He leans down, his lips gently caressing mine. "I don't think I could ever be ready for you, baby," he says against my lips before intensifying our kiss and pulling me tight against his body. "There's no way a man can prepare for the likes of you."

"The likes of me?" My hand glides down the front of him, grabbing his length through his jeans. "Hmm... you seem prepared to me."

"Get that one-track mind of yours out of the gutter, woman." The heat of his breath on my ear hits me right where he intended it to. What I wouldn't do to rid this house of the ghosts who still haunt it.

"You love my one-track mind," I say without thinking.

He stills and brings his eyes to mine. All playfulness gone. "I do. More than you could ever know."

His lips devour mine before I can reply, and then, in the blink of an eye, he has me bent over the arm of the leather chair as he takes me from behind. Ghosts be damned!

Just as he reaches his climax, he growls, "There's no way I could have ever been prepared for you, Charlotte. Never."

If he only knew how hard I was falling for him.

Who am I kidding?

I fell weeks ago, and I have no intention of getting up.

Chapter Twenty-Seven

Charlotte

"**A**nything else need to be taken out to the table, Sharon?" I ask Callen's mom.

"If you can grab the salad dressing, I'll get the rolls, and we should be all set. Thanks, darlin'."

"Sure thing."

Walking through the kitchen of Callen's childhood home and out to the back deck, where everyone waits to start Sunday night dinner is surreal.

Yes, it's fascinating to be in one of my biggest client's family home, but it doesn't compare to the curiosity I have about my boyfriend.

As odd as it is at thirty-two years old to say I have a boyfriend, that's exactly what he is. Well, he's much more *man* than boy, but *manfriend* doesn't really work. It's been two weeks since the Fourth of July party, when I made it clear to Callen that I had no desire to share him. The same party where he introduced me to his mom. I had met her outside the store, but that meeting had nothing on being introduced as his girlfriend... two minutes after having her son's rooster in my mouth.

Yes, I called it his rooster. I can't even think of the other word when I remember that introduction. It was the most embarrassing moment of my life. No, there weren't any outward signs that said, Hey! Nice to meet you. I just gave your son a blowy, but the entire moment still felt so wrong.

And Callen loved every excruciating second of it.

At one point, when someone interrupted our conversation, he looked at me and rubbed the corner of his mouth, making me believe I had something on my face. My heart stopped. A sheen of sweat accompanied the red-hot blush that followed. I reached up to wipe away any lingering mess but felt nothing. He gestured to the other side, and I fell for that as well.

Nothing.

By the time Sharon's attention was back on us, he was bent over laughing so hard he was crying, and I was bright red.

I. Could. Have. Died.

Now, here we are at Sunday family dinner. That dreadful yet admittedly hilarious moment a memory, and Callen, with Ruby lying at his feet, waits for me at the head of the table, where I take the seat to the right of him. Happy to be by his side and loving the company and the incredible view of the vast ranch behind me, I settle into my chair. Somewhat disappointed my back is to the gorgeous landscape, but I'm hoping I'll have many more chances to experience the view. Everywhere the eye can see is part of McKinnon Ranch. It's incredible. What it must have been like to grow up here.

"Hey, baby. I missed you."

"I was just in the kitchen for two minutes. How are you going to handle three nights without me at your place?"

We've spent every night together since the Fourth, and it has been divine.

"Ruby and I will be lost without you."

"I think you'll manage."

"Be that as it may, I still plan to pry all of your deepest, darkest secrets out of Karissa while she's here."

"Good luck. She's a tough cookie."

"What are you two lovebirds talking about over there?" Daisy interrupts.

"Charlotte was just telling me she doesn't think I'll be able to get her secrets out of her friend when she's here this week."

"Like I told you before, she reminds me of you," I say in her direction.

"She's right then, son. You don't stand a chance," Sharon says, with her arm outstretched, hand opening and closing. "Now pass your mother the salad."

"Ha!" I giggle, not looking at Callen because I'm too focused on the cornbread I'm slathering with honey butter. "Your mother is a wise woman."

I've just handed the breadbasket to Daisy when, out of nowhere, a hot, wet breath passes over the side of my face, causing my hair to blow with it. I jump out of my seat, unsure what in the world is going on and feeling so gross.

"I told you, you were bound to meet Bernadette. Charlotte, this is Bernie..." Callen reaches through the wood slats on the deck to rub the adorable blond cow's head. "And Bernadette, this is Charlotte, but you can call her Charlie, if you like. She's one of us, so please play nice."

Grabbing my napkin, I wipe my face off and then reach through the deck railing and give her a scratch, too.

Once our introduction is over, my attention is back on Callen, and oh, what a sight he is. He's beaming. There is something about seeing this often too-serious man smile with abandon.

"What?" I ask quietly.

"You, that's what. You make me smile."

"Right back atcha, cowboy," I say, only for him to hear.

"Alright, you two. Get up and wash your hands before you touch any of this food. We'll wait."

We do as instructed and are back in our seats in a flash, the smiles never leaving our faces.

"You two are too cute," Mia says.

Nobody disagrees with her, but quiet chuckles float around the table as we pass the food, and dinner begins.

Being here with him. With his family. Well... it's easy.

Comfortable.

Sharon, Daisy, Angus, Mia, little Sawyer in his high chair, and Callen feel like home. Since day one. They don't treat me like the new person in town. They treat me like... well... they treat me like family.

Angus and Mia catch my eye as they have on more than one occasion tonight. They're supposed to be just friends, but I can't be the only one who sees the spark between them, can I? Am I just so happy I'm projecting my feelings onto the two of them? I really don't think so. Watching him bounce Sawyer on his lap, sharing his potatoes with the toddler, there is no denying the affection between the three of them.

There is more than meets the eye going on there. I know there is.

Conversation flows. The food is delicious. We joke and tease, and then I somehow ruin it all over a compliment about apple pie.

"Sharon, this pie is amazing."

"Thank you, honey. It's Callen's father's recipe. Baking was one of his many specialties."

"Oh yeah?" I smile, then fill my mouth with another tasty bite.

"It's true. Baking was just scratching the surface for him. There wasn't anything my Aidan did that he didn't excel at."

Sharon's love for her husband is beautiful. I turn toward Callen—sure he must be smiling at his father's memory, but I couldn't be more off the mark.

He places his fork on his plate and pushes his half-eaten pie away. I feel for him. Losing my dad has been the hardest thing I've ever been through. The grief comes in waves and when you least expect it.

Taking his hand in mine, I give it a squeeze, letting him know I've got him. At times like this, there isn't much else anyone can do. In my experience, just knowing Karissa is there when I need her means more than any words she could say.

"The way the whole town counted on him and the store. You know, he built it from scratch. Started small and over the years, it grew leaps and bounds, becoming one of the most trustworthy businesses in Goose Hollow."

Callen's leg bounces with irritation. Tension that wasn't there two minutes ago radiates from him.

"Mom, you better not let Knox hear you talk like that. He thinks he's Goose Hollow's golden child. Don't want him to think he's not your favorite," Angus jokes.

"You kids are an entirely different category, and there is no such thing as a parent having a favorite."

"C'mon, Mom. It's okay, you can admit it." Daisy puts her hands under her chin and bats her lashes. "I'm your favorite, right?"

"Don't be silly."

"It's okay, Mom. We know Cal's the hero of the family. Taking over for Dad and filling his shoes. You can say he's your favorite."

Callen clears his throat. "Mom, dinner was superb, but Charlotte and I need to get going."

He stands and wide-eyed, I stand with him. His hand squeezes mine, holding on for dear life.

"Dinner was terrific. Thank you so much for having me again."

"Dude, you aren't really leaving, are you? It was a compliment." Angus looks as confused by his brother's mood swing as I feel. "What did I miss?"

Ignoring his brother, Callen leads me to his mom's end of the table and bends to kiss her cheek.

"Is everything okay?" she asks, holding on to his shoulders.

"Everything's fine, Mom. I have an early morning is all. I'll call you tomorrow."

"Sounds good."

He takes my hand again, and I wave my goodbyes and follow him through the house. Outside, he opens the truck door for me, but before he lets go of my hand so I can get in, I bring his knuckles to my mouth and place a kiss on them. Hoping to express how much he means to me and that I'm here for him when he's ready to talk about whatever just happened.

He drops my hand to hold my face and leans in for a gentle kiss. Then, with his forehead resting against mine, his breath tickles my face when he whispers, "I'm sorry."

Shaking my head, I tell him the truth. "I understand. It's hard for me to talk about my dad, too."

He kisses my forehead and helps me in.

He's quiet all the way back to his place while I spend the drive replaying the day in my head. After our afternoon quickie on the couch, he showed me the rest of the house and the massive outdoor space. It seemed endless. Trees that went on forever in one direction and open pastures with grazing cows in the other.

It's absolutely beautiful.

On the way to his mom's house, we stopped by the barn, where he introduced me to Mabel, his sweet horse who also acts as his therapist during their morning rides. She was beautiful, but I couldn't take my eyes off Honey.

It was love at first sight.

Honey is small, yet elegant, with a golden coat and a white-blond mane. Drawn to her as soon as her flaxen head popped out of her stall, I left Callen's side and if I'm being honest, I didn't hear much of what he said while I rubbed her velvety soft nose. There were seven horses in the barn, but before we left, I made a stop at her stall again. When she nudged me with her nose for one last pat, Callen promised we'd come back later this week to go for a ride.

After we left the barn, he introduced me to the chickens and goats. It was nice to see him in his element, dressed in a tight T-shirt, perfectly fitting jeans, and roughed up boots. He looked positively delicious with the ranch in the background.

The fluidity with which he moved around the land he knew better than the back of his hand made me realize why the pressure of keeping the finances for the family in order meant so much to him. This land has been an integral part of his life, and he'll do anything to keep it that way.

It was nice to see this side of his life and, most importantly, start to piece together a little more of the puzzle that is Callen McKinnon. I could have stayed out there with him all day, but sadly, we had to leave the peace of our wandering to head to dinner with the family.

Once we reach his house, he goes through the motions of letting Ruby out and watering the flowers in the backyard. He's in his head, using the space to clear his mind. I know enough to know it's not me personally he's trying to get away from, so I let him be.

Sometimes you just need a moment to let the grief wash over you. He'll come back in when he's ready. And I'll be here waiting for him.

I slip my shoes off and curl up in the big chair in his bedroom, intending to use my book as a distraction, but I don't see a single word on the page. A memory of my dad and I dancing in the living room to Hall & Oates plays like a home video in my mind. It's a relief to be taken by surprise by a happy memory and not the ones I usually have of him taking his last breath as I sat at his bedside holding his hand.

Closing the book, I reach back into my bag, grab my phone and earbuds, and push play. "You Make My Dreams Come True" fills my ears. Closing my eyes, I envision me and my dad dancing in the living room. The memory warms my heart. The song ends, and just as the opening beats of "Rich Girl" begin, I notice Callen leaning against the doorframe where he's watching me.

"Hey, you," I say, pulling out my earbuds and wiping a stray tear away.

"Hey." He pushes away from the door and walks toward me and my favorite chair. He scoops me up, and even as comfortable as I was, there's nothing like being in his arms.

I feel safe.

Cared for.

Needed.

Wanted.

He's slowly but surely been planting seeds around the hole in my heart, and I think something beautiful may be blossoming.

He lays us down on the bed. We're both still dressed and on top of the covers as he holds me. Holds me like I'm his lifeline. Like if he lets go, he may just float away.

"You okay?" I ask softly.

"I am as long as you're here."

The thought that this big, beautiful bearded man could feel this way about me makes me all warm and fuzzy inside, but he isn't himself right now and I'm worried about him.

"Wanna talk about it?"

"No comment."

"What am I, the press?"

"If you are, you're the prettiest reporter I've ever seen."

"Stop it. What happened tonight? Was it too hard to talk about your dad?"

He takes a deep breath and buries his face against my neck. His facial hair tickling my skin.

"You know you can tell me anything. Nobody knows what you're going through more than I do right now."

"That's just it." He sighs into my neck. "Nobody understands because nobody knows."

"Knows what, sweetie?"

He releases a heavy sigh.

"Turns out my dad's not so perfect. At least not when it comes to running a business."

"How so?"

He rolls onto his back and brings me with him, pressing me to his side. My chest rests against his ribs, and my leg tangles with his. Reaching my arm around him, I give him a squeeze, letting him know I'm here for him when he's ready.

"My dad, you know the... what did my mom say?" His fingers gently run up and down my arm as he speaks. "That's right, the most trustworthy businessman in town. Well, it turns out he didn't like to pay his taxes, but he did like to keep a second set of books with all the shady handshake deals he made."

Well, *shit*.

I place a kiss on his shoulder, staying quiet.

"Apparently, making me executor of his will and leaving me to run the family business wasn't enough. He had to stick me with a one point three million dollar tax bill on top of everything else."

Lifting my head to look at him, I know I must have heard him wrong. "What?"

"One million, three hundred seventy-four thousand five hundred twelve dollars and three cents, to be exact."

"How did you find out?"

"Let's just say when I filed last year's taxes in April, the IRS was very happy to hear from me."

"And nobody knew until now?"

"Nope, and I've made sure they don't. He left me in charge. That makes it my problem. Nobody else's."

"But isn't it a family business? Don't all the family members make money from the store?"

"I'll figure it out."

"How?"

"Not sure if you remember me telling you about the plot of land I was in the process of buying when we met?"

"Of course, I do. You were going to build your dream house on the south side of the lake because the view of the sunsets was best from there."

Please don't say what I think you're going to say.

"God, I'm glad you came back into my life." He kisses me on the head.

Okay, that is not what I thought he was going to say.

"I've put the five acres up for sale."

That's what I was afraid he was going to say! Dammit!

Untangling myself from him, I sit up so I can look him in the eyes. "You can't."

"I don't really have an option." He shrugs calmly, already resigned to the facts in front of him.

"You can't just throw your dream away."

"My dream is just sitting there in limbo. I stopped plans

when Dad died. Things were really getting on track, too. The well and the electric were in. I had cleared some trees, drawn up the plans, and laid the foundation. There were no bones to the house, but we were almost there. When we lost Dad, it was sudden. My world became a whirlwind of grief and paperwork. It was like being thrown into the eye of a storm. A storm I was ill-prepared for. Once I found out about the taxes, I knew I couldn't move forward with my plans."

"Why haven't you told your family? I'm sure they would be more than happy to help. Knox would—"

"No. I'm not telling the family." He cuts me off, but his tone is steadfast rather than angry. His mind is made up, and he seems to have made peace with his decision. "It would crush Mom and tarnish everyone's memory of Dad. I won't be the one to do that."

"But you know none of them would want you to give up your dream."

"Charlotte, that store is the heart of this family. Hell, it's the heart of the community. I would rather sell my land and never build my dream house if it means saving it. And my mom... God, she's been through enough. She can't lose any more than she already has. I want to do everything I can to handle this on my own."

This man's heart is so big and so stubborn. And I couldn't love it or him more.

It hits me right in the chest, and my fingers tremble as my mind catches up with my heart.

I. Love. Him.

Shit.

When did this happen?

There's a difference between *falling* for someone and knowing you are *in love* with that person.

And I know. At this very moment. I am in love with this man.

It feels good yet terrifying at the same time. For now, I'll keep it to myself. He has enough going on. So, I tuck my emotions away and hope my trembling doesn't give me away.

"What can I do to help?"

"Nothing. You being here is enough." He pulls me back down to his chest and wraps me in his arms. "I have a meeting with my tax guy next month. Until then, I just want more of this."

"Wait, I have a better idea."

"Is that so?"

"Get your head out of the gutter, McKinnon."

I sit up and adjust my pillow settling myself against the headboard. "Come here." I pat my lap. "How about a head rub? You once told me I was pretty good at it."

He cuddles up to my lap, wrapping his arms around my waist. My fingers weave through his thick, dark hair, eliciting moans from him when I add pressure. He nuzzles himself deeper into my lap, offering me more access to the rest of his head. My fingers alternate, soothingly gliding through his hair and across his scalp and gently massaging his temples and tight jaw muscles.

His body grows heavy against my lap, and every time I think he might be asleep, another moan slips out, making me smile.

Taking care of him feels natural.

Like something I want to do for a long time. Maybe even forever.

Sitting here in the dark with this beautiful man, I work in quiet, slow motion as my fingers relax him. All the while, my mind races with everything he's confessed to me tonight. Thinking of how I can help him or, at the very least, get him to understand that he should lean on his siblings and not take on everything alone. It's a family business, and the family should work together to figure out a solution.

Grieving through the loss of a parent is hard enough without all the additional stress and disappointment he's feeling.

I would love to help heal his heart the way he's beginning to heal mine.

He was so certain I was *his* as soon as I came back into his life. His overbearing possessiveness is annoying and sexy at the same time. The way he supports me in following my passions makes it impossible not to fall for him. Most surprising, is the way he knows what I need even when I don't. And, of course, the way he cares for me.

He keeps planting seeds and taking up more and more space in my heart.

Almost like fate brought Callen back into my life when I needed him most.

Chapter Twenty-Eight

Callen

Sam Hunt sings about breaking up in the '90s from the amphitheater stage as the setting sun casts an orange hue across the Central Oregon horizon. Charlotte is in my arms as we sway back and forth, singing along to one of her favorite artists, and all is right in the world.

Since the Fourth of July, my life has flipped upside down, and God, I hope I'm never right side up again.

Her possessiveness that night showed me a new side of Charlotte. One I understood all too well because I feel the same way about her. Every time she's introduced to a new person in town and that person happens to be a man, I have visions of ripping their arm from their body cavity so they can't shake her hand. If she had an ex-husband I had to come face-to-face with... well, I'm not sure I would have handled myself with the grace Charlotte did when she met Kacey.

But in that laundry room when she declared that she didn't want to share me with anyone else. Now, that was something to see.

That impulsive moment was one of the most impactful of my life. The way she took control of the situation and made her intentions clear. I've never felt so wanted by anyone.

The confidence in her eyes is more breathtaking than the sight of her on her knees.

And it was the sexiest thing I had ever seen.

Knowing she felt as absolute in wanting me... wanting us... as I did in my need for her gave me a security I didn't know I was lacking.

It wasn't until we walked out of the house with my arm around her that a slight weight lifted from my chest. My insecurities about what it meant for her to be here, in my hometown, but not really mine after dreaming of her for so long, had been weighing me down more than I had known. But they drifted away on the summer winds that night.

As embarrassed as she was to meet my mom right after she gave me the best blow job of my life, the timing was hysterical. She fell for it every time I would give her the signal that she had cum on the corner of her mouth, and she was furious with me. But all was right when we went home and shared the hell out of each other.

Since then, we haven't spent a single day apart. I've stayed at the cabin a few times, but we mostly stay at my place in town. Our sexual chemistry is off the charts, but what's happening between the two of us is a lot more than that, it's intense and fun. And downright perfect. She has become an essential part of my day. I must see her. Talk to her. Touch her. For fuck's sake, I need to smell her every day.

I've never been big on mundane conversation. But I'll be damned if I couldn't listen to her talk about paint drying and find it captivating. She makes me want to share every thought that pops into my head with her. Having her to confide in about my struggles with the mess Dad left me has made it possible to breathe again.

I've found my person. I feel it in my bones.

Everything she does is enchanting, and I could make watching her live her day-to-day life a full-time job. Nothing makes me happier.

Okay, being buried deep inside her is phenomenal. My skin against hers... that's my real happy place.

The way she lit up when I took her to the ranch to ride last week was just about the sweetest thing I'd ever seen. The thing is... with Charlotte... even when she's sweet as pie, she's still hot as hell. If it hadn't been broad daylight with workers going in and out of the barn, I would have taken her right there in front of the horses on one of the hay bales.

We've done Sunday dinners at Mom's, and Mom is just as smitten with her as I am. Charlotte has taken to my family easily, and I'll admit it's nice that she doesn't have that starry-eyed image of my big brother. His fame is inconsequential to her unless it's work-related.

She's a fucking unicorn.

And she's mine.

"Hey, man. I'm gonna go for another round, and I need another set of hands. Think you can let her go for five minutes?" Owen yells in my ear.

Pulling her tight against my chest, I get close to her ear. "Be right back. Gonna help Owen with beers. You want one?"

She turns and puts her arms around my neck. "Nah, I'm good. I'll miss you, though. Don't dillydally."

"I promise there will be no dillying or dallying. I'll be back as soon as the beer line will allow."

I love you.

It's right there on the tip of my tongue, but I keep it to myself and kiss her instead. I wonder if she can feel my love for her in our kiss.

Because damn, do I love her.

Like ass over boots love her.

She is the only key that fits.

The missing piece of the puzzle.

You name a cliché about love, and that's what she is. That's what we are. And I wouldn't want it any other way.

I love her so much it hurts to even consider the possibility of her returning to California. Every night I lie in bed with her in my arms, racking my brain for ways to make her stay. When she's wrapped up in me, and her heartbeat drums a lullaby against my ribs as the steady rhythm of her breaths does its best to lull me to sleep, it is almost impossible not to panic.

Why haven't I told her how I feel?

What's holding me back?

"Hey, Charlotte?" I yell, just as the crowd applauds the end of the song.

"Yeah, baby?"

"I fucking love you!" I yell over the cheering fans.

"You what?" Tears glisten in her eyes, and a smile lights up her face.

She heard me, but I've taken her by surprise.

Shit, I've taken myself by surprise. Cradling her face, I

reiterate what I've just said. So close there's no way she doesn't hear me. "I said, I love you. I. Am. Fucking. In. Love. With. You." I press a small kiss to her lips, not giving her a chance to reply. "I'll be back."

When I turn around to catch up with Owen, he's waiting for me with a shit-eating grin.

I smile right back, not embarrassed at all that he heard our conversation.

We push our way through the crowd, doing our best not to walk on the blankets and rented chairs littering the general admission area of the amphitheater. It's a sold-out show, and the ladies of Central Oregon are all dressed to impress. Daisy Dukes and low-cut shirts appear to have been the preferred dress code, but when I have a woman like Charlotte waiting for me, nobody else compares.

We've reached the beer line, and mercilessly, only a handful of people are in front of us.

Owen slaps me on the shoulder and spins the lid of his baseball cap to the back. "So, my asshat of a friend has finally found *the one*. You really do love her, don't you?"

"Done and dusted, my friend." I follow him as we move up in the line. "If I tried to deny it, I'd be lying."

He crosses his arms in front of his Alabama T-shirt, looking perplexed. "Let me get this straight. That intelligent, funny, beautiful woman who has her own money and likes to build furniture has fallen for a small-town cowboy who runs the local hardware store and is, well, you?"

"Maybe she's not as intelligent as she appears," I kid, but it's just as flabbergasting to me as it is to him.

The line is moving at a steady clip, with only one person

in front of us. "Has the topic of how you plan to navigate a long-distance relationship come up?"

"Not really. We're taking it day by day. But she's hinted that she's considering a move."

"What do you mean, day by day? You just told her you loved her."

"Because I do."

"And when you say she's considering a move, I assume you mean a move to Goose Hollow."

"Yes. But I haven't pushed her. I don't want to pressure her."

"Have you offered to move to LA?"

"It's not an option."

Owen gives me a look that questions my sanity before turning to place our order. "Six EBCs, please." Turning his baseball hat around, he dives back into his questioning. "Why is it not an option?"

I really don't want to talk about this. With you or anyone.

"I have too many responsibilities."

"Dude, you need to figure out how to delegate. You're the boss. You can run things from afar and visit often."

"There's too much going on for that and you know it."

"Okay, maybe not today, but once shit gets figured out, it could be an option."

"Here you go," the bartender interrupts, hopefully ending the conversation.

"Thanks," I say, stuffing tip money in the jar.

Owen turns his hat back around like he's preparing for the battle ahead as we fight through the crowd to get back to our spot. And an unexpected battle it turns out to be.

The first shot is fired not two steps out of the beer garden we're sidetracked.

"Hey, Cal. Hey, Owen. How's it going?" Skye, an old friend of mine from Prineville, says, stopping us in our tracks.

"Good to see you, Skye. Got beers to deliver. See ya soon," Owen says, as he walks away.

I'll never know how Owen gets off with being politely rude because I'm never so lucky.

"Yep, great to see you. Hope you and the kids are doing good. Give them my best," I say, desperate to get back to Charlotte.

Following Owen's lead, I try to walk away, but my former friends with benefits isn't letting me off so easily. Skye is one of the few women on my *friends with benefits* list I once told Charlotte about. We haven't explored those benefits in years, and I have no intention of hooking up with anyone other than Charlotte ever again.

She walks her fingers up my biceps, to my shoulder, where she braces herself and lifts on her toes to whisper in my ear. "Haven't seen you in a while, Cal. We should fix that, don't ya think?"

"Sorry, Skye—"

"C'mon, don't say no," she interrupts. "I have an Airbnb for the night, and you know we always have a good time."

I gently shrug her off my shoulder, doing my best not to spill the beers. "Sorry, but I'm—"

"He's in a relationship." Charlotte pops up out of nowhere, taking a beer out of my hand. "Here, baby. Let me take one of those for you, and you can introduce me to your friend."

Surprised, Skye removes her hand from my shoulder, but

it still hovers in the air like she's not sure what to do with it or what to say.

"Skye, this is my girlfriend, Charlotte. Charlotte, this is Skye."

"Girlfriend?"

"Nice to meet you, Skye. We have to go, though. I've memorized the set list, and some good ones are coming up and we would hate to miss them." She walks in front of me, her jean short-covered ass swinging with extra sass, her pony-tail swaying to the same rhythm.

All I can do is shake my head and chuckle as I watch her little show.

She looks over her shoulder to make sure my former *friend* is watching and gives her a wave of her fingers before turning her attention to me. She gives me a wink and purrs, "C'mon, baby."

Wherever you're going, I'm going, sugar.

"See ya, Skye," I yell over my shoulder.

I follow Charlotte back to our group, where we deliver the beers. Falling back into sync with the crowd, we sing along for a couple of songs before she turns to face me, lifting to her toes to kiss me.

The slow and seductive press of her lips seems to have a purposeful meaning. She isn't drinking, so her hands are free, and she wraps them behind my neck. Her breath tickles my cheek when she yells over the noise of the show. "She was one of your friends with benefits, wasn't she?"

The mere hint of jealousy from her is such a turn on I have an instant erection. "She was."

"She was a little too touchy-feely, if you ask me."

"I agree. That's why I was about to tell her I was in a relationship, but you cut in before I had the chance."

"I didn't like it."

"I get it." I give her a small kiss and try to change the subject. "What were you doing out there, anyway?"

"You told me you loved me and then walked away without letting me reply. I wanted to fix that."

Her face glows like a star in the clear, dark desert sky when the lights from the show pass over her features. It's crowded, and although the heat of the day is behind us, it's still humid out, making our shirts stick to our bodies. The beat of the music competes with the pounding of my heart as I wait for her reply.

"Chip, I love you too! I love you so much, you're pretty much all I think about anymore!" she yells at the top of her lungs over the music.

"Yeah?"

She's beaming with love and happiness when she nods her reply. "I was just waiting for you to catch up to me."

Sam starts singing a new song, and I lose her when Karissa screams in her ear. Charlotte jumps back around, her hair slapping me in the face. One of her arms goes around her friend's shoulders, and the other is in the air as they sing along. When the beat picks up and the chorus begins, they jump up and down together.

I guess this is their song.

It's nice to see her like this. Letting go of the grief she tries so very hard to keep tucked away. Out of sight, as if she hasn't suffered the biggest loss of her life.

This moment for her is pure joy. Which means it is for me too.

Anymore, my happiness depends on hers.

Today, she is happy, and all is well.

The song ends, and a slower one begins. She reaches her hand behind her, searching for me, and I take it. I drink the last of my beer and drop the cup to the ground to put both arms around her and hold her tightly.

Her hands latch onto my arms, and she presses her ass against me, bringing my dick to life once again. Only this time, the moment isn't here and gone. Her ass is relentless.

"You better be careful, sugar."

Her reply is to turn and kiss me, but her swaying doesn't stop. She tortures me through this song and the next.

"I'm not sure you know what you're doing, Charlotte. We're in public, but you push me much further, and they're going to arrest us for lewd behavior."

She kisses me again, and I think she's going to test just how far I'll go when "Ex To See" starts. Karissa turns to her, smiling ear to ear, and I release her from my embrace so she can sing and dance with her friend.

This seems to be a favorite for everyone as I watch Daisy, Owen, Angus, and Mia sing along with their arms up, accentuating the lyrics.

This group of people makes up my family. They may not all be blood, but they are my people. Knox and my mom are the only ones missing. I would do anything for all of them, but Charlotte is quickly becoming my entire world.

Chapter Twenty-Nine

Charlotte

"So, what do you think?" I ask Karissa as we rock back and forth on the porch swing at the cabin. Drinking our morning coffee in our sweats, hair up in matching messy buns, we peacefully take in the warm, earthy scent of the fresh air we could never even dream of back home.

The wind whispers through the trees as a piece of driftwood rolls in and out, riding the small lapping waves of the lake. In the distance, float a couple of ducks not far from a small fishing boat.

"It's beautiful, Charlotte," she replies, gazing over the lake that now feels like it belongs to me and me alone.

"Right?"

"This place suits you."

"It does, doesn't it?" I couldn't agree with her more.

"Couldn't be more different than your place back home, but it's strangely perfect."

"Is it crazy that I've imagined this being my new *regular* life?"

She takes my hand in hers. "No, not at all. He's a great guy."

"I meant Oregon."

"Sure you did."

I sigh. There's no need to pretend she's wrong. The thought of leaving Callen hurts my heart.

"He is pretty great."

"You two are great together and let's face it... the man worships the ground you walk on. The way he watches you. Girl, what I wouldn't give to have a man look at me like that."

"But is now the time for me to fall into a serious relationship? It's what I want, but is it smart?"

"What in the world are you talking about? Now is the ideal time."

I release a big breath and share what's been going through my head since Callen and I became an *us*. "I've never done anything truly on my own."

"What?"

"I went to my parents' alma mater."

"But you earned the grades to get accepted, and you took the classes and earned your degrees. Not your parents."

"Yes, but I didn't even consider any other schools."

"So?"

"Then I went to work for my dad's firm."

"But you lived on your own, paid your own way. It's not like he was footing the bill."

"Of course. Come on, you know what I mean."

"I really don't."

Is she making this hard on purpose?

"You do too. You're just—"

"Not telling you what you want to hear?" she says, cutting me off.

"Karissa, I've always done what I thought everyone wanted me to do. Or at the very least, what everyone hoped I would do. I've never made a big life decision based solely on what I want. If I sell the business and leave the only city that's ever been home and move here, it can't be for a man, can it?"

"Why the hell not? You want to be with him, don't you?"

"More than anything."

"So? *He* is something you want. Choosing to move here would be something you want, too. Something you would be doing for you and nobody else. Well, except it would be for Cal as well."

"True."

"I really don't understand why you won't let yourself have this. To let yourself be happy. There has to be another reason."

She's right. I just haven't wanted to say it out loud.

"I refuse to follow in my mother's footsteps," I share reluctantly.

"Oh, Char. Never. You could never be like your mom. Please tell me you know that."

"But moving for a man is something she would do."

"She would, but only because she needs their money and their giant house and expensive cars. You don't need Callen for those things."

"No, I don't."

I don't really even need to work again; with the money I've saved on my own and now inherited from my dad, I'm pretty much set. But I can't imagine not doing something to earn a living.

"Then we agree. No more comparing yourself to that woman."

Taking a sip of my coffee, I stare out at the lake and think about how much I'll miss Callen when I leave.

"Has he asked you to move here?"

"He hasn't come right out and asked, but he has made it clear he doesn't want me to leave. Is that the same thing? Am I getting ahead of myself?" I set my mug on the ground so I can hide my face in my hands. "He hasn't even asked me to move here yet, and here I am, struggling over whether I want to change my entire life for him."

"Remove the man from the picture. Can you see yourself living here?"

I take her question to heart and answer her honestly. "I can, Karissa. I really can. I could live right here in this cabin and wake up to this lake every day. Every night, I could watch the sunset over the water and never get tired of it. I love it here."

"It is pretty dreamy."

"Isn't it?"

"I don't think Knox will let me live here forever, though."

"Buy your own damn lake house. It's not like money is an issue. You can take your time and build tables for Daisy when she needs you to and figure out the logistics along the way."

"You make it sound so easy."

"It's because I know you. Which means I know how

exceptionally capable you are. You can do anything you set your mind to."

I rest my head on her shoulder. "Thanks."

We enjoy the beauty of our surroundings and sit in comfortable silence for a few long moments.

"I'll admit, I'm sad it's my last night. I've loved it here." She throws an arm around my shoulder and squeezes me to her side. "Most of all, I've loved seeing you so happy. I swear, you're more yourself than you've been in years."

Chapter Thirty

Charlotte

"Daisy, tell me again, how in the world are you single? What is wrong with the men around here?" Karissa asks, gazing adoringly at Daisy.

It's Karissa's last night, and she and I are having dinner at Matador in Redmond with Daisy before we meet Callen at The House. Our drink order was just taken, but you'd think we were already three or four deep with the laughter and silliness on the drive over.

I knew the two of them would hit it off. But their friendship was set in stone when the Spice Girls came on the '90s channel playing in the car. We found our Baby Spice to go with our Ginger and Scary Spice. We are three, not two peas in a pod.

"They're all from Goose Hollow, and I've known everyone here my entire life. I think I need a stranger. Somebody who hasn't known me since I was running around the kiddy pool in nothing but my diaper."

"You know, none of the men in this town see you that way, right?" I cut in. "You have quite a hold over many of them. I've seen it with my own eyes."

She chuckles, then leans in conspiratorially. "That may be true, but I still see them like snotty little kids. When you know everything about them, everyone they've dated, every idiot thing they've done and I've done, it takes away the fun. I'm not interested in any of them."

"You're telling me you see the Adonis that is Owen, with his fine ass dimples, as a snotty little kid?"

"Well, I'm not blind, but he's basically family. Dating him would be too weird. Besides, his goal in life is to torture me at every turn."

"You mean like pulling your pigtails on the playground because he actually likes you?"

"Uh, no. Nothing like that."

"So what you're saying is you need some *strange*. Got it," Karissa exclaims, and we all burst out laughing.

We chat a little longer, and when our margaritas arrive, we hold our glasses up and toast. "To us!"

But before our first sips are down, Daisy grows serious. "Okay, so before the tequila has set in and we're still sober, I have to talk to you about something."

She looks deadly serious. My heart sinks, and my mind instantly goes to Callen. Is she about to tell me something that could disrupt everything? Something that could potentially change my life forever?

"Is everything okay, Dais?" I ask, reaching across the table to squeeze her hand.

"Yes, but I think they could be better." Her smile eases some of my concern.

Karissa leans in. "Do tell."

"Well, I know you're still figuring things out, and you haven't said for sure if you're moving here, but I can't imagine you or my brother being apart from one another for more than twenty-four hours, let alone dating long-distance."

"This is about me and Callen?"

"No. As much as all three of my brothers love to be the center of attention, this is about you and me and the beautiful relationship we could have."

"Oh, this is getting good," Karissa coos, rubbing her hands together.

"You're scaring me, Daisy." I chuckle, but it's not a lie. This is Daisy. You never know what's going through her head.

"Hear me out." She tightens her grip on my hand when I try to pull away from her. "I may have brainstormed this in my head and have even outlined a business plan and name, but we would do this as a team. I mean, I guess we could do it long-distance, but it would go a lot better if you were here in Goose Hollow."

"What are you talking about?" Karissa and I both exclaim at the same time.

"I love to design and plan. You love to knock down walls and build shit. Let's do it together. As much as it saddens me, this area is growing in leaps and bounds. Old homes are being updated to become rentals, and there's a ton of new construction going in. Let's flip and remodel houses. Design and build the furniture for the rich people moving here from California." She gives me a wink. "I know you're still trying to figure out what to do, but if this idea helps you decide to stay, I wouldn't be mad about it."

I don't even give it a second thought.

"I'm in."

"You're in?" Karissa and Daisy ask in unison.

"I'm in." I hold up my salt-rimmed glass, and they follow my lead. "Let's build shit!"

Our glasses clink as they touch. Daisy's smile couldn't be any wider, and my best friend's eyes shimmer with unshed tears. Tears of joy. For me. Because she knows I'm taking control of my life and am about to follow my dreams.

* * *

"C'mon, babe, they're playing our song," Callen says as he pulls me onto the dance floor at The House.

"We have a song?"

I've heard the song, but never felt any particular attachment to it. The beat is slow, and he wraps his arms around my waist, swaying. "Every song is our song, if it means I get to dance with you and have you all to myself." He leans forward and places a sweet kiss against my lips.

"Aw, you've missed me, haven't you?"

As much as I've loved having my bestie here with me, I've missed falling asleep in Callen's arms every night.

"I've been to the ranch to shovel shit every morning."

"What?"

"I guess you could say I've needed the distraction."

"Distraction?"

"Charlotte, I meant it when I said I don't like to share."

"You've seen me every day, you maniac." I lightly smack him on the arm.

"I missed waking up to you. You're quite addictive, sugar."

My heart trips over itself as I continue to fall head over heels for this man.

I asked Daisy to let me be the one to share our news with Callen. Wanting to gauge his reaction when I tell him my plans.

"I'm glad to hear that." I make sure he's fixed on me as I breathe in a long breath and then release it. "How would you feel about being able to feed your addiction on a daily basis for the foreseeable future?"

Our swaying stops. His eyes grow wide as he looks at me, clearly confused. "What are you saying?"

"I've decided it's time to sell the business to Richard. As soon as I've tied up all my loose ends back home, I'm moving to Goose Hollow and going into business with Daisy. We're gonna flip houses and build shit."

His smile is big and beautiful. "I'm so damn happy for you. Your dream is coming true." He pulls me into his arms, kissing the top of my head.

Nausea swirls in my belly, and it's not the tequila. His response to my news is not at all what I had hoped it would be. Did I expect him to sweep me off my feet? Maybe. Maybe not. Gah! I don't know. But I expected more than him being happy for me. What about us? How could I have been so off base?

My chin quivers as my emotions get the best of me.

He gently grips my chin with his thumb and forefinger. "Hey, what's this all about? This is great news."

"You said it was great news for *me*, Callen? I guess I just thought... I mean, maybe I should have talked to you about it first?" *Suck it up, Charlie. Just say what's on your mind.* "Callen, how do *you* feel about me moving to Goose Hollow?"

"Shit, baby. I'm over the fucking moon."

He kisses me gently again.

"It's not too soon?"

"Charlotte, yours isn't the only dream coming true." He twirls me out in front of him. "I thought you knew." He twirls me back against his body. "I only wanna dance with you."

Chapter Thirty-One

Charlotte

I'm in the zone. In my happy place.

Well, one of many new happy places. The lake, The House, Callen's bed, and here in the back warehouse at McKinnon Hardware and Lumber, where I've been building the tables for the job Daisy got me.

With only two more to finish, I'll be able to stain and seal the tables for the wedding ahead of schedule. I've pushed myself to finish since I leave for LA in five days, and I don't know how long I'll be gone.

My goggles are firmly in place as I use the power saw Callen has set up for me. Dust from the wood covers my old-school '90s overalls and Dr. Martens. Hall & Oates plays in my earbuds, and memories of my dad teaching me how to use a saw just like the one I'm using tonight put a smile on my face.

In the past, these same memories would have left tearstains on the wood. But today, all I feel is lucky to have happy thoughts of my dad. Mom may have taken off, but she couldn't have left me in better hands.

In some ways, my dad was my best friend. I always had Karissa, but Dad had to be both mother and father to me. He may have been building his business and making a name for himself, but I never felt second on his priority list.

I never felt obligated to become a lawyer and work for Dad's firm. It was my decision. I was a dedicated student who was accepted into an excellent school and thought my dad hung the moon. Of course, I wanted to be just like him. So, I became a lawyer.

I'm damn good at my job.

My clients trust me.

I make a lot of money, but it doesn't make me happy.

As crazy as it may seem to people on the outside, I would rather be in the back of a lumberyard warehouse building tables for a fair wage than drafting contracts and making statements for narcissistic clients for an obscene amount of money.

I'm at peace for the first time in years.

It's not every day a person is on the verge of not only fulfilling their professional dreams but also their personal dreams.

Callen McKinnon is everything I never knew I needed. I got a glimpse of the man he was back in Los Angeles, but I was just scratching the surface of all that he is. He's loyal and kind, funny and sexy, and he sees me.

Supports me.

Encourages me.

Ruby startles me out of my musings when she appears out of nowhere and sits at my feet like the good girl she is, with one paw on my boot. Knowing the man I was just daydreaming about will be right behind her, I stop the saw, lift the goggles to the top of my head, and drop my earmuffs to my neck.

"Hello, sweet girl." I bend down to pet her. "What have you and Daddy been up to today?"

"Work and missing you." The deep timbre of his voice carries over the night air all the way to my belly. It somersaults at the mere presence of him.

When I turn to greet him, the view is one I'm not sure I'll ever get used to. How could I with the way his gray T-shirt hugs his torso in all the right places? Or how his tan biceps are no match for the cotton shirt trying to contain them? Then there's the way the corded veins on his forearms scream for attention. Don't even get me started on the well-worn jeans straining against his thighs or the banged-up wellington work boots that give me butterflies every time I hear them coming my way.

I'll never get used to Callen McKinnon. Never.

Instead, I'll admire the beauty of the man and thank my lucky stars that he's mine.

Even though I know there is no way to make myself look presentable in my current state, I dust off my overalls and take off my gloves just in time for him to reach me.

"You missed me?" I ask, just like I always do.

Him saying he missed me and me acting surprised has become one of our many little things. I'm sure we're annoyingly adorable to those who have to hear it all the time.

He pulls me into his arms. "Don't pretend not to know that every minute away from you isn't pure torture."

"I missed you too."

"Yeah, how much did you miss me?"

Hands on the small of my back, he presses me closer.

"If only I could show you."

"What's stopping you?"

"Uh, we're in the middle of the warehouse."

"So?"

"What if one of the guys walks in and catches us?" I whisper, like *the guys* are close enough to hear. "Unless you're into your employees watching?"

"I would rip their eyes from their sockets."

"I know I should take your penchant for violence as a neon red flag, but your caveman antics turn me on."

"Do they now?" He unclips one of the straps on my overalls.

"Everything about you turns me on, Callen."

He brings his lips to mine, kissing me at a slow, methodical pace. His tongue traces my upper lip as his hand dips under my black tank.

"No bra?" He pinches my nipple.

"What are you doing? Hoping to rip some eyes out of sockets?"

"Sugar, it's already after eight. Nobody's here."

He rolls my nipple between his fingertips. "So, no eyes to worry about then?"

"Nope."

He snaps his fingers and points, and Ruby takes her position at the door to keep watch.

"Come here," he says, making his way to a pallet stacked high with boxes of vinyl flooring. He blows on the top boxes, but his brow furrows, unsatisfied with the results. Before I know what's happening, he pulls his shirt over his head and lays it on the boxes, then guides me until I'm standing in front of the pallet.

"What are you doing?"

"I'm going to fuck you, Charlotte. Right here and right now."

I start to remove my goggles from my forehead, but he stops me. "No, just like this."

"Callen, I'm a mess."

"You're fucking beautiful. Seeing you like this, doing what you love. That's what turns me on. Leave it all."

I'm speechless, giving over to him, as I almost always do.

He unhooks my other shoulder strap and lets my overalls pool at my feet. The hammer he gave me, that I keep in my thigh pocket, thuds against the concrete floor. His fingers wiggle into the sides of my panties, and he pulls them down my legs, stopping to place a kiss over my pelvic bone. I'm aching for his touch, and my legs instinctually open for him as wide as they can with my clothes bound around my ankles.

"I love you, you know that?" I sigh, watching him as he moves down my body.

"I do, but I'll never get tired of hearing you say it."

Taking a knee, he finds my eyes, penetrating deep into the part of me that was made for him. Only him. Even here in this dusty warehouse, surrounded by pallets of wood as he prepares to fuck me, I know it's more than that. I know my heart is his, and his is mine.

Fingertips gently open me up, and he sucks my clit into

his mouth. I want to close my eyes and throw my head back, but his eyes order me not to.

Tongue darting over my most sensitive spot, he circles it at a mad pace. My need to orgasm builds when he stops and licks my pussy from top to bottom like an ice cream cone. I'm soaked for him, and his throaty growl vibrates through my core, all the way to my heart.

Wordlessly, he stands. His hands find their way under my tank and travel over my stomach, rib cage, and breasts, lifting my shirt as his fingers blaze a trail up my torso. He tucks my shirt under the earmuffs at my neck and then lifts me up, carefully placing me on his T-shirt.

Leaning back, one of my hands braces my weight, my most private parts bared to him as he slowly inspects my body. The heat in his eyes is dangerous. Taunting.

Taking my turn to admire him, my gaze blatantly roams over his broad chest and the ripples of his abs. The V that disappears into his waistband is a teaser for the perfection that lies behind the denim of his jeans.

When my more than approving appraisal finally makes its way back to his face, I focus on his mouth, watching his tongue dart out over his full bottom lip.

"Fuck. You have no idea what it does to me when you look at me like that." His voice is low. Carnal.

"Like what?" I ask coyly. Acting as though the thrill of being spread out before him, essentially naked in a public space, doesn't have me ready to combust.

"Like you may just want me half as much as I want you."

Sitting up, I reach for his pants and pull out the condom I know will be in his front pocket. Carefully, I place the edge of the wrapper between my lips. We've been having so much sex lately that he's sure to always have one on him since we never know when the mood may strike. I undo his pants in a flash, and his cock is in my hand before they thud against the floor.

"Put it on, sugar."

"So impatient," I mumble around the package.

He tugs the condom out of my mouth. "If you could see yourself right now, you'd understand. I've never seen anything so fucking hot."

He leans down and sucks one of my nipples into his mouth, rolling the rubber on at the same time. My hands rake through his thick hair, my back arching, needing to be as close to him as possible.

His hands grip my ass, scooting me and his shirt to the edge of our makeshift table. His length nudges against my center, and I want to open my legs wide enough to wrap around his hips. If only my current overalls around the ankles situation wasn't limiting my mobility.

He slowly inches his way inside me, filling me nearly to the point of pain. Nearly.

He's in no rush, leisurely thrusting in and out of me. He knows this pace keeps me right on the edge. Cruelly, never quite reaching the tempo he knows I'm aching for.

"So tight, baby. So. Damn. Tight."

"Mm-hmm." Is all I can get out as he rocks me in a sweet rhythm only he can create.

All my concentration focuses on finding the bliss I've only ever felt with Callen.

The bliss that comes when I give up control.

Control I've only ever given up to him.

"Tell me what you want, sugar."

"Faster."

His thrusts grow harder. Deeper. Our bodies slapping against each other fills the chilly space around us. But even with my hands on his ass trying to dictate our rhythm, he doesn't pick up his pace.

Why does he ask me if he's not going to give me what I want?

Because he knows what he's doing, and he knows it's not time.

"Never." *Thrust.* "Deep." *Thrust.* "Enough," he growls.

I drag my hand from his ass to touch myself, but he intercepts my wrist, stopping me.

"No."

"Please," I beg, needing to find my release.

"You wanna come, Charlotte? Is that what you want?"

"Yes! God, yes!"

He finally grants me my wish, and with his newfound speed and the force of his body hitting my clit, I'm close. So. Close.

"I will never get enough of you. Never." His words, spoken through gritted teeth, are all I need for stars to cloud my vision and my soul to leave my body.

I ride his heavenly pounding through my orgasm, and when I open my eyes, I'm so glad we didn't finish at the same time. I love watching him come. The veins in his neck strain, and his brow creases, but he never takes his eyes off me.

Finished, he doesn't pull out right away. Instead, he presses his forehead to mine and whispers, "I love you, Charlotte Carruthers."

"I love you too, Callen McKinnon."

My stomach growls, ending the romantic moment.

"Did you forget to eat again?"

"No. Well, wait... maybe?"

"Come on." He kisses me for five heartbeats. "Let's feed you."

He pulls out, disposes of the condom, and pulls his pants back up. Next, he lifts me off the boxes and sets me back on my feet. He shimmies my underwear and my tank back into place, then fastens my overalls.

"You take such good care of me." I sigh against his chest.

"It's all I want to do, baby." He shakes his shirt out before sliding it over his head. "I'm not just here to fulfill your sexual kinks."

"Kinks?"

"Listen, if dirty warehouses full of sawdust are your thing, who am I to judge? I am just here to serve, milady." He bends into a silly mock bow.

"Oh, whatever. This was all you, you freak!"

He pulls me into his embrace and kisses me senseless. His beard is abrasive, but I couldn't care less.

"Shit, you're all red. I need to trim this down, don't I?"

"I don't mind. It's sexy."

"Not if it hurts you."

"I think I'll survive."

My stomach begs for attention again.

"Woman, you have to stop starving yourself when you're working back here. Let's go eat."

"No, I have a few more things I want to do before I leave. I'll eat later."

"If you won't leave, I'll bring the food to you."

He calls Angus at The House and puts in an order for my

favorite House burger with cheese, no mayo, no onions, and a side of tots. The man knows me so well.

"Thank you," I say against his lips as I kiss him goodbye.

"Be right back."

Once he and Ruby have vacated the premises, my goggles and ear protection are back in place, and I return to what I was doing before he so pleasantly interrupted me.

Chapter Thirty-Two

Charlotte

Callen sits atop the stack of flooring we got down and dirty on a mere thirty minutes ago as he watches me eat. My food sits next to him, and I'm perched on a wheeled stool I've raised as high as it can go, like I'm sitting at a table.

"You sure you don't want me to go with you?" he asks before popping one of my tater tots in his mouth.

"It's not that I don't want you to come, you know that. I've just got so much to do. I won't have time to spend with you. Besides, you would distract me like you did tonight, and I won't get anything done."

"You love my distractions."

"I do." I smile around my mouth full of food. "I really do."

God, the way he looks at me. I've never felt wanted like this. I've never wanted to be distracted like I do when he's around.

"The sooner I can get things done; the sooner I can make Goose Hollow my new home."

A smile stretches across his face. "Sure do like the sound of that, sugar."

"Me too." I smile, downright giddy from his excitement over my relocation.

"Speaking of you moving here... I've been doing some thinking."

My heart drops, unsure what he could have been thinking about that we haven't already discussed.

"What's that?"

My phone vibrates in the front pocket of my overalls.

"Shoot, one second." I check the screen, but it's not a number I recognize. I hold it up to him. "Unknown caller. Could be a client. Could be spam." I shove it back in my pocket. "If it's a client, and it's important, they'll call back or leave a message. Right?"

"Right."

"I can't wait until I don't have to worry about clients calling from their burner phones in the middle of the night because they've done something stupid. Now, what were you saying?"

"Well, I was thinking, why go back to the cabin when you come home from Los Angeles? Instead, move in with me."

My heart swells with joy to know he wants me to take the next step with him. I've thought about this scenario many times, and as much as I want to say yes, a part of me knows the right thing to do is say no. "You want me to move in with you?"

"I do."

My joy is short-lived because I'm about to turn him down.

I stand between his legs and rub my hands up and down his jean-clad thighs. "Callen, I want nothing more than to fall asleep in your arms every night, but I think I need to do part of this on my own."

"But you aren't on your own. You have me."

He's keeping his cool, but there's a hint of irritation in his voice.

"I know I do, and you have been and will be there every step of the way. But I've always done things on the back of someone else. This is the first time I'm doing something on my own. I mean, I'm starting the business with Daisy, so I have a partner, but you know what I mean."

I sound like a broken record, having just given this same excuse to Karissa a few days ago.

"But that's business."

Shoot, he's got me there.

"I know, but just until things are off the ground. It may not make sense, but I need to do this. I need to rely on myself."

I place a soft kiss on his lips. Thank goodness he kisses me back.

"I hear you. I don't agree with you, but I hear you. Just tell me you'll think about it."

"I promise I'll think about it, but I'm not really sure if your neat-freak tendencies can handle me and all my shoes."

"Nice try."

I give him a wink.

"I still hate that you're leaving."

"I know, but it won't be forever."

He kisses me again and then rests his forehead against mine. "As long as you come back to me."

"Always."

Chapter Thirty-Three

Charlotte

Eyes beaming with pride, Karissa holds up her champagne flute. "Cheers on your big move and to you and Daisy on your new business venture. I am so damn proud of you."

"Thank you, but I'm going to miss you so much!"

Karissa and I clink our glasses together, and she blows me a kiss. I savor the tickle of bubbles on my tongue. I'm exhausted, but the stress of the last two weeks will all be worth it. Besides, I'm never too tired for Nobu. This is where she and I celebrate all the big things. Can't lie, I'm gonna miss nights like tonight.

"So, the office is all settled?"

"As much as it can be. Dad made everything easy since he had all the paperwork written up, and Richard has been great. Since I started the process while I was in Oregon and had already met with the staff to let them know their options, the past two weeks have been about reaching out to clients."

"It's so great that Richard is going to take over the lease. What a relief not to have to move things." Karissa takes another sip of her bubbly. "That would have been so stressful."

"I know. Besides the name change, it should be pretty seamless. Only one person is leaving. Everyone else is opting to stay. Since he didn't have the room to move everyone to his offices, he's opted for a second location. It works out great."

"And your clients? How are they taking the news?"

My phone rings with an unknown number, and I decline the call. "Stupid spam calls."

"They probably want to tell you your car warranty is up. They're so annoying. Anyway, back to your clients. How are they taking it?" she asks as she pops a crispy Brussels sprout in her mouth.

"For the most part, they've been great, some not so much. I think we'll lose about a third, which is to be expected. Most love their teams and won't leave, but no hard feeling to those who do. They were loyal to me and Dad. Richard accounted for the reduction in business, so he's not concerned."

"So, give me the dirt," Karissa says, with a devious smile. "Who didn't take it well? Who was the star of this edition of celebrities behaving badly?"

Leaning over the table, I lower my voice so I can't be overheard. "To be honest, it was more like managers and agents behaving badly. In reality, we work with them more often than not, and many of them lost their minds. Dan Jones on Nicolette Gwen's team threw his napkin on his plate, walked out of Tower Bar, and never came back."

"You're kidding?"

"Nope, but Nicolette stayed, and we chatted for another hour. She is so sweet. I'm gonna miss clients like her. Josh West and his team took things well. He really thought his career was over after he came out, but it just shows that good things come to good people because his career and love life are soaring right now, and I couldn't be happier for him. I'll miss Josh and Nicolette the most."

"I'm assuming the Hollow Knocks took things well, seeing as you're part of the family now."

"Well, let's not rush things."

Already giving him special treatment because I love his brother, I don't mention my meeting with Knox earlier today. Client privilege and all that.

"You're moving your whole life to be with Callen. I think we're way past rushing things."

"Still. One step at a time."

"Char, what are you talking about? That man is in love with you. You know he wants you to have his babies, right?"

"Shut up."

"Have you two not talked about what comes next?"

"Well, he asked me to move in with him when I get back to Oregon."

"And you said...?"

"I told him no."

"You what?"

"I don't know. In the moment, I had flashes of my mom and freaked out. I told myself I couldn't. Not because of him, but because I thought I had to prove something to myself that *I* can move to another state and start a new business on my own without relying on anyone but me and my business partner."

I don't tell her I've second-guessed my answer every day. That I wish I had said yes.

"I will never know where you got this distorted view of yourself, but you worked hard for everything you have accomplished." Karissa takes my hand in hers. "You don't need a man to succeed, but you deserve to be loved. You haven't lived a fairy-tale life. Girl, since you were a kid, you have been through it. You." She points at me with her free hand. "Deserve happiness. You deserve the security and comfort that Callen can provide you."

This is why she's my best friend. She cares about me like nobody else. Knows everything there is to know about me and only wants what's best.

"I know I deserve all those things, but I also know deep down this is something I need to do for myself. It won't be forever. Just until I find my footing in my new life. Right?"

"Well, if this summer is any indication, you've already found your footing, and it looks pretty damn good on you."

I sit back in my chair and strike a pose. "It does, doesn't it?"

We're both chuckling when our black cod with miso arrives. "You know you're going to miss Nobu."

"True. But after all the breakfast, lunch, and dinner meetings I've had in the past two weeks, some home-cooked meals sound pretty nice right about now."

"But you don't cook."

"No, but my man does." I wink.

"See, another reason you should take him up on his offer."

She's right; I was an idiot to refuse him.

* * *

"Hey, baby. How was your day?" Callen smiles, and my heart skips a beat.

It's so nice to see his face, even if it's just on the small screen of my phone.

"It was shit because you're still gone."

"Stop it. Seriously, how was your day?"

"I'm being serious. Nothing feels right when you're so far away."

"I know. I feel the same. But we're getting close." He sits down on the couch, and Ruby jumps up next to him with a big smile. "Hi, sweet girl."

"She misses you too."

"Well, she won't be missing me for long." I flip the phone around so he can see the stacks of boxes all over my living room. "I've made a decent dent in the packing. The movers will be here the day after tomorrow to finish and move it all to the storage unit in Bend. The house will go on the market Monday." I can't believe I'm selling my house. I love this house. "I have one last meeting in the morning, and then I'll pack up my office. Kristen is coming over tomorrow afternoon to take pictures. Things are moving right along."

"So if the movers are taking your stuff, that means you have no choice but to put your butt on a plane and come back to me."

Oh, how I love this man.

"Early next week, if all goes well. The plan is to book my flight home tonight. But not before I get through the stacks of mail I came home to. I'm sure most of it's junk, but I've been putting it off. It's amazing how much junk mail still goes out. All my bills come to me electronically, but you never know when something important will show up. So it must be done."

"Don't forget to put in your change of address while you're at it."

I know what he's getting at, but I don't broach the subject of moving in with him. Because it's on the tip of my tongue to tell him I've changed my mind about his offer. After my conversation with Karissa, I promised myself I would sleep on it one more night and if I couldn't come up with better reasons than the lame excuses I gave to my best friend, Callen may just get his wish after all. I really want to blurt out my plans right now, but one more sleep.

"Thanks for the reminder."

"Did you need me to send you my address?"

And there it is.

"Nah, I'm all good. I set up a P.O. Box back home."

"I like the sound of that."

"P.O. Boxes turn you on?"

"Sugar, your box is the only one that turns me on." He winks, a wry smile on his face.

"You are so stupid."

"I was referring to you calling my hometown *your* home-town. It's music to my ears."

"It does sound good, doesn't it?"

"Okay, little lady. No more procrastinating. Sit your ass down and talk to me while you open your mail."

I aim my camera phone at the mound of dead trees on my dining room table. "There is a shit ton. Not sure you'll be able to stay awake that long."

"We'll see. Now prop me up somewhere and get busy."

"Ha! I can hear you saying that when you're a hundred years old. Just prop me up and get busy."

I move a vase into the middle of the table and rest my phone against it to free up my hands.

"Sugar, as long as it's you propping me up, I'll always want to get busy."

"Well, if I have my way, you'll be a very busy hundred-year-old."

I start a pile of flyers and obvious junk mail. Another for official looking items.

"Woman, you are saying all the right things tonight. Well, with the exception of admitting you've changed your mind about moving in with me."

He's killing me right now. I'm on the verge of telling him he's right, but for some reason, I don't. One more night. I just need one more night.

"Cal, we've been through this."

His voice turns serious. "Only my friends call me Cal, Charlotte."

"Good grief," I say as I open another envelope. "Don't get your panties in a bunch. I'm tired. I was just saving energy."

"Well, maybe if you were using a letter opener, you wouldn't be using so much energy ripping those envelopes to shreds. Dear Lord, woman, have you never opened mail before?"

"How old are you? Who uses a letter opener?"

My heart stops when I pick up the next envelope. My body breaks out into a sweat, and I think I may be sick.

Callen is still giving me a hard time when he stops mid-sentence. "Baby, what is it?"

"I don't want to open it."

"Open what?" When I don't respond, he adds, "Talk to me, Charlotte."

"It's from the California Parole Board."

His relaxed posture with his arm draped around Ruby changes abruptly as he moves to the edge of the couch.

"I'm here, baby."

I rip open the envelope to find one lone piece of paper inside. The date at the top of the page is a little over a month ago.

"Let's see... it says William Davies is up for early release. I have until fifteen days from the date of this letter to participate in a parole suitability hearing."

"When is the hearing date?"

I scan the document, searching for the date, and as soon as I do the math, the paper in my hand begins to shake.

"Charlotte?"

"Last week. Callen, it was last week."

"It was just a hearing. How can we find out the board's decision?"

"There's a website here. Let me grab my laptop. Hang on."

"Take me with you. And make sure the house alarm is on, baby."

With Callen in my hand, I make sure the deadbolt on the front door is in place and turn on the front porch light. With shaky fingers, I set the house alarm and flip each switch I pass, turning on all the lights as I jog down the hallway and grab my computer out of my bedroom.

"Hey, slow down. You're okay."

He's right. Don't panic, Charlie. It was just a hearing. Do. Not. Panic.

But no matter how many times I tell myself to stay calm, the sense of dread creeping its way into my psyche has a mind of its own. By the time I'm back at the table, it feels like I'm outside my body watching what's happening like a slow-motion scene in a movie.

"Okay, there," I say as I prop the phone back up. "Thank you for putting up with my silliness."

"Don't thank me. I'll always want you to take me with you."

His sexy little wink doesn't do me in like it usually does, but I appreciate the effort.

I log in and grab the letter to find the website details, but the paper is shaking so much I can't read it.

"Hey, sugar. Just breathe for me. Look at me and breathe."

Setting the letter down, I release a big exhale and meet his beautiful brown eyes.

"There she is. You need to breathe with me?"

I nod.

"Listen to me, Charlotte. I'm here, and you got this." Ruby jumps off the couch and puts her head on his leg. Just seeing her face on the screen is a comfort. "I want you to inhale for the count of four and then exhale for a count of four."

Without hesitation, I follow his instructions and take a deep breath in.

"That's it. One. Two. Three. Four. Now, release it slowly."

I exhale, and he counts me through it again.

"There you go. Feeling any better?"

"Better, but I feel kinda silly. I'm sure I'm overreacting."

"You're being completely rational. Do not apologize. Now, why don't we see what's up before we worry too much more?"

"You're right, Okay, let's do this."

I focus on my laptop and navigate through the site, enter William's details, and wait.

When the information appears on the screen, the fear that had lost its stranglehold on me two years ago comes flooding back. The loosened knots in my stomach tighten.

"Baby, what does it say? You look like you've seen a ghost."

"They let him out three years early."

"Fuck," he says to himself. "It's going to be okay. You're coming home in a few days, and he likely can't leave the state. Once we get you here, you'll feel better. In the meantime, go stay with Karissa, and I'm gonna get on the next flight to LA."

"You don't need to do that. I'll be fine."

"You may be fine, but I won't be. It's not up for discussion."

He's walking through his house, and soon, I see him in his kitchen, where I know he charges his computer. He props the phone up and begins typing away.

"Callen, you can't just leave. What about the store? What about Ruby?"

"Ruby can stay with Angus, and I have staff who can handle the store."

I want to argue, but I'm so damn relieved I can't. My body slumps in my chair. "Okay, thank you."

"Shit. The only direct flight from Bend left forty-five

minutes ago. But there's a five thirty flight in the morning that will get me to Seattle, and then a connecting flight from there will get me to LAX by ten to eleven."

"Callen, you don't need to get up that early and take two flights to get here. That's ridiculous."

I'm being polite, but I want nothing more than for him to get on that early flight.

He pulls a credit card out of his wallet. "Don't you know I'd do anything to get to you? Getting up early and taking two flights is nothing if it means you'll be in my arms in less than fourteen hours."

"I love you, Chip."

"Nowhere near as much as I love you." He lets out a small sigh. "Okay, as much as I hate to do this, I'm gonna let you go so you can call Karissa and have her bring that cousin of hers and meet you at your place. Then I want the three of you to leave together in one car back to her house. I'm gonna call Angus and Loten and get things arranged, and then I'll call you back and stay on the line with you until they get there. Sound good?"

"Sounds great. Thank you again. Talk to you soon."

"Bye, talk to you in a few minutes."

His face vanishes from my screen, and wrapped in Callen's love, I dial my best friend. As I fill her in on what's happening, I'm scared as hell. But having a person in my life who drops everything so he can be by my side—when I'm likely overreacting—as if it's nothing at all, is incredibly comforting.

He cannot get here soon enough.

Chapter Thirty-Four

Charlotte

I've been useless this morning.

More than once, I've completely spaced out while someone was talking to me. My mind has been an exhausted whirlwind, flashing scenes from last night into my thoughts on a constant loop. First the letter, then the information I found on the website. Callen trying to calm me through the phone until Karissa and her cousin Jimmy showed up.

The level of fear that had taken over my body on the walk from the house to Jimmy's car would have brought me to my knees if Karissa hadn't been there to hold me up. The entire drive to Karissa's place, I kept turning in my seat to make sure no one was following us. It was overwhelming.

Rage churns in my chest. I'm so mad at myself for letting this piece of sheet overtake my mental well-being again. I told myself I would never let anyone control me like this again. And here I am.

Callen offered to stay on a video call until I fell asleep, but I crashed in Karissa's bed and didn't want to keep her up. Besides, he needed to get what sleep he could before his early morning flight. Jimmy was kind enough to sleep on the couch, and I got through the night knowing that Callen would be here by lunch.

He's been texting me since he woke up, keeping me posted on his location. He texted before he got on each of his planes. When his flights landed, he texted. When he got in his Lyft to my office, he texted.

When I'm not thinking about William Davies, I'm thinking about Callen.

At the moment, I'm speaking with my soon-to-be former assistant about where to forward my messages and mail after I've moved when my phone pings and an electric jolt shoots through my body because I know what it means. He's here!

CALLEN

Walking into your building now.

CHARLOTTE

Yay! On my way down. I'll meet you at the front desk.

CALLEN

Yes, ma'am.

With no shame in my game, I sprint down the hall at a breakneck speed and push the down button for the elevator five more times than necessary. The rest of my conversation with Lara will have to wait until later.

When the doors open, I slide in with the three people

who also must be going to the lobby, since that's the only button pushed, I use the fourteen-floors to check my reflection in the elevator wall. The woman behind me gives me a little smile while the two men to her left continue to scroll on their phones.

When the elevator pings on the lobby floor, I swear it zaps my heart because it's beating like I've just run for miles on the treadmill. The doors are barely open when I turn sideways to get out and rush toward the entrance of the building.

When I see him, a gasp escapes me at the sight of his clean-shaven face.

"Callen, what have you done?" I squeal, rushing past Ernie at the front desk and into Callen's muscular arms. He wraps them around me, lifting my feet off the ground.

"You don't like it?"

He places me back on my feet, and I grab his face, kissing him hard. "I love you any way I can get you."

The woman from the elevator passes by with a grin.

"I love you too, baby. And we are never... ever... going two weeks without seeing each other again."

"Never." I caress his face with my fingertips.

He leans into my hand. "It's good to see your face."

"Yours too, but if I'm being honest, this new look of yours reminds me of this guy I once knew."

"Is that right?"

"Yep, his name was Chip," I whisper in his ear. "He was a beast between the sheets."

He chuckles and gives me a gentle slap on the butt. "C'mon, Miss Carruthers. Show me your big fancy office."

Chapter Thirty-Five

Charlotte

We're following my real estate agent, Kristen, as she takes pictures of the house I've lived in for the past five years. Since Callen has never been here, I'm attempting to give him a tour at the same time. We've only made it as far as the living room. With Kristen busy getting what she needs, I hope and pray she hasn't heard or seen anything that makes her uncomfortable because my gentleman from small-town Oregon is being anything but gentlemanly.

At the moment, his tongue is taking a tour up my neck to my ear.

"I can't wait to make you come in every room in this house. I'm gonna start by bending you over your couch."

Doing my best to keep my giggles at bay, I push him off playfully and whisper, "Shh. Kristen is in the other room!"

He ignores me. "Then the kitchen counter, the shower, and, of course, your bedroom."

"You do know the movers will be here to pack tomorrow at nine o'clock, right? That's a lot of ground to cover in the next sixteen hours."

"Baby, you know I love a challenge. Besides, I'm always hard when I'm around you, so it shouldn't be a problem."

"What in the world has gotten into you?" I step out of his arms and back my way out of the room, but don't take my eyes off him for fear he'll pounce if I turn my back on him. "You're like an eighteen-year-old at his first frat party."

"Charlie?" Kristen calls from the other room.

"Saved by the bell." I aim at him before calling back to her. "Coming."

She's moved on from the kitchen and is snapping pictures of what is by far my favorite room in the house. We're listing it as a den, but it's my heaven. The room has exposed beams, floor-to-ceiling bookshelves, a gray overstuffed couch with a chaise, and too many throw pillows to count. The one window in the room takes up the entire back wall and looks out over the city.

Before I escaped to Goose Hollow, I thought my view from the hills here in Los Feliz was the best money could buy, but give me my lake-view swing at the cabin over this multi-million-dollar view any day.

"What's up?"

"So these shelves didn't come with the house. You added them, right?"

"I did."

"Even though these aren't built-ins, you know they will still need to stay with the house. Honestly, if anyone is on the fence about making an offer, all we need to do is show them this room, and I think it will make the decision for them. It's absolutely perfect."

"Whoa," Callen says, joining us in what used to be my happy place. Now it's anywhere he is. "She's not lying. This room is something else."

"Thanks. It took some time, but I didn't want to compromise. This is exactly what I wanted when I designed the room. It's my favorite space in the house. I can't lie, I'm gonna miss it."

"You built these shelves, didn't you?"

My heart melts that he recognizes my work.

"I did."

Kristen gasps, "You what?"

"She built them," he answers for me. "She's pretty damn talented, isn't she?"

"Holy cow, Charlie. I had no idea. My mind is blown."

My cheeks hurt from the stupid grin beaming across my face.

He wraps his arms around my waist, bending down to rest his chin on my shoulder. "I can see why you're gonna miss this room. You still sure about this? You're giving up a lot."

I reach up and stroke his cheek, now scruffy with afternoon stubble. "I'm gaining much more than I'm giving up."

He kisses me on the cheek. "I love you."

"I love you, too."

Kristen clears her throat. "So, just so we're on the same page, you're okay with leaving the bookshelves?"

"Yep."

"Okay, well, I think I have what I need. I'll edit and

upload these pictures, and we'll be ready to list the house on Monday."

"Thank you for everything. We're flying out on Sunday afternoon, but you know I'm always available. Just call or text."

"Perfect. I'll leave you lovebirds alone then. I'm sure you have a lot to do before you leave."

"You have no idea," Callen jokes. His arms still wrapped around me.

There's no hiding my blush that likely gives away his meaning, but we don't faze Kristen one bit. In fact, her smile only broadens, and her eyes soften. "I'm happy for you both. I'll see my way out."

Pushing his hands away, I step out of his warm embrace. "Don't be silly. I'll walk you out."

"It was nice to meet you, Callen," she says, extending a hand to him.

He shakes her hand. "You as well."

Kristen and I walk through the house, and when we get to the front door, she turns to me with a solemn look in her eye.

"I'm gonna miss you, but I'd give it all up for a man who looked at me like that man looks at you. I'm thrilled for you."

A twinge of irritation spikes through my veins to think she assumes I am just moving for a man. "Yes, he's pretty great, but I'm also starting a business with his sister. I'm not just moving for him, Kristen."

"Come on, we both know if he wasn't in the picture, you wouldn't be leaving all this to build furniture in Oregon. And that's okay. There's nothing wrong with moving for love."

Is she right?

If Callen didn't exist and I had just met Daisy on a trip to the cabin, would I move everything just to start the business with her? Would Goose Hollow still be the place I now call home?

Irritated with the doubt she's put in my mind, I open the door, letting her know I'm done with the conversation.

"Come here." Kristen's arms open, expecting a hug.

A hug I give her because she's one of my oldest friends, and I can't stay mad at her. She doesn't know about the struggle going on in my head and heart because I haven't shared it with her. Her smile is genuine, reflecting the happiness she feels for me. How could I stay mad at that?

We hug and I thank her again.

Once she's gone and I've locked the front door, I stroll through the house on my way back to Callen. Taking in everything I built along the way. I'm proud of myself for being able to purchase such a luxurious home as this one. I've worked hard and sacrificed my personal life because of my work, and this house was my reward.

Peeking into the den, there he is. My favorite person in my favorite room. Pillows litter the floor and he's lounging on the chaise, shirt and shoes off, and the top button of his jeans undone.

"Why are the pillows all over the floor, Chip?" I ask, stopping in front of the couch where he's laid out and looking magnificent, his defined arm muscles stretched above his head. The light sprinkle of auburn curls scattered over his broad chest and that damn V of his is pure decadence. "And why are you posing like Kate Winslet in *Titanic*? Am I supposed to paint you like one of my French girls?"

"Maybe later. I've decided we're starting in this room." He scoots to the edge of the couch.

"Starting what?"

"Sugar, don't be coy." He looks at his watch. "We've only got fifteen hours and forty-three minutes to get to every room." Hooking a finger in the front of my pants, he tugs me closer, unzipping them and kissing my now exposed lower belly. "And it's a big house."

He helps me out of my jeans, and I pull my shirt over my head.

Standing before him in nothing but lace, I say, "You know you're about to turn thirty-six. You're no spring chicken."

"Oh, honey. You've just laid down the gauntlet."

He hooks his fingers into the side of my panties and ever so slowly pulls them down my legs. Standing, he towers over me as he reaches around and unhooks the clasp of my bra. He growls as his gaze hungrily rakes over my naked body.

I've been wet and ready for him since I walked into the room and found him shirtless and waiting for me, but that look.... It makes me squeeze my thighs together. Returning the favor and desperate to get him inside me, I pull him to his feet and help him out of his jeans. Once he's naked, I don't ask. I tell him to sit back down.

He does as instructed, and I crawl onto his lap. His cock rubs against my clit and it feels so good to be skin on skin, with nothing between us.

I feel him reach for his jeans to get a condom.

"Baby, I'm on birth control, and there's been no one but you." I circle my hips to make sure I have his attention. "I want to feel you. Just you."

His hands grip my hips, and his expression turns hopeful. "You sure?"

"I am." I lift myself above him. Taking him in hand, I line myself up, ready to sink onto his erection. "Are you?"

"Fuck yes."

I slide his length across my wetness, readying him before I slowly sink down. Hands gripping his hair, I adjust to his length. This position is always so intense. I move up and down, sinking deeper with each motion, until he fills me to the hilt.

We set a leisurely pace with his hands on my ass, helping guide our rhythm. My arms now cradle his head as he takes my breast in his mouth. I ride him in pure bliss. He is so deep inside me; the feeling is all-consuming. The rest of my body reverberates from the pleasure of his touch.

Releasing my nipple, he brushes his lips over my heart. "I love you so fucking much."

I can't even begin to reply because his thumb rubs my clit, and he changes our cadence ever so slightly, hitting my G-spot and sending me screaming his name as I fall over the edge.

And I take him with me.

We fall, and we fall.

* * *

The loofah feels good against my body. Callen washes me, and after only four hours of sleep and my most sensitive parts sore from all of our lovemaking, it feels nice to have him take care of me.

He moves the loofah between my legs, and I hiss from the tenderness.

"Sorry, baby."

He drops it on the shower floor and uses his soapy hand instead, gently cleaning me. He takes the showerhead down and guides my leg until my foot is on the shower seat. Opening me up to him, he rinses me with hot water. As tender as I am, it feels good. So good, in fact, that by the time he lowers himself to his knees, I'm throbbing with need for him. No matter how tired or tender I am, I still want him.

Need him.

"The movers are going to be here in thirty minutes. You can't keep me in this shower all morning."

"I promised you I was going to fuck you in the shower, and I am not a man who breaks his promises."

"Honestly, I'm not sure if I can handle anymore fucking. She's tired," I say, patting my tender bits.

His eyes don't leave mine as he lifts my hand so he can lean forward and lick me from my opening to my clit. "Sugar, I'm going to fuck you with my tongue and this," he says, holding up the showerhead.

Aiming the water at just the right angle, he adjusts the settings on the showerhead. The clicking sound that accompanies each adjustment sends a shiver of excitement through me. When my knees buckle, he knows he's found the right setting.

"Oh, this is gonna be fun."

No longer meeting my gaze, he appears mesmerized as he watches the water bounce off my body, sending me into an almost instant orgasm. It won't take long, thanks to the sensitivity caused by nonstop climaxing over the past fifteen hours.

"Callen... oh my God..." My hands brace the wall, afraid

my legs may give out and I'll fall. "I'm close... now, baby... now... "

He knows exactly what I'm asking for, and he gives me what I want. Dropping the showerhead, he grabs my ass with one hand while his finger presses at my entrance and he sucks my clit into his mouth. His sucking matches the throbbing that takes over my body as the world goes dark and I see stars.

My body stiffens as I black out from the pleasure. He relentlessly rides the wave with me and doesn't stop until my body goes limp.

Lowering my foot to the shower floor, I right myself, yelping when he picks up the showerhead and nonchalantly aims it at my center one last time before putting it back in place and shutting off the water.

He steps out first to grab a towel and begins to dry me off, ignoring himself. Water drips from his hard body that I know better than my own. Learning what turns him on and gets him off is something I hope to explore till the end of time.

I want every bit of this man, and I want to give him every bit of me.

Once I'm dry and wrapped up in my towel, he dries himself off and ties his towel around his waist. "Don't go back to the cabin. Move in with me."

Since he arrived yesterday, we haven't discussed the real reason he's dropped everything to get on the first plane here. William's name hasn't been mentioned, but I think him asking me repeatedly to move in with him is his way of saying he's worried and thinks I'll be safer if I'm with him. Instead, we're subconsciously choosing to live in a fairy-tale bliss where I don't have a stalker. Convincing myself he's simply here to help me move is preferable to the truth.

"Callen, I still need to prove to myself that I can do this on my own."

I spray my hair with product, then run my hands through it before rinsing them off.

"What does living with me have to do with starting a new career with my sister?"

God, I know he's making sense. I was so close to changing my mind and agreeing to move in with him. All I wanted was one more sleep. But then I opened that letter, and my fears took over, snatching my night of reflection away from me. If I say yes now, will it only be because I'm scared? Would I be accepting his offer for the right reason or because William Davies is controlling my life again?

"I know it doesn't make sense to you, but right now, I need to be in control of my life. I need to know that the decisions I'm making are because of what I want and need and not for a man."

"But you'll live in my brother's cabin? It makes zero sense, Charlotte," he says sternly from behind me, watching me in the mirror as I rub in my moisturizer. Frustration creases his brow.

I'm going about this all wrong. Why can't I tell him that having my stalker out on the streets makes me feel like I'm losing control of my life again? That I've promised myself I would never let William or anyone else control my life. Callen isn't trying to control me. I know this. Why am I dying on this hill when, deep down, I want nothing more than to live with him? My dad was right. I am stubborn. And often for the wrong reasons.

"I'm not staying at the cabin forever. If it makes you feel better I can find a rental. I'll start looking as soon as we get back."

"But why?" He moves in close and wraps his arms around me. Chin on my shoulder, he continues to talk to me in the mirror. "You aren't moving to my town and not sleeping in my arms every night. Why cause us both the hassle?"

Because I'm an idiot.

"It won't be forever, I promise."

"I need to know you're safe."

"The cabin is like Fort Knox. I couldn't be safer there. Besides, you leave for your birthday trip in a few days. The cabin is safer than your house if you aren't home. How about we talk about it when you get back?"

"Please don't find a rental."

I don't reply, and he hops up on the counter next to me.

I really don't want to find a rental. We want the same thing. So why am I so stuck on this?

"Do it for Ruby. You know how much she loves you."

"Really, McKinnon? Using the dog as leverage? You're better than that."

"I'm really not."

Chapter Thirty-Six

Charlotte

"Here's to a bright future and a beautiful partnership!" Daisy says as we clink our glasses together.

"I can't believe we're doing this! Gah! I'm so excited!" I say, stomping my feet on her plush rug in exhilaration. Not minding at all that I'm toasting to my future, yet again.

Daisy and I are celebrating on her couch with a charcuterie board and champagne for two. It's official. I have signed on the dotted line to begin my first project with High Desert Designs.

"Girl, it's going to be great! *We* are going to be great! You know you're good at this, you know you love it, and if you don't love it so much in the end, no harm, no foul." She's right. She's always right.

"I can't thank you enough," I say with sincerity. "I really

can't. You and your family have come to mean so much to me in such a short period of time."

"Sweetie, you know we love you too. We couldn't be happier to have you as a part of our family now."

"I owe your brother so much. Okay, well, maybe I owe your brothers so much. Knox for being such a good friend and lending me his cabin which inadvertently sent me to Goose Hollow and Callen. And a new beginning. It wasn't his intention, but I'll never be able to thank him enough. And Callen... there are no words for how grateful I am for him."

"Every now and then Knox does get something right, but like you said, rarely on purpose." She chuckles before she takes my hand in hers. "And trust me, Cal feels the same way. He loves you so much."

Tears trickle down my cheeks before I even realize it. They're happy tears, and they take me by surprise.

"Whoa. Sorry." I giggle, pulling my hand from hers to use my palm to dry my face. "I don't know what's happening right now, but I swear these are tears of joy."

"You have nothing to be sorry about. You're in love and taking big steps in your personal and professional life. Emotions are to be expected. Just no walking away this time."

I look up at her ceiling, hoping the waterworks will slide back into my tear ducts. Once I've gathered myself, I rest my hand on hers. "Daisy, I love Callen more than you could possibly know. I will forever be grateful for this second chance with him. I promise you, I have no intention of walking away. Yes, it's soon, and I don't know exactly what our next step is, but I know whatever step I take, it'll be by his side. In fact, I'm not sure why I've been so stubborn about moving in with him when it's what I want. In fact, I need to tell him now before I talk myself out of it again!"

I pull my phone out, excited to have finally decided to get out of my own way.

"Now that's what I'm talking about. The two of you together—"

The front door flies open, likely leaving a dent in the wall, and Callen thunders into the house, adding a raging storm to the atmosphere. Our celebratory vibe crashes to a halt.

Worried about him, I stand to go to him.

"How could you?" he bellows, his finger pointing at me.

Stunned silent, Daisy asks the question I can't get out. "What in the world are you going on about?"

Callen ignores his sister, all of his fury aimed at me.

"I told you about the business in confidence! I trusted you, and you ran to Knox so he could sweep in and save the day! What the actual fuck, Charlotte?"

"Callen... I... I... " I stutter, trying to find the words. How could I have been so stupid to think this could have waited until tonight?

What have I done?

When I met Knox for lunch in LA, he said he would need a few days to set up a meeting with his accountant. Later that night, I opened that damn letter that sent my world into a spiral. Waiting until we were home, away from the stress of LA, seemed the best course of action. Never thinking Knox would come through so quickly. I thought I had time.

"Why?" Callen asks, disappointment almost replacing the rage in his eyes. Almost.

He must know I only went to Knox because I love him. How could he not?

"Because it shouldn't only be your burden, Callen." I've found my voice but don't raise it, doing my best to keep calm. I'm scared shitless to see him this angry. Not because I think he'll hurt me, but because it's clear, *I've* hurt *him* so badly.

"I trusted you!"

I reach for him, but he pulls away and I swear I can feel the piece of my heart I've saved for him all these years fracture.

God, how it hurts.

"You weren't leaning on your family," I continue, trying to make him understand. "You were giving up your dream to protect your father's legacy. That may be the honorable thing to do, but baby, it's too much for one person to shoulder."

"It wasn't your place," he spits, no longer yelling, but the low rumble of his voice is worse. Cruel even.

"I'm so sorry, Callen. I thought I was helping. I really did."

"You should have told me. Instead, I had to hear it from my fucking lawyer. Not you. Not my superhero brother who swooped in to save the day, but my God-damned lawyer." He looks at me with pure disgust.

The champagne we'd been celebrating with now sours in my stomach.

"What are you two talking about?"

Neither of us answers Daisy as the distance between us grows until it feels like we're miles apart. He drips in the pain I've caused with what he must see as my betrayal. I hope I haven't done us irreparable harm.

"What. Is. Going. On?" Daisy tries again.

His eyes not leaving mine, he replies through gritted teeth. "I'll let Charlotte fill you in on *our* family business."

He turns and leaves, slamming the door behind him as hard as he flung it open just a moment ago.

Daisy turns to me. "What the hell did you do?"

"I clearly made the wrong decision and involved myself when I shouldn't have. I just love him so damn much. And I knew the solution to his problem and... and... I messed up." My stomach churns. "Oh, God. I think I'm going to be sick."

Holding my stomach, I pace back and forth. Once the tears begin to stream down my cheeks, there's no stopping them. Plopping down onto the couch, I cover my face with my hands to hide my shame from her.

My tears of joy replaced by tears of heartbreak.

What have I done?

What. Have. I. Done?

Daisy sits next to me and rubs soothing circles on my back. "Hey. Talk to me. What's going on?"

"Daisy, I swear I thought I was doing the right thing."

But I should have known better.

"Charlotte, please tell me what's going on, and we'll figure this out."

"After his reaction, I'm not sure he wants to figure anything out. And I don't think it's my place to tell you anything. I've already done enough."

Oh my God. Have I lost him?

"Daisy, I'm so sorry, but I have to go."

I grab my bag and practically run out her front door. I need to get the hell out of her place before I speak out of turn and tell her everything.

What was I thinking?

As soon as I'm in the SUV, I dial Callen's number. After the second ring, he sends my call to voicemail.

He rejected my call.

This cannot be happening.

Panic takes hold, the knots in my stomach wrapped in nauseous guilt and fear. Have my actions ruined us before we even had a chance to get started? Dialing his number again, I put the phone on speaker, wrapping my arms around my middle.

The phone doesn't even ring before his voicemail kicks on, so I text him.

CHARLOTTE

I'm sorry.

Can we please talk?

Do Not Disturb appears on my phone.

He's turned off his notifications.

I know I should take the hint and give him some space, but I can't. I need to fix this.

Fix us.

Steeling myself, I take a long breath in for the count of four and then let it out for a count of four. I repeat the technique he taught me less than a week ago until my breathing stabilizes and the tears have dried. Using a napkin from the glove box, I pat my face dry. With the band I keep around my wrist, I yank my hair into a ponytail and pull it tight, as if preparing for war before putting the car in gear.

I just need a chance to talk to him.

Maybe if he hears me out, he'll understand that I only got Knox involved because I love him. I was trying to help.

The first place I go is the store. I don't see his truck, but I go inside anyway, just to be sure. He could have parked around the back.

"Hey Charlie, what brings you in today?" Livvy chirps in welcome. "Boss man isn't here. Are you coming in to work on your tables?"

"You sure he isn't here?"

She notices me wringing my hands, and her cheerful tone changes to one of concern. "I haven't seen him all day. Is everything okay?"

No, everything is not okay!

"If you don't mind, I'm gonna check out back to make sure."

"Of course. I don't think you'll find him, but if he comes in or calls, I'll be sure to tell him you're lookin' for him."

I'm already pushing out the door when I yell my appreciation over my shoulder. Rushing back to the lumberyard, I run up and down the rows of wood, but there is no trace of him or Ruby. But I check the warehouse just in case.

He's not here.

Shit!

Jogging back to my rental, I mentally piece together what I want to say when I see him. I broke his confidence, but if he hears me out, I can only hope he'll understand my motivation was pure.

I'm white knuckling the steering wheel when I pull up in front of his place. His truck isn't in the driveway, but I jump out and knock on the front door anyway. He doesn't answer. I knew he wouldn't, but the worry gripping my heart doesn't care as it tightens its hold.

"Where in the world did he go?" I mutter to myself as I pace in front of his front door.

Not watching where I'm going, I trip on the cowboy boots he has propped up beside the door. He never wears them inside the house. His neat freak compulsion would never allow that.

His boots remind me of Mabel. Mabel is where he goes when he's stressed. The ranch is where he went when he was missing me. It's where he goes to clear his head.

I could be very wrong, but my gut tells me I'm right.

My head is a dizzying mess of thoughts as I rush to my SUV. Thoughts I try to organize like a PowerPoint presentation in my mind, not wanting to miss any important evidence that would help me plead my case. My brain whirls with the same practicality I use drafting a deal or negotiating a contract for one of my clients.

But today, I'm the client, and I'm representing myself.

And I *have* to get this right.

My mind has been so busy that I'm turning off the highway and on to his parents' property in what feels like seconds.

The dirt road past the house seems even bumpier than usual today, like I'm being tossed around a dryer and my stomach doesn't know which way is up. My already sweaty palms turn clammy like they do on the rare occasion I actually have to appear in court.

Pulling around to the side of the barn, I'm relieved yet scared shitless when his truck comes into view. I park next to it and give myself the briefest moment to gather my thoughts and emotions. I wipe my palms on my pants and tighten my ponytail once more.

"You are going to go in there and state your case."

Checking the rearview mirror, I'm not surprised to spot pink blotches all over my face. I'm not a pretty crier, and my eyes are as puffy as I expected. Not exactly the look to convince a man whose confidence you broke that you're worth sticking around for. But in the grand scheme of things, my looks aren't why he loves me.

"Be clear. Be concise. Do not let your emotions get the best of you."

Quickly, I lean in front of the AC vents to help contain the nervous sweat I have going praying he hasn't been watching me sit in my car while I talk to myself.

Turning off the engine, I jump out and enter the barn with my head held high.

It's eerily quiet. The only sound is the slapping of my flip-flops against the hard ground toward the barn.

Mabel's stall is empty.

Shit.

He's out on a ride and he's usually out for a couple of hours when he rides.

I debate going back out to the car to sit in the AC or waiting right here in the barn until he gets back. One thing is certain. I'm not putting this off.

Honey whinnies, catching my attention.

"So how was he when you saw him?" I ask her. "He was pissed, right?"

She shakes her beautiful blond head and moves closer, so I rub her velvety nose. Memories of the day he took me for my first ride on her play on the projector of my mind. We laughed and loved, and it was perfect.

The reckless, desperate side of me wants to be the

woman in the romance novels who saddles up the horse she's only ridden once before and gallops off to find her man. It would rain, and I would fall off my steady ride, only for my hero to come save me, and we would live happily ever after.

But this is my story, and in my story, I wouldn't get the saddle on correctly, and it would slide off somewhere out where not even the cows frequent. Of course, I'd break a bone. And since Honey knows her way home, she'd take off, leaving me to my own devices. I'd have to hobble back to the barn in my flip-flops. And instead of rain, I would get a blistering sunburn or collapse from heat exhaustion. Or, likely, both.

As dramatic as that would be, it's not the option I choose. I think it's best for both me and Honey if I sit here and wait. I wander through the barn and admire the other horses. A couple of them are friendly enough that I offer my hand, and they sniff, hoping for a treat. Once they realize I'm empty-handed, most step away, but a couple let me rub their noses.

I end up back at Honey's stall, where she nuzzles up to me, asking for attention. However, I have this sneaking suspicion she can sense my need for comfort. She and I bonded the moment I laid eyes on her.

She gets me.

Her soothing presence keeps my nerves at bay. My mind has slowed and is no longer frantic. I know what I want to say, and hopefully, he'll hear me out.

My stomach is still twisted into a bunch of knots, but the feeling is more about the anxiety of what's to come and less the worry of my champagne from Daisy's ending up on the barn floor.

Honey and I are standing in companionable silence when

wheels crunch on the gravel outside the barn. A truck door slams shut, but the footsteps are so light I have to strain to hear them.

Logically, I know it's not Callen because he's out with Mabel. But for some reason, my instinct is to duck into Honey's stall and hide, but my rental is outside, and whoever it is knows I'm here. Hiding would make me look like a hot mess. Well, a bigger one than I already am.

Much to my surprise, Sharon walks into the barn, her face beaming when she spots me.

"Fancy to find you here. I thought I saw Cal ride off a bit ago. But then I saw your car and thought I would pop down and say hello."

I meet her in the middle of the barn, and she takes me in her arms in one of those mom hugs that's like being wrapped in a warm blanket. They comfort you and tell you you're going to be okay. No words needed. I love this woman's hugs. I think I might actually love her. Her whole family, for that matter. God, I hope I can fix things with her son.

Sharon's embrace reminds me of all the hugs I missed growing up. All of my mom hug experience has come from Karissa's mom and my grandmother. My mom would have had to have been around to wrap me up in her love, but I still consider myself lucky to know what it feels like.

"Hi, Sharon. How are you?"

"Well, I'm just fine, sweetie. How about you?" she says, letting me go.

Looking down at the ground to hide my red eyes I try to sound as natural as possible when I reply. "Oh, I'm good. Just waiting for Callen."

"You may be waiting a while, darlin'. When he takes off

on Mabel like he did today, he'll likely be gone for some time."

"I don't mind waiting."

"Everything okay between the two of you?"

Keep your mouth shut, Charlotte. Of all the people in his family, his mother is the one person who can never know!

"Well, we've had a bit of an argument, and I came here hoping to talk to him."

"I'm sure everything will be fine. He's been under a lot of stress lately. I'm sure it's not anything you've done."

I wonder how much she knows? Could she be as oblivious to the store's problems as the rest of the family?

"No, I'm afraid it is over something I've done."

Her brows lift in question. "Is that so?" she says, her voice lowering. Almost stern. Her mama bear instincts flipping into place like a switch.

"Oh, goodness, nothing like that. Sharon, I love your son. I am *in love* with your son. I would never betray him like that."

She doesn't say anything but keeps her eyes on mine, as if searching for the truth.

"I know what Kasey did to him, and it makes me sick to think of the pain he must have felt. I promise you, I would never hurt him like that."

Her hand palms my face. "I'm so glad you found him."

"Me too. He's a pretty special man."

"You know, he loves you, too. He told me as much."

My cheeks grow hot with embarrassment. Hope blossoming in my chest.

She pulls me into another hug.

"You have got to be fucking kidding me!" Callen's voice roars through the space. His rage bouncing off the high beams of the barn.

Sharon releases me, turning her attention to her son.

"Callen, I was hoping we could talk." I can hear how shaky my voice is, but his reaction to seeing me here is so abrasive. So severe.

He and Mabel stand in the middle of the barn.

"First Knox and now my mother! Is nothing sacred to you?"

"Son, what in the world are you talking about, and why are you speaking to Charlotte this way? I raised a gentleman, not a bruiser."

He looks between the two of us. Realization paints his features, and he knows that he's the one letting the cat out of the bag, not me.

"Callen, I didn't—"

"Not now, okay?"

"Can we just talk?" I say, walking toward him.

He lifts his hand and gives one slow shake of his head. "Not. Now," he grits through his teeth.

"Callen Brian McKinnon. What has gotten into you?"

"Mom... I... I don't know where to start."

"How about the beginning?"

"Yes, ma'am."

The desolation in his voice nearly breaks me. All I want to do is run to him and take care of him like he's been taking care of me. To wipe away the pain I know this conversation with his mother is going to bring him. But I know this moment isn't about me. I need to give them space.

He knows where to find me when he's ready.

Not saying another word to either of them, I leave without looking back. Giving them the privacy they deserve.

Chapter Thirty-Seven

Charlotte

I walked out of the McKinnon barn four and a half hours ago and haven't heard a word from Callen or any of his siblings.

His silence is deafening.

His phone is still on *Do Not Disturb,* but I know he'll see my missed calls and texts from before our run-in at the ranch.

To calm myself, I'm swinging on the front porch listening for his truck tires on the dirt road, but all I hear are the geese honking, the frogs croaking, and the crickets chirping around as dusk approaches.

All I want to do is call and text until he picks up. Acknowledges me. Hears me out.

Instead, I swing.

I hold on to my phone like a life jacket, keeping me afloat, and I swing.

It's not like I didn't think going to Knox without talking to Callen about it first wasn't going to be an issue. But I thought we could have a rational conversation where he would listen to my side of things, and everything would be fine.

I've never been so delusional.

The thing is, Knox is, well was, my client, and he and all the members of the McKinnon family deserve to know what's happening with the store. It impacts them all, not just Callen. Of course, I also knew the tax bill would be completely in Knox's budget. The band makes enough to cover the back taxes with one week of T-shirt sales. Even though he's in a band and not all the revenue goes to Knox, he can certainly afford to help the business.

When I met with him the day before Callen arrived in Los Angeles, I told him his brother needed him and that he should call Howard, the family lawyer. I didn't technically tell him about the tax bill, but telling him to call Howard was basically the same thing.

He warned me that his little brother didn't like to accept help from anyone, especially him, and that he was going to be pissed. I believe his exact words were for me to "prepare for a shitstorm when he finds out."

I had planned on telling him on the phone the night after the meeting, but then opening that damn letter scared it right out of my brain. Then he showed up at my office without his beard, and it was like a time warp back to the Sunset Marquis. Then we were busy with packing up my office and getting the house on the market. And, of course, all the sex.

Things were stressful and busy, yet having him there by my side made it all kinds of wonderful. He played the role of my personal assistant *with benefits* and kept my mind off thinking about William Davies roaming the streets again.

He was my knight in shining armor.

We were both so tired on the plane that by the time we got back to Goose Hollow late last night, we passed out as soon as the bed came into view.

My plan was to tell him over dinner tonight.

Now he's not speaking to me, and he leaves in the morning for his annual McKinnon sibling retreat to celebrate the birthdays of all four McKinnon children. They were all born in August and all have the same middle name. Brian for the brothers and Brianna for Daisy. I guess every family has their oddities.

They usually go away somewhere fantastic, keeping the destination small enough that Knox can have some peace. This year, they should have gone to La Paz. However, because of his worry for me and his insistence on remaining nearby, he asked Daisy, Angus, and Knox if they could move their trip to Fort Rock Park, which is only a ten-minute drive from Goose Hollow. None of them batted an eye.

They may be staying in a brand-new private luxury lodge, but there will be no beaches to walk on. No waves to surf and no infinity pools with the view of the Sea of Cortez. He asked the three of them to give all of that up... for me.

And I betrayed him.

At least that's how he sees it.

I remember everything about the night he confided in me because it's the night I realized I had fallen madly in love with him. I can recall every word spoken as we lay in his bed, and he told me what had him so stressed out. I've replayed the conversation over and over in my head to make sure I wasn't actually breaking a promise of any kind. Yes, it's just semantics, and I understand how he sees what I've done as a betrayal, but the truth of the matter is he never told me *I* couldn't say anything to Knox.

"Why haven't you told your family? I'm sure they would be more than happy to help. Knox would—"

"No. I'm not telling the family," he cuts me off, but he doesn't seem angry. He's resigned. His mind is made up, and he seems to have made peace with it. "It would crush Mom and tarnish everyone's memory of him. I won't be the one to do that."

"But you know none of them would want you to give up your dream."

"Charlotte, that store is the heart of this family. Hell, it's the heart of the community. I would rather sell my land and never build my dream house if it means saving it. And my mom... God, she's been through enough. She can't lose any more than she already has. I want to do everything I can to handle this on my own."

He specifically said *he* wasn't telling the family and wanted to handle it on his own. He didn't ask *me* not to tell anyone. Yes, I know it was implied, but sometimes when you love someone, you cancel your family trip to make your person feel safe. And sometimes you tell their ridiculously wealthy brother that the person you love needs their help. We've both done some extreme things for each other.

When my phone simultaneously pings and vibrates—of course, I wasn't leaving missing his call or text to chance—it scares the bejesus out of me. My phone fumbles at the tips of my fingers for a couple of sweat-inducing moments before I turn it right side up and see a text from Callen has come through. Before I have time to read it, my phone vibrates with another message, as though he's hitting send with each new thought.

CALLEN

> I need some time and space to think. I'm not ready to talk.

> Charlotte, I love you, but what you've done is not something I can easily forgive.

> Please set the alarm. Knox and I will have access to the outdoor cameras, and we're just a phone call away should something happen. We're heading up to Fort Rock in the morning.

His number still shows *Do Not Disturb,* so I assume he likely won't take my call if I were to try. I force myself not to call him, even if I'm dying to.

But he did say he loved me.

He also said forgiving me wouldn't be easy.

Instead of feeling better after hearing from him, that sick feeling intensifies until all I want to do is crawl into bed and cry.

With this objective in mind, I go inside and lock myself safely in the cabin. I set the alarm and wait for another text. But it doesn't come.

After five minutes with no more contact, I message him back.

CHARLOTTE

> I understand.

> I'm sorry for hurting you. But I'm not sorry for trying to help you and your family.

> I love you. I'd do anything for you. I hope you know that.

Maybe I shouldn't double down on my lack of apology for what I did, but if he gets to keep his land and build his dream house, it was worth it. As long as all he needs is temporary space and nothing more than that. I'll leave him alone while he's away, but if he hasn't talked to me by the end of the week, I'll find a way to prove to him how much I love him.

Let's hope it doesn't come to that.

Chapter Thirty-Eight

Callen

"So, are we really gonna keep sitting around this place like things aren't awkward?" Knox says from the other side of the kitchen table in the luxurious rental house we're staying in. "We've been here for five hours, and shit is off with all of us. I didn't plan to take this week out of my tour and fly home from Europe to sit here and have an emo party with the three of you."

I've had a raging headache since my phone call from my lawyer telling me that Knox paid the store's debt to the IRS. I found the awkward silence we ate our lunch in much preferable to hearing my egotistical big brother's voice. Not that I was able to eat even half of my food. I'm too angry to eat. "Thank you for the reminder. We almost forgot how very important you are. You honor us with your presence."

"Fuck off, Callen."

"Fuck you, Knox."

"Both of you, fuck off!" Angus yells. His fist slams against the table as he stands, taking his plate and mine to the kitchen.

Deafening silence fills the room.

Each of us sifting through our own thoughts and feelings.

The past week has been the highest of highs and the lowest of lows. Watching Charlotte turn ghostly white as she read the letter telling her that her stalker was free was like a living nightmare. Sitting at home with her so far away, knowing *he* was out there, nearly did me in.

I was a powder keg ready to explode.

My need to get to her all-consuming.

She handled the situation better than I did. But once she was in my arms again, all was right in the world. I kept my promise to her and made her come in every room in her house. However, I hadn't convinced her to move in with me, but I was close. I know I was.

I was riding so high I didn't think I would ever come down.

But then I got the call from Howard, and everything changed.

Charlotte's betrayal cut so deep it was as though she had broken through my ribs and ripped my heart right out of my chest. After the hurt, came the blind rage that sent me to Daisy's, where I knew I would find her.

I haven't talked to her since my blow up, and as angry as I am, and even though I'm not ready to forgive her, I miss her. Like an addict, I can't stop checking the security app on my phone. The camera feed outside the cabin hasn't changed, the last fifty times I've checked it, but I power on my phone to look anyway. She said she feels safe there, but I feel itchy without her near.

"So, we gonna talk about the elephant in the room or what?" my sister asks.

"Great question, Dais," Angus chides as he loads the dishwasher. "Time to put down your goddamn phone and have an adult conversation."

Ignoring Angus, I continue to stare at my phone. "I don't really feel like talking about it."

"Sorry, bro." Angus leans over the table and knocks my phone out of my hand. "But right about now, you don't have a leg to stand on."

"Forgive me for trying to keep everything together, so the rest of you didn't have to be burdened with any of it."

Angus joins us back at the table. Taking his seat, he immediately gets to the point. "You had no right to keep things from the three of us."

"I was the one he appointed executor of the will. I'm the one he tasked with cleaning up his shit show."

"That's bullshit, and you know it. That store belongs to all of us," Angus spits.

"Then why weren't all of your names listed under that part of the goddamn will?"

"Cal, come on, you know you should have told us," Daisy says, her calm voice notably missing the venom of my little brother.

"She's right," Knox says from the head of the table.

"Why, so you could come in with your lifestyles of the rich and famous money and save the day?"

"Why not? I had the funds. It was nothing."

Grabbing my phone, I bolt out of my seat, sending my

chair flying. "Well, how nice that one point three million dollars is nothing to you! Must be a thrill for you to get to be the big city celebrity who can always sweep in and save the day!"

"Man, shut up," Angus says, standing to step between the two of us.

"Says the hometown hero!"

"What the hell has gotten into you, Callen?" Angus asks. Brow furrowed, and a confused look on his face.

"Nothing. Just forget it."

I storm past them and out the back door, pulling it closed behind me, only I never hear it shut because, of course, my asshole family is hot on my heels.

"Nice try," Daisy says. "Talk to us, you idiot."

"What do you want me to say?"

"Well, for starters, why didn't you tell us what was going on as soon as you found out?"

"Sounds like a great place to start," Knox agrees with her.

I can feel their gazes burning into the back of my head and know there's no way to avoid them. I take a deep breath, exhaling slowly before facing my siblings.

Knox stands the closest with his hands in his pockets. His boiling anger from moments ago is now more of a slow simmer. Angus and Daisy's expressions are soft, filled with concern.

"I didn't want you to know."

"We've established that. Come on, sit down and talk to us." Angus pulls out a chair at the huge wooden table under the covered outdoor kitchen space.

When I take a seat, they follow suit, sitting in silence, waiting for me to explain myself.

"I was so mad at Dad when I discovered all this tax bull-shit and his second set of books. I should have been grieving him. Instead, I was angry and disappointed. It was like I never knew him. And well, shit. I didn't want that for the three of you and, most of all, Mom."

Daisy takes my hand. "Cal, as much as we appreciate that you were trying to spare our feelings, we can't keep secrets like this from each other. Besides, why deal with it on your own when you have us?"

"Dais, no offense, but what were you going to do about it? Why put you through that when there was no way you could help?"

"Because it's our store. Our business. We all deserve to know, even Mom," she replies softly.

"I disagree." I stand firm.

"Of course you do." Angus huffs.

"What about me?" Knox says, leaning back in his chair with his rock star bravado on full display. Shoulder length hair tucked behind his ears and arms and hands covered in tattoos. He thinks he's so damn cool.

"What about you?" I retort.

"There was something I could have done about it."

"I didn't need you to swoop in and fix it."

"Why?"

"Dad left me in charge. I took it as his way of telling me he wanted me to take care of it."

"Why the hell am I touring the world, leaving everything and everyone I love behind for two years at a time to make millions if I can't even help my family when they need it the most?"

"You've worked hard for your money, Knox."

"What's mine is yours."

"He's right, Cal. You can't keep shit like this from us. You can't take care of everything for everyone," Angus agrees with him.

Daisy gets up and hugs me from behind. "Yep, what he said." She releases me, then kisses me on the cheek. "Now repeat after me. I, Callen McKinnon."

"Are you serious right now?"

"Say it," Angus and Knox say at the same time.

"The three of you are ridiculous."

"Say it!" they yell in unison.

"I, Callen McKinnon."

Daisy continues. "Swear to never keep secrets from his family when it pertains to them or when they can help."

Before I have time to repeat her words, Angus and Knox both moan. "Say it."

Clearing my throat, I repeat her words. "I, Callen McKinnon." I look between my brothers as they rest their cheeks on their hands as they gleefully watch our sister torture me. "Swear to never keep a secret from you idiots."

"Mom too," Daisy interrupts.

"Okay, fine. I'll never keep a secret from you three idiots or Mom when it involves you or when you can help."

"There you go. Was that so hard?" She smacks me on the back of the head. "Now, how are you gonna fix things with Charlie?"

"What did you do to Charlie?" Knox questions, defensive without even knowing what's happened.

"Knox, you should have seen him. He barged into my place screaming, his face all red, and pointing his finger at her, yelling, 'HOW COULD YOU?'"

"What the fuck, dude?"

"She knew I didn't want you to know, Knox."

He leans back again. "For some reason, which I cannot figure out, that woman loves you, and she couldn't stand the thought of you selling your land and giving up your dream house when there was an easy fix."

"It wasn't her place."

"No, it wasn't." Angus taps the table thoughtfully. "But when her idiot boyfriend was too stubborn to do the right thing, she felt she had to step in."

"Thanks. Nice to know whose side you're on."

He shrugs.

"She betrayed my confidence. How do I trust her again?"

"Did you specifically ask her not to say anything?"

I begin to answer, but pause to think back to our conversation, realizing I never specifically said those words. "No, but it was implied. She knew how I felt."

"And here I thought you were the smart one out of the four of us."

"Thanks a lot, Gus," Daisy says, flipping him off.

"You know what I mean. Charlie loves the hell out of him."

"You don't have to tell me. Right before shithead over here barged in screaming at her, she had just been in happy tears telling me how in love she was with him."

I'll be damned if hearing my sister recall her conversation with Charlotte doesn't have me itching to ditch my siblings and drive my truck to the cabin. If only she hadn't gone to Knox.

"She can tell herself she's moving here to start a new business with me all day long, but we all know she wouldn't be uprooting her life if it weren't for you."

"If that were true, she'd be moving in with me."

"Get over yourself, Cal. Just because she doesn't want to live together right now doesn't mean she never will. She just lost her dad. She just closed her dad's firm and left the only job she's ever known, moving away from the only town she's ever lived in. Give the woman some time to adjust to the upheaval. Let her be in charge of her own destiny. It doesn't mean she doesn't love you. You big baby."

My little sister makes a fair point, but I'm not ready to concede. "I get that. I do. But things are different now. That asshole is free. If she's not with me, how can I protect her?"

"Was she with you last night, or were you still shutting her out?"

"I watched the cameras outside the cabin all night long."

"So you haven't talked to her since you left my house?"

"I told her I needed space."

"How did she take it?"

My phone's still in my hand, so I check the cameras again before pulling up the text. "She said she was sorry for hurting me, but not sorry for helping the family."

Daisy's eyes widen. "Wait, you texted her?"

I don't reply.

Angus throws his head back and asks the sky, "What is your malfunction?"

"Fuck you, Gus."

Daisy snatches the phone out of my hand and walks away from the table, reading my messages out loud. "I need some time and space to think. I'm not ready to talk. Charlotte, I love you, but what you've done is not something I can easily forgive."

Knox rubs his hands over his face. "What the fuck, dude?"

"Please set the alarm. Knox and I will have access to the outdoor cameras, and we're just a phone call away should something happen. We're heading up to Fort Rock in the morning."

"Maybe I'm stupid, but this doesn't make any sense." Knox cocks his head to the side, a confused expression on his stupid face. "You're so freaked out about her stalker being released you move our trip from Mexico to basically down the street to protect her. You shaved your beard off because the asshole who just got early release from prison has a beard and you don't want to remind her of him. But you aren't even speaking to her?"

"Thank you, guys, for moving the trip. I appreciate it. Sorry if I didn't say that before."

"Doesn't matter where we go as long as we get together." Knox means it. His eyes can't lie and he really means that. "It's fine and not the point."

"What is your point?"

"My point is, you would move heaven and earth for this woman, yet the first time there's a conflict, you text her and say you aren't ready to forgive her, but you haven't even heard her out. I know you're pissed, but she deserves a conversation."

He's right. I know he's right.

All I want to do is jump in my truck and drive to her, but we have rules about our annual trip, and they'll never let me leave.

I run my hand through my hair. "I fucked up."

"You did," Knox agrees.

"But again, how can I trust her? I may not have forbidden her to discuss it, but she knew how important it was to me to keep it my problem."

"She was trying to help you, and you know that." Angus releases a frustrated breath. "What you see as a betrayal, we see as her playing a role in saving the family business and stopping you from doing something you'd regret later. I understand where you're coming from, but deep down, you know you can trust her."

"Gus is right. She deserves a phone call, at the very least," Daisy agrees.

As I study the three concerned faces staring back at me, my anger subsides, and I begrudgingly have to admit how grateful I am to call them my family. I should have treated them as such and included them when I got the call from the IRS. I've messed up in multiple ways.

"I'm sorry for not telling you about Dad and the taxes. I was just trying to spare you the disappointment I felt. It won't happen again."

"Thanks for looking out, but we're a family, and we go through this kind of shit together from here on out," Angus says. Nothing but sincerity in his voice and brotherly love in his eyes. "I'm still unpacking the dad shit. We're gonna save that for tomorrow. This is all new information for the three of us. We'll sleep on it and then the four of us need to talk to Mom."

I nod my understanding to Knox. "Noted." My phone lights up with a calendar reminder for the next day. "Did you know that Charlotte and I share a birthday?"

"No way!" Daisy squeals.

"You were gonna leave her alone, not knowing where things stood between the two of you, on her birthday? Dude, get in your truck and drive your ass to the cabin and make things right. Bring her back with you, since it seems like we have another sibling to add to the August birthday mix."

Knox's offer causes my chest to tighten. All these years I've resented him and his lifestyle when the truth is he's still the brother I grew up with. The brother who would do anything for me, and I would do the same for him. He's a damn good man.

"Nah, we made rules long ago. It would always be just the four of us."

"That was before one of us fell in love with someone who already feels like family and has an August birthday." Angus pounds his fist on the table in excitement. "Go get her!"

They don't have to ask me twice.

I've been miserable without her for the past twenty-four hours.

"Thanks, guys. I'll be back, and hopefully, she'll be with me."

I'm running through the house to the front door when Knox yells from the back yard. "Don't come back without her!"

I fucking love my family.

I'm in my truck on my way to her in seconds flat.

I can't get to her fast enough.

Chapter Thirty-Nine

Charlotte

My fingers tremble as I tape down the last corner of the wrapping paper on Callen's birthday gift. Considering he's asked for space, my gift may be presumptuous, but I won't be giving up on us anytime soon.

I've checked my phone a hundred times and am disappointed every time I do. I get that he's pissed, but we haven't gone this long without speaking in weeks, and the lack of communication is taking its toll on me. I don't feel comfortable in my own skin. I've spent countless hours staring into space, my brain somehow spinning a million miles an hour, yet being completely blank at the same time.

Everything feels off.

I haven't called Karissa to tell her what's going on. Subconsciously fearing that voicing my concerns for our future will make it all too real. I refuse to believe we're over. He said he loved me and that has to mean something.

A couple of hours ago, I gave myself a pep talk and came up with a plan of attack.

I started by unpacking and getting settled into the cabin. Then I worked on his gift, and now, as I tape the card to the front of the package with my still shaky fingers, I feel good about what's inside. I can only hope that after he takes the time he needs, this gift will reassure him.

My phone vibrates on the table, and my heart leaps in my chest at the hope that it's Callen. Much to my disappointment, it's not him. Instead, it's news from my friend at the DA's office. Mark and I met in college and have remained friends. I reached out to him the morning after I found out about William's release, and he said he would look into the case and keep me updated.

MARK GOLDSTEIN

Hey Charlie. Hope your move to Oregon is going well. I have an update for you. Davies checked in with his parole officer yesterday morning. So he hasn't skipped town.

A wave of relief washes over me, knowing my stalker is a twelve-hour drive away. I needed some good news.

CHARLOTTE

Thanks for the update. I appreciate the peace of mind.

MARK GOLDSTEIN

Anytime. I'll keep checking in each week to make sure there is no deviation. I'm sure it's hard knowing he's out, but at least we know he was in California as of yesterday morning.

CHARLOTTE

Thanks again, Mark.

With this one weight off my shoulders, I feel more determined than ever to begin my new life. To make decisions that make me happy. To move forward with the man that I love.

Tomorrow is his birthday and mine, and space or no space, I will be wishing him a happy birthday.

Until then, I need to get rid of the nervous energy wreaking havoc on my body and am hoping the exertion of a couple of miles in the kayak will do just that.

Leaving the wrapping paper on the table, I take his gift with me to the bedroom to change my clothes. Feeling a newfound strength within myself, I decide to replace some of my anxiety with determination and excitement.

And with that thought, I bound outside, ready to take on the rest of my day.

Chapter Forty

Callen

Eighteen minutes later, I turn onto the dirt road leading me to the cabin and the woman I love.

The late summer sun is high in the sky, but the canopy of tall trees all but blocks it out, providing a shady cover as the truck bounces side to side over the unpaved road littered with pine needles.

Driving a little faster than I should, I have to hit my brakes about halfway down the road.

A car I don't recognize is pulled over into the greenery, partially blocking the road. The car, an older model Jeep Grand Cherokee, has California plates and isn't one I've seen around town.

What the fuck?

An overwhelming sense of dread floods my senses. I veer around the out of place vehicle and floor it.

My gut tells me something isn't right. Rounding the last bend before the cabin, I change my approach, slowing down and driving as quietly as possible so I don't announce my arrival. The cabin comes into view, and I fucking hope I'm jumping to conclusions. I don't see any activity from my vantage point, but I sure wish I had brought Ruby with me.

I climb out of the truck, gently pushing the door shut. Since I parked closest to the back of the house, I make my way through the trees and across the lawn to the back sliding glass door. I peer in and consider knocking, but that uneasy feeling won't go away.

At first glance, everything inside seems fine. Gift-wrapping supplies are spread out across the kitchen table. No signs of a struggle. There are empty broken-down boxes on the kitchen floor. It seems Charlotte's been busy unpacking. I'm not sure how I feel about that. I'm still upset with her, but I need this woman in my bed at night.

Movement from the living room catches my eye. The hair on the back of my neck stands up and I know in my bones it's not Charlotte.

Everything inside me is screaming William fucking Davies.

Blood pressure spiking, I pull on the slider door handle. Much to my relief and surprise, the door slides open. I let myself in, barely breathing for fear of making a noise. The hammer I gave Charlotte sits on the kitchen counter just inside the door, and I pick it up as I make my way into the house.

The sound of someone walking on plastic only a few feet away stops me in my tracks. I take a long breath in, hoping it will quiet the beat of my thundering heart, but I don't get to the count of four before footsteps walk across the plastic again, heading down the hall.

Peeking around the corner, I feel sickened by the scene before me. It can't be real. It's like something out of a movie. Furniture has been moved to make room for the large green tarp spread across the living room floor. Next to it lay zip ties, duct tape, a gallon of bleach, a syringe, and tools I don't identify because I don't want to. It's too much.

But what sickens and outrages me the most is the image of a man in black walking down the hall with glove-covered hands and blue shoe coverings on his feet. A man intending to use all of this on Charlotte.

William. Fucking. Davies.

Walking around his demented psychopathic setup, I follow him, the sound of the shower filling my ears as I watch him open the bathroom door. Steam billows out and the sound of the shower fills the air.

Hell no.

Running after him and into the bathroom, my world becomes a living, breathing nightmare as I watch him pull open the shower door and Charlotte's scream fills the air.

Chapter Forty-One

Charlotte

With my face tipped upward, my eyes are closed, luxuriating in the rain showerhead. There's only one bathroom in this house, but Knox knew what he was doing when he had it installed. I let it take away the stress and worry of the day, grateful for the first taste of calm I've had since Callen nearly broke down Daisy's door.

When the skin on my fingers begins to pucker, I take it as a sign I've been hiding in here way too long, enjoying the relaxation and avoiding coming face-to-face with the reality of an empty cabin.

No Callen.

No Ruby.

Just the quiet of the house.

Begrudgingly, I reach for the knobs to turn off the water,

but before my fingers touch the metal, the shower door slams open and a surge of cold air rushes over my body. Stunned, I look at the door.

No.

It can't be.

But it is.

William Davies stands in front of me with a wicked smile and malice in his eyes.

My bloodcurdling scream cuts through the silence, bouncing off the tile walls. He seems to get some sick thrill from my reaction because his wicked eyes dance and his smile grows even more sinister. He reaches for me, but I push myself into the farthest corner of the shower. He opens his mouth, but before he can speak, there's a blur of motion behind him. Everything that happens next plays out like snapshots in my mind.

First, there's the blood.

So. Much. Blood.

It splatters against the shower door and drips down William's face heartbeats before he crumples to the tile floor.

I scream again. Or, at least, I think I do. But it feels like I'm in a dream trying to scream, but nothing will come out. Subconsciously, I hear it almost as though in the distance.

Then I hear someone else.

Callen.

He's here.

But how?

I'm still screaming when he wraps me in a towel after turning off the water.

"Baby, I've got you."

I scream again.

His face is in front of mine. "You're okay. I've got you."

It's really him.

He's here.

He's got me.

"I need to get you out of here, baby." He picks me up and carefully steps around the fallen body on the bathroom floor.

"William," I mutter, still unable to believe my eyes. "He was... he was here." I try to get a look at the body, but Callen tucks my head against his shoulder.

"It's okay. I got you."

He carries me to the bedroom and lowers me to the bed, keeping my back to the door, but his eyes dart toward the hallway. My heartbeat races as he steps away from not wanting him to leave me alone. Looking over my shoulder, I watch as he stops in the doorway, then bends over, placing his hands on his knees and taking a few steadying breaths. Flooded with relief, I face forward because he's partially closed the door and is staying in the room with me.

"Here, sugar," he says, picking up my robe that was already on the bed. "Let's cover you up."

He uses the corner of the towel still wrapped around me to wipe the blood from his hand before helping me into my robe. My brain refuses to process his actions the same way that it looks past the specks of blood on his face.

There was blood everywhere.

I say nothing as I piece together the images in my mind.

William is here.

Callen is here.

"Charlotte. Baby. Look at me." He's on his knees in front of me. "Stay right here. I'll leave the door open, but I need you to stay in the bedroom. Okay?"

I nod.

He takes my face in his hands and presses his forehead to mine, breathing out a heavy sigh. "You're okay."

I can't tell if he's trying to reassure me or himself, but the feel of his breath on my face barely registers through the numbness that's taken over my body.

"Be right back. Please stay here."

I register him leaving the room and hear him on the phone in the hallway calling for help, but my focus stays on the dresser across the room. I stare at the knob on the second drawer on the right as my mind spins and my chest tightens.

Is William dead?

Did Callen just.... Did he kill a man? To protect me?

What does this mean for Callen? Will they arrest him?

As much as I wish my stalker dead, I don't wish that heaviness or guilt on Callen. He doesn't deserve to carry that burden because of me.

I can hear Callen moving around in the bathroom. There's a ripping noise followed by running water. But I stay where I am, just like he asked me to. My body is so numb I'm not sure if I could put one foot in front of the other if I tried.

I have no clue how much time has passed when Callen re-enters the room. I know he's left the door ajar because I don't hear the click of it closing.

He sits down on the bed next to me. "Come here, let's dry your hair." He gathers my hair behind my shoulders and uses a fresh towel to pat it dry. "The police are on their way. Why don't we get you dressed?"

He places a kiss on the top of my head before pulling clothes out of the dresser. Finally, it hits me. Callen's really here. The feel of his lips against my head is what I needed to wake me up out of my stupor.

"You came."

He's on his knees again when he confirms. "I came." He holds up my favorite oversized McKinnon Hardware sweatshirt. "Let's take off that robe and put this on, shall we?"

I nod, untie the robe, and take my arms out. He pulls the sweatshirt over my head, and once my gaze is back on his handsome face, the worry in his eyes breaks my heart.

Only breaking our locked gaze to study the hands still gripping the bottom of the sweatshirt, his knuckles turning white. Forcing him to release the shirt, I take his hands in mine and meet his gaze. "Thank you."

A kiss to my forehead is his only reply.

He's here, taking care of me. But he's not talking to me. Maybe he's not really over what he sees as my betrayal.

"I'm so sorry I went to Knox."

He gives a small shake of his head before brushing his thumb over my cheek. "Not now, sugar." He stands and unfolds a pair of sweatpants and a pair of boy short undies. "Here, step into these."

He helps me into my clothes as he watches the hallway. I start to look over my shoulder to see what he's looking at, but he stops me. "Baby, don't."

"Why can't I leave the bedroom? What don't you want me to see?"

"Sweetie, I—"

"Callen," I interrupt him, knowing he's trying to protect me but needing to know why I have to stay in the bedroom. "I'm going to find out as soon as the police get here, and I would rather hear it from you."

"Baby. Don't make me."

"Please. I need to know."

Several seconds pass as he struggles to find his words, but he reluctantly does. "When I came in, there was... shit... I think I might be sick." Holding his stomach with one hand, he paces in front of me, arm gestures flying as he continues. "There's a fucking tarp laid out in the living room, Charlotte. And duct tape and a syringe. Fuck! And other shit I can't even think about right now."

I've gone cold at with the description of the plans William apparently had for me. My body is shaking like I've been left naked in the snow.

He squats down with his hands in his hair. "If I had gotten here seconds later...."

"But you didn't. You saved my life." My voice trembles.

Callen's head pops up, his focus narrowing in on me.

"Shit, you're white as a ghost. I'm sorry. I shouldn't have... Shit!" He rushes to me, sweeping me into his arms and sitting down with me on his lap. "You're safe now, baby. I won't let anyone hurt you."

"You saved my life," I repeat. He's so damn warm I burrow into him.

"Sweetie, I think you've got that backward. You showing up in my store two months ago saved mine."

"I'm so sorry."

"Everything happens for a reason. If things had happened any other way, I may not be holding you in my arms right now. None of this is your fault. There is nothing for you to be sorry about or to be forgiven for."

He sways us in a soothing motion as we sit on the bed,

both trembling, taking in what's happened as sirens sound in
the distance.

Chapter Forty-Two

Charlotte

Over the next hour, the police arrive, along with the county DA to take our statements and log evidence. Still breathing yet unconscious, with a bloody head wound from the hammer Callen used and from his fall, William Davies is driven away in an ambulance. Luckily, the cabin's security system is top-notch, and we're able to give the authorities video footage of him disarming the alarm and carrying in the tarp and his other tools while I was in the shower.

Owen is on duty and arrives a few minutes after the sheriff's office. While Callen is interviewed, he sits with me. When I mention my concerns for Callen, he reminds me that William is in violation of his parole. His parole states he has to stay a certain feet's distance from me, but he also crossed state lines and broke into the house with malice intent. He assures me Callen has nothing to worry about legally. I couldn't be more grateful to have him here.

After Callen and I give our statements, we're left alone in the bedroom with the door open while they snap pictures of the scene and bag up evidence. We haven't spoken in several minutes, our minds still reeling with the knowledge that I could have died today. We can't seem to get close enough, seeking comfort in one another as we lie on the bed. The adrenaline that kicked in when I saw Willian has faded, leaving me hollow and exhausted inside. I'm afraid if I open my mouth, sobs will spill out.

Feet shuffle in the hallway and Owen appears, knocking on the doorframe. "Hey, you two. Ready to get out of here?"

"We're clear to leave?" Callen asks, sitting us up.

"Not to leave, but to wait outside until we get the all clear. The rest of the McKinnon clan is out back, and being a pain in the DA's ass, basically demanding to lay eyes on the both of you."

Callen stands, lifting me up with him. "Thanks, man. Do you think we'll get to leave soon?"

"Yep, it shouldn't be too long now. I'll walk you out when you're ready." He steps back into the hallway, giving us a moment.

"Can I stay with you tonight?" I blurt out. There's no way I'm staying another night in this house that had been my refuge the last couple of months.

"Charlotte, that's not even a question. I'm not letting you out of my sight ever again."

He pulls me into his arms, and I rest my head against his shoulder, breathing in his scent and reassuring myself that I'm okay. I'm safe.

Despite his declaration, I can't shake the image of him angrily walking out on me at Daisy's. "You sure?"

He uses his finger to lift my chin so we're eye to eye. "Am I sure? What are you talking about?"

"We haven't really talked about yesterday."

"We'll talk about it later, but I know you were only trying to help." He kisses my forehead. "I love you."

My body sags in relief, my heart caught in my throat. I swallow, as I now struggle to speak. "I love you, too," I whisper.

"How about you pack enough clothes for a week, and then we'll go see my siblings before they all get arrested for harassment."

I want to ask him if I can pack for forever, but right now isn't the time for life-changing conversations. We've been through a lot, and emotions are high. Instead, I nod and fill a suitcase with my essentials and his birthday present. We'll figure out long-term living arrangements later.

Hand in hand, we follow Owen down the hallway, carefully stepping around the yellow numbers marking logged evidence. In the living room, I come face-to-face with the tarp and tools Callen struggled to describe. My heartbeat thumps like a bass drum, and I feel like I'm outside my body watching my worst nightmare unfold in slow motion.

Callen's hold tightens on my hand as he tucks me against him. "Don't look. You're fine. I've got you, sugar."

And I know he does.

He's said it countless times today, and it's been true each and every time.

He's got me just like the three people sitting on the picnic table in the backyard waiting for us have got him.

They watch us limbo under the police tape, labeling the back door as a crime scene and meet us on the grass. Daisy plows into me with tears in her eyes, which makes me cry for the first time all day.

"Don't cry, I'm fine. Callen got here just in time."

She releases me and then hugs Callen as soon as Knox releases him to take me in his arms.

"I'm so damn glad you're okay. My brother loves the fuck out of you, you know that?"

"And I love him right back."

"Good. He deserves someone like you in his life."

Angus hugs us next, and when he steps out of his brother's arms, Callen keeps ahold of him so they're standing side by side with his arm draped over his little brother's shoulders. "I don't even want to think what would have happened if you three hadn't pushed me out the door when you did. You all saved her life today, which means you saved mine. I'll never be able to thank you enough."

We're interrupted by barking. A car door closes, and Ruby makes a beeline for her daddy.

Sharon's not far behind her. "You two get over here right now," she orders.

Callen takes my hand in his and we, along with Ruby, walk across the grass to meet his mom halfway. Once she reaches us, she pulls us into her arms as Ruby tangles herself between our legs. "Angus called and told me what happened, and I couldn't get here fast enough." She pulls back, looking me over. "They said you're okay but are you really?" she asks me.

"Yes." I shake my head, because I wasn't physically hurt, but emotionally I'm a mess. "Well, I will be."

She turns her attention to her son, patting his face with her hand, her voice soft. "And you? You okay, son?"

"I'm fine, Mom. You don't need to worry. We're both fine."

"Cal, you nearly killed a man tonight because he was about to hurt the woman you love. Don't try to tell me everything is fine."

First Knox and now Sharon. Hearing his family talk about his love for me so casually eases some of the fear and anxiety I've felt since he burst into Daisy's place full of rage. Crazy that I'm still thinking about our fight after everything that's happened, but Callen McKinnon has become everything to me. To think that I could have messed that up or, worst of all, hurt him is almost scarier than what happened here today.

"We're both still in shock, but we'll get through it."

Her gaze bounces between us, assessing us with a mother's knowing eye. "As long as you lean on each other and those who love you, I know you will."

"Thanks, Mom." He pulls her into another hug. "I love you."

She's putting on a brave face, but when they embrace, her facade falls. Concern paints her features and tears fill her eyes as she holds her son. Blinking rapidly, she steels herself and pulls back from him, her emotions schooled and a glint back in her eye.

Taking me by the shoulders, she meets my gaze. "If you need anything at all, you call. You got that?"

"Yes, ma'am. Thank you."

"When you're up for it, come over and I'll make

pancakes." She links an arm with each of us, and we walk back to the table to join the others.

"I've heard about your pancakes."

"I bet you have. A stack of my pancakes always does the trick." She winks.

Once we reach the table Daisy, Angus, and Sharon sit on one side with me between Callen and Knox on the other side. Callen and I hold on to each other for dear life. For a couple of minutes, the bustling of the police officers and detectives leaves us all in an awkward silence. But Knox, being Knox, takes it upon himself to lighten the mood.

"Nice table," he says, bumping his shoulder gently against mine. "Who knew you were hiding a secret wood-working talent under that lawyer exterior of yours?"

"Got to keep you on your toes, McKinnon," I say, forcing a smile.

"Isn't that my job? To keep my lawyer on *her* toes."

"You certainly have done a good job of that over the years. My thoughts and prayers go out to your new repre-sentation."

His family chuckles, and Knox gasps in feigned shock. I appreciate him adding a bit of levity to the situation. Just like the rest of his family, Knox has always been thoughtful. Even when he's gotten himself into hot water, and I'm scolding him about his predicament and working to get him out of it. He's always kind and respectful, and I owe him so much.

I owe this entire family so much.

Quietly, speaking only to Knox but knowing they all can hear me, I say something I've wanted to say for quite some time. "All joking aside, it has been a pleasure working with you all these years. Truth be told, you and the rest of the band are my favorites. But if you tell any of my other clients I said that, I'll deny it."

"Sorry, but I have witnesses," he replies. A mischievous grin on his face.

"But on an even more serious note, thank you for bringing me to Goose Hollow. If you hadn't seen a friend in need and offered your place to me, I never would have had a second chance at love. You not only brought me back to Callen, but you unknowingly led me to Daisy and a shot at following my dreams. I'll never be able to thank you enough."

Tears slide down my cheeks as my emotions get the better of me. Callen turns to straddle the bench and pulls me as close to him as humanly possible, kissing me on the head.

This small gesture of affection that he so often does is one of the most grounding, loving things I've ever felt. It's my new favorite thing. I lean into the kiss, closing my eyes.

"Hey, y'all," Officer Hibbs interrupts. "You're free to go. We'll be in touch with both of you very soon, so please keep your phones on and stick around the area."

As we all stand from the table, Callen asks, "Any updates from the hospital?"

"Davies is alive, but still unconscious. Not only does he have head trauma from the hit to the back of his head, but he cracked the side of his skull when he landed on the tile floor. Don't worry. We've got an officer watching him around the clock. He won't be getting out of his hospital bed for a while, but when he does, he'll be escorted back to California."

"Thank you for the update. Please let us know if things change," Callen says, relaxing against me.

Tension leaves my body, too, exhaustion creeping back in.

"Of course. I'll be in touch." He turns and walks back to the cabin.

"Where do you guys want to go?" Angus asks. "I'll give you a ride, since neither of you should be driving right now. You wanna go to your place or back up to the lodge?"

Callen nudges my shoulder. "You wanna go back to my place, sugar?"

"Yes, please."

Chapter Forty-Three

Callen

Charlotte hasn't spoken a word since we climbed into the back seat of Gus's truck, and I have no intention of pushing her. As long as she's in my arms, everything is as okay as it can be for the time being.

Today was the culmination of all of her worst nightmares coming true.

Mine too.

When I entered the house this afternoon and found that tarp laid out on the living room floor, everything went red. But when I saw him at the end of the hall, I knew what would happen next, and there could be no hesitation on my part.

He wasn't going to lay a hand on her. I had to stop him by any means necessary.

Sitting here in the back of the truck, I can still feel the hammer twirling in my fist as I rushed down the hall.

As I entered the bathroom, her scream cut through my chest and split my heart in two. If only that had been the worst of it, but nothing could have prepared me for the sight of her naked body cowering in the corner of the shower, her eyes wild with primal fear.

At that point, Davies became an obstacle I had to get through to reach her.

Fueled by adrenaline and fear for Charlotte, I didn't think twice about swinging the hammer into the back of his head. The blunt force of impact radiating down my arm barely registered in my rush to get to her. The sound of William's head slamming against the shower floor sent a sick feeling through me. But she was all that mattered.

Once she was in my arms, I had to get her as far away as possible from the monster on the floor. I was so focused on settling her in the bedroom I didn't even realize blood had splattered across my face.

With Charlotte recovering in the bedroom, I went to check on the asshole motionless on the bathroom floor. He was breathing, but not moving. To play it safe, I borrowed the fucker's duct tape and taped his ankles and wrists together. It was then that I caught my reflection in the mirror above the sink and saw the blood. Dread that she saw me like this seized me. As I scrubbed the blood from my face, I wondered what she thought of me. Would she see me differently after what I've done? Would she replay this moment in her head every time she looked at me?

The hours that followed were a blur. My worry for Charlotte was always at the forefront of my mind, while the nagging worry that I may have killed a man came secondary. I stand by my actions, but a life in prison means a life without Charlotte, and that would be a death sentence.

Having Owen as a buffer gave us a bit of comfort, but my family waiting for us outside nearly brought me to tears. Tears I didn't shed because I needed all my strength to support the woman sitting next to me in this truck.

I'm grateful Angus offered to drive us to my place. I could have driven, but Charlotte needs me. Her grip on mine tightens as we pass Davies's vehicle, now covered in police tape. As we drive through town toward the house, she stays cuddled against me, forgoing her seat belt. Normally, I would insist she put it on, but we both need her in my arms right now.

We pull up to the house, but she doesn't budge. I kiss the top of her head and whisper, "We're home, sugar."

She looks up at me with tired eyes. "I don't want to stay at the cabin anymore."

At once, hope springs in my chest that she means what I think she means. A murdering psychopath attacking her isn't exactly the reason I wanted her to agree to move in, but I meant what I said. I can't let her out of my sight.

"Like I said, baby. We're home."

Angus walks us to the front door. "If you need anything at all, I'm just a call away. And when you two are ready, join us up at the house. We'll be there the rest of the week."

"Thanks." He pulls me into a hug. "I'll call you."

Charlotte gives him a wave, and he leaves us on our own.

I let us into the house where she takes me by the hand, leading me to the bedroom. Much to my surprise, she pulls my missing gray Eastlyn Brewing T-shirt out of her bag.

"Have you had that since our weekend?"

She smiles but still doesn't speak as she removes her sweatshirt and covers herself in my T-shirt. She pulls back the bedding. "Lay with me?"

"You don't have to ask me twice," I say, pulling my T-shirt over my head and stripping down to my underwear.

We climb into bed, and she wraps herself around me, placing a kiss over my heart.

"I love you, Callen."

"I love you too, baby."

"It's over."

"It's over, baby."

"I'm so tired."

"I know, sugar."

"I haven't slept soundly since I opened that letter."

I was on the video chat with her when she opened *that* letter. I watched as her face paled and the fear took hold of her. What I didn't see was the fear she had buried below the surface every day since then. She did an exceptional job of hiding her fear from me. Letting me think my presence was enough to give her peace of mind.

What an arrogant prick I've been.

How did I miss it?

"I'm so sorry, Charlotte."

"Don't be. I'm free now. It was easy to tell myself I felt safe because he was behind bars, but he was always there in the back of my mind. It was like there's always been this internal countdown to his release and the knowledge that he'd have the opportunity to find me again. Whenever my brain wasn't busy, it was counting down."

Fuck if she isn't breaking my heart.

"Then to have that day come sooner than expected was a

lot. This has been the happiest time of my life, but the day I got that letter, he took some of that happy away from me."

She places another kiss over my heart.

"But now, thanks to you, I'm free to be completely joyful without his dark cloud hanging over me. Thank you, Chip."

"Please don't thank me. There isn't anything I wouldn't do for you, baby. Now go to sleep. I've got you."

It only takes a couple of minutes before she's asleep, but with it not even being eight o'clock and the events of the day racing through my head, it takes what feels like hours before my mind tires and lets the sandman in.

Chapter Forty-Four

Callen

I realize Charlotte's no longer in my arms when I feel the bed dip beside me. Soft lips brush over mine, and she playfully whispers, "Chip. Wake up. It's your birthday."

As I slowly open my eyes and stretch myself awake, I'm greeted by her radiant smile, which usually implies she's up to no good. She's kneeling beside me on the bed and the low light from the lamp on the bedside table makes her look like a goddamn angel. Like my angel.

"Well, if it's my birthday, it's your birthday too," I grunt sleepily.

"How right you are. And for my birthday, I want to give you your gift."

"Babe, it's still dark outside. What time is it?"

"It's a little after four."

"In the morning?"

"We went to sleep a solid eight hours ago, besides I thought your secret identity was as a cowboy. Don't you all get up early to milk the cows?" She giggles, pleased with herself.

"Since when are you so sassy at this time of day?"

"Since I woke up and realized it's your birthday and I can give you your present."

Beaming ear to ear, she reveals a box wrapped in chocolate chip cookie wrapping paper. I'm not sure if I've ever seen her so happy when she says, "Sit up, sleepyhead."

"Not so fast." I throw back the covers and cross the room to my closet to grab a couple of things from the top shelf. "I have a present for you, too."

She scoots to the edge of the bed. "When in the world did you have time to shop?"

"Before I flew to Los Angeles last week. How about you?" I kneel on the floor in front of her, bringing us face-to-face.

"Yesterday morning."

Yesterday, before her worst fears came to life. Before I nearly killed a man.

"Look at us both, planning ahead."

"Here. You go first," she insists, pushing the box toward me. "But read the card first."

"Man, you're bossy!"

She just smiles, and I notice her T-shirt... well, my T-shirt, again. It looks much better on her than it ever looked on me.

"I can't believe you stole my shirt."

"Before I came back to Goose Hollow, I slept in it a couple of days a week. But once we started our little slumber parties, I tucked it away so you wouldn't try to take it back from me. It's mine now. You can't have it."

"I wouldn't dream of it." I lean forward and kiss her as I slide the card from the envelope.

The card matches the wrapping paper. "You really have a thing for chocolate chip cookies, don't you?"

"You're my Chip." Her cheeks turn rosy, and I finally shake the last of the sleep from my head and laugh. "I knew you'd like it." She winks. "Read it out loud."

"Yes, ma'am."

I clear my throat and read.

"Dear Chip,

I've been head over heels in love with you since the first night I met you. You were a perfect stranger, and you saw me. You listened to me. You were curious about my hopes and dreams, and you made me feel like they were all possible.

If your offer to shack up and live in sin is still on the table, please ask me again after you read this card.

I hope you have a very happy birthday.
All my love,
Charlotte."

Swallowing past the lump in my throat as I silently reread her words, my heart swells, and my stomach flips all over itself with joy at the knowledge I never have to go another day without her. When my eyes finally meet hers, there's expectation in her gaze. She's almost giddy, waiting for me to ask her to move in with me again.

Instead, I place the gift bag in front of her. My heart trips when sadness washes away her glee. She looks down at the bag and tries to hide her disappointment.

With my index finger under her chin, I gently lift her face and bring her eyes back to mine. "Trust me, sugar."

As I watch her remove the tissue paper, my nerves kick into high gear. Needing to do something to release my nervous energy, I shift and readjust to one knee.

Charlotte eyes me.

"This floor is murder on the knees," I explain.

"Well, get up here then." She pats the bed next to her.

"Nah, I like the view from here."

"Suit yourself." She sticks her tongue out. "You sure do like tissue paper."

"You wrap your gifts and make them look all pretty. I bury mine in a bag full of tissue paper. It's the thought that counts."

She gasps and covers her mouth when she pulls the black wood frame out of the bag. I'm surprised by her reaction because there's a note covering the framed gift. When I see her skimming the paper, I put my hand over it to stop her.

"Out loud."

Her eyes are glossy when she reads.

"Charlotte, I'm not sure what you've done to me, but whatever it is, I hope you never stop. I know you aren't perfect, what with your love of cheesecake and dislike of coffee, but my love for you is strong enough to overlook your shortcomings." She chuckles. *"Because you are perfect to me. You are everything to me.*

I love that you don't need me to follow your passions, and you have the strength to make all of your hopes and dreams come true on your own. As long as I get the honor of being by your side as you journey through this life and the next, that's good enough for me."

She pauses, and my heart just about stops.

"But you're not the only one with dreams. To quote the great Hall & Oates, "you make my dreams come true." So I will wait as long as you need me to. And when you're ready to move in, I hope you'll also be ready to be my wife.

Happy birthday, Charlotte. I'll be here waiting. You know where to find me. Love, C."

Slowly, with my life hanging in the balance, she lifts the piece of paper and comes face-to-face with the Bob Dylan keycard from our amazing weekend.

A tear slides down her cheek as she beams a watery smile in my direction. "You kept it?"

I don't think she's put two and two together. That I'm before her on bended knee.

"I did. Charlotte—"

"Open your gift." A lone tear glistens down her face and falls from her chin.

"But Charlotte—"

"Please?"

"Of course, baby," I say, trying to hide my disappointment as my knee digs into the ground that is quickly beginning to feel like concrete.

I rip off the paper, and shock hits me square in the chest. "You've got to be kidding me."

In my hand is a matching black frame and in the center is the same hotel key. She has added the hotel name at the top and the day we met at the bottom, so she wins, but we gave each other the same birthday gift.

Isn't that just the shit?

"It's crazy, right?"

"So crazy, it's not crazy, if you ask me."

She scoots closer to the edge of the bed, so she can sit directly in front of me. She takes my face in her hands and kisses me. So long and so slow, the pain in my knee becomes a distant memory.

She pulls back just enough to look me in the eye. "Did you mean it?"

"Mean what, sugar?" I know what she's asking but want to hear her say it.

Her cheeks pink and her fingers shake along with her voice. "Did you just ask me to be your wife?"

Now my fingers shake as I put the small box I've been hiding under the bed on her leg. She stills and looks down.

As she releases me to take the box in her trembling hands, I swear my heart stops pumping in anticipation. It's one thing to move in together, but we've never discussed marriage.

She opens the box, and the smile gracing her lips when she sees the tiny diamond on a simple gold band activates my heart once again.

Her eyes are glossy with unshed tears when they meet mine.

"It was my grandma's. I promise we'll upgrade."

"It's perfect."

"Yeah?"

"Best birthday ever." Her fingers tangle in my hair, and

her forehead rests against mine. "But, Chip, we're gonna need to build a bigger closet."

"Well, you see, I was thinking we could build a bigger house. Think you can manage with what we got here a little while longer?"

"Will you be here?"

"Yes, ma'am."

"I think I can manage."

Chapter Forty-Five

Callen

Four months later...

en! Nine! Eight!

"One sec. I have to get my glass!" my wife yells, sprinting to the table on the side of the dance floor to grab her champagne flute as we count down to midnight.

That's right. I said, *my wife.*

Today, I married my best friend, and the only woman I wanna dance with for the rest of my life.

If someone had told me a year ago that life could be this good, I would have told them to shove their positive affirmations up their ass. But here we are, and life is fucking fantastic!

"I'm back. Did you miss me?"

Four! Three!

"Always, sugar. You know that." My arm wraps around her waist, pulling her into my side.

"Two! One! Happy New Year!" The two of us cheer, holding our glasses in the air as our voices blend with the voices of those we love the most.

My wife turns in my arms, blinding me with her mega-watt smile. "You gonna kiss me or what, Chip?"

Not wasting another second, I plant my lips on hers for the millionth time tonight and it's just as perfect as every kiss that's come before it. I've been trying to sneak her out to the other barn to consummate our vows in the tack room, but obstacle after obstacle has gotten in my way. The horse barn may not be the most romantic, but it's worked before and it'll do.

"God, I can't wait until we're alone," she says against my lips.

"My thought exactly. I bet we can slip out and be back before anyone notices we're gone," I offer, hoping she's as desperate for me as I am for her.

She looks around the party, then back at me, excitement in her eyes. "Yes, please. But I need to grab something real quick."

"Make it snappy, woman. I'll wait by the side door." I give her ass a pat, and she kisses me on the cheek, downs her sparkling cider, and dashes away.

She said she didn't want to forget a thing about our reception or to be too exhausted to ravish me when we got home so she only had one glass of champagne before sticking to the sparkling cider. Since I'm fully onboard with her ravishing plans, I'm not complaining.

Keeping my head down to avoid eye contact and any

obstacles that threaten to come between the two of us getting a few naked moments alone, I can't help but think back to August 23rd. Our shared birthday and the day Bob Dylan helped me propose.

The hours that led up to my proposal may have been a nightmare, but our wedding day came together like a dream. Some, not all, of those closest to us worried that getting engaged after such a traumatic experience may not have been the best idea. I can see their point. It does seem extreme, especially since I hadn't been speaking to her the day before I asked her to be my wife. The thing is, I'd decided to ask her to be my wife before that shitty day in August. I'd already asked Mom for Granny's ring and everything. Sure, Charlotte and I had some shit to work out, but even when I was upset with her, I knew she was it for me.

Our hearts were ready.

Charlotte suggested the county courthouse, but I wanted her to have a night like tonight. This is my second-and-last-wedding, but this will be her only, and I wanted to make it special. But we didn't need a year to plan. Shit, in my mind we've been married since the day she moved in. Well, she moved in what she could. My small two-bedroom house is nice enough, but Charlotte was right, it is nowhere near big enough for all her shoes.

I may not need a piece of paper to tell me I'm hers and she's mine, but there's no denying tonight has been a quite the celebration. How could I not celebrate how fortunate I am to get a second chance at love? I'm glad we did this. For her and for me.

"Why you hidin' over here by the door, brother?" Knox

asks, as he saunters my way and wraps his arm around my shoulders. "Planning your escape?"

"Nah, was just hoping to sneak off with the Mrs. for a couple of minutes but she's doing something over there." I nod my head in the direction of Charlotte, who is in the corner going through her bag, looking for something.

"Got it. You're hoping to get freaky on your wedding night. Understood. Please do not elaborate."

My reply is a chuckle and a shake of my head. Other than our birthday week, he hasn't been around to see the two of us together. He's still adjusting.

"I'm happy for you, Cal." He pulls me tighter to his side. "You got yourself one hell of a gal."

"I sure did. Have I thanked you in the last hour for bringing her back to me and for this amazing party?"

"It's been a couple. You're slackin'."

"Well, thank you."

"Stop thanking me."

He relaxes his hold on me, but keeps his arm draped over my shoulders. "Fine. But you didn't have to do all this." I wave my hand in front of us.

Knox sent his event planner to the stars to our sleepy little town, and she transformed the barn into a winter wonderland. Chandeliers hang above the long tables where an elegant dinner was served. There are huge flower arrangements on every available surface and tiny white lights everywhere. Charlotte says it's magical and she's right, you wouldn't know that a couple days ago the space was full of hay and heavy equipment. I'm sure all this magic cost Knox a pretty penny. All we had to do was relocate some tractors and clean things up and his planner did the rest.

"Yes, I did. If Charlie was gonna get married in a barn, we had to class up the joint. You know you married yourself a lady, right?"

"Maybe in the streets, but in the sheets–"

"Nope," he cuts me off before I can finish. "Huh, uh. Don't wanna know."

It's so much fun getting under his skin like this. And it's a first. Knox has never been one to shy away from sex talk.

"Since when did you get so squeamish?"

"Since you married my friend."

Point taken.

"Well, getting married in the barn was Charlotte's idea. You know I would have given her whatever she asked for."

"I know, but it's my gift to you."

We would have been married months ago, but there was no way we were doing this without Knox. He *had* to be here. But I didn't want him to fly in one day and out the next. We had to find a time when he could be here for the days leading up to the ceremony and that meant the band's holiday tour break. There would be no us, without my stupid big brother, so of course, we waited.

And it was worth the wait. New Year's Eve dancing with our friends and family, drinking champagne at the best barn party I've ever been to with the woman I love on my arm. What more could a man ask for? Well, besides five minutes alone with his new bride.

"Thank you for playing double duty today too. I appreciate you stepping in for her dad."

"Of course, it was my honor. Her dad was a great man."

Originally, the plan was that Charlotte would walk herself down the aisle. She said she couldn't imagine anyone but her dad doing the job. But at the last minute, as Knox, Angus, Owen and I were getting settled at the altar, Knox got a call from Charlotte asking him to do the honor of walking her down the aisle. He didn't hesitate and I fought back tears as he jogged out of the door to get to her, wishing it was me running to comfort her on such an important day.

There was no keeping my composure when I watched my brother, who was also my best man, enter the barn with her on his arm. Walking toward me, with tears in her eyes, was the love of my life. Even with my own tears blurring my vision, she was breathtaking in her long-sleeved, formfitting white lace gown. Her hair down in waves, looking like an angel sent to earth just for me. It took all my willpower to stay in place and not run to her.

When Charlotte and Knox reached me, it felt like a full-circle moment. Of course it should be him. He was the one who brought her into my life to begin with. And today he was the one who put her hand in mine as we stood before Mayor Reyes and pledged ourselves to one another.

We've danced to Hall & Oates and the best man has brought out all his big moves on the dance floor. Mom has cried, Sawyer—looking sharp in his tuxedo—has boogied with all the ladies, we've had our fill of cake, and now I need a piece of my wife.

"Well, I'll leave you to it then. Don't take too long though. It's after midnight and we might all turn into pumpkins soon." Knox leaves me on my own, waving to Charlotte as she crosses the room.

"Hey, Chip," she says, as her arms round my middle, and she hugs me from behind.

"Hey, sugar. Where did you sneak off to? And why didn't you take me with you?"

"Sorry, but I had to go get your present."

"Present?"

"Yep." She beams.

"What in the world are you up to, woman?"

She releases her hold on me. "Take me somewhere private and you'll find out."

I shrug out of my suit jacket, place it over her shoulders and quietly open the door. The sky is dark but with lights strung around the barn and the bright white snow on the ground lit by the moon, it's easy to see. It's been snowing all day, but we can still make out the paths we had shoveled to take us from building to building.

I've taken two steps out the door and am preparing to pick Charlotte up and carry her to the other barn when I see a someone else already doing the same thing. "What the fuck?"

"What's wrong?" she asks, taking a step out into the frigid air.

"Am I seeing things or is that Angus carrying Mia to the barn? The barn I was supposed to be getting you naked in."

"No, you're not crazy." She giggles. "I've told you for months there's something going on between them, but you refuse to listen to me."

"But... I don't understand... It's Mia. Mia Powell. She's like a sister to me. That's just wrong. Gross actually."

"Yes, but she isn't your sister now, is she?"

"You're a mean woman."

"Facts are facts. And we need to keep this to ourselves.

We didn't see a thing. You got that? They'll tell everyone when they're ready."

All I can do is watch them disappear into the barn. Completely shocked.

Charlotte pouts. "We aren't getting any sexy time until we get home, are we?"

"Sorry, baby. I'm not sure I could get it up if I tried. Not after what I just saw."

"Oh, I don't know about that." She rubs her hand over my cock and she's right. I get a semi instantly.

"You are insatiable," I growl, putting her my hand over hers increasing her pressure.

"What are you two doing over here, trying to escape?" Karissa interrupts, poking her head out of the barn.

Stepping back in, I close the door and do my best to also black out what I just saw. "Nope, just cooling off," I say, hoping I don't sound suspicious.

"Well, Daisy is trying to get one last group photo for the night. We've got you two. Now we just need to find Mia and Angus and we've got everyone.

"Oh, uh..." Charlotte stutters. "I think Mia ran to the house to use the bathroom. I haven't seen Gus." There's a twinkle in her wide eyes when her gaze locks with mine.

I know her well enough to know, she loves having this secret. And she loves, love. Let's just hope she's getting ahead of herself and there is a logical reason for what we just witnessed.

Karissa pulls on Charlotte's hand, and I follow them to the dance floor. Standing in the middle of the crazy cast of characters that make up our family, be it by blood or because we chose them, I'm right where I want to be. I fucking love every person here. Well, maybe not Owen's date, who I've never met before, but she seems fine.

I'm basking in my happiness when I glance down at my wife, who has that look in her eye. A look that says she's up to something and takes my mind far away from what's going on in the other barn.

"I found the bride and groom. Let's get some shots while we wait for the other two," our maid of honor announces.

Everyone around us is abuzz, posing for pictures with their tongues out or giving each other devil horns, but Charlotte and I stand with our arms around each other, looking into each other's eyes.

"Thank you," she says, for only me to hear.

"For what, baby?"

"I never thought I could be this happy. That life could be this good. I guess I'm thanking you for giving me you."

"Charlotte McKinnon, you are my everything. There is no me without you. All of me is yours. You know that, right?"

"I do." Her hand that had been around my waist slips into mine and she places something into my palm.

"What's this?"

Holding a finger to her lips, she shushes me.

Looking down at my hand, I find a pink and white plastic stick.

Logically, I know what I'm looking at, but my brain has been shocked silly and is refusing to function.

Looking back up to her, I'm met with bright blue watery eyes.

"Is this what I think it is?"

She nods, taking the pregnancy test out of my hand so she can stash it in my pants pocket. Lifting to her toes, she whispers in my ear. "Shh... Don't tell anyone, but you're gonna be a daddy."

Dumbfounded by her news, Charlotte doesn't have to worry about me telling a soul, because words aren't adequate for the joy and the fear and the excitement I'm feeling.

She watches me process the information with wide glowing eyes. "You okay, big guy?" she asks because I still haven't spoken.

"Never better."

It's true. I have never been happier than I am right here, right now.

Acknowledgments

To my husband... Where do I even begin? Only Wanna Dance With You is my 11th full-length novel and you are still my ride or die. There really aren't any words to say what your support means to me. You know the joy writing these stories about love and romance makes me, even if they haven't let me quit the day job yet. You keep pushing me to do what I love, and your excitement with each new release is something I will never take for granted. Thank you for EVERYTHING. I love you so much more.

To every reader, reviewer, blogger, and influencer who has shared your love of my books, you mean the world to me. I wouldn't still be getting to do this if it weren't for you. Thank you, thank you, thank you!

Harley Stone... Is there another person out there in the world who cares about others as much as you? You are one of a kind and I'm so grateful to call you my friend.

Jenny at Editing4Indies... Thank you for putting up with me. I know I put you through it with my inability to use a comma properly. Well, that and so much more! I appreciate you!

Jillian Liota at Blue Moon Creative Studio... You were an absolute dream to work with! I am giddy over all four covers for this series and can't wait to share them all with the world! Thank you so much!

And finally, to all of my friends and family who have supported me on this journey. And I don't just mean those of you who have read my books. I know you aren't all into the spicy romance (But I swear if you try it, you'll love it!), but still you don't judge me and I love all so much for that.

What To Read Next

Standalone Novels

Disregarded Heart

Blackbird

Series

The Only in Goose Hollow Series

Only Wanna Dance With You

The Only Heart That Matters

The Only Thing That's Real

It Could Only Be You

The Between the Pines Series

Raised On It

Bottle It Up

Click here for your FREE copy of We Are Tonight! A Between the Pines Prequel

The Gorgeous Duet

Gorgeous: Book One

Gorgeous: Book Two

Lisa Shelby is a USA Today bestselling contemporary romance author, a self-proclaimed love geek and cake-pop addict. Born and raised in the Pacific Northwest, this is still where Lisa calls home with her husband and their dogs. When she isn't sitting in a coffee shop writing her next happily ever after, you can find Lisa with her husband likely eating tacos, traveling, listening to live music, or binging way too many TV shows.

Join Lisa's Reader Group: Lisa Shelby's Love Geeks

9 798869 221179